Lust & Philosophy. A novel

The Exact Unknown and Other Tales of Modern China

Massage and the Writer: Essays on Asian Massage

At the Teahouse Café: Essays on the Middle Kingdom

American Rococo: Essays on the Edge

The Kitchens of Canton. A novel

Confucius and Opium: China Book Reviews

THE MUSTACHIOED
WOMAN OF SHANGHAI

A NOVEL

ISHAM COOK

Magic Theater Books

Published in the United States by Magic Theater Books

ISBN 13: 9781732277441
ISBN 10: 1732277443

Cover design by Wang Chen, based on a painting by Zhang Daqian.

THE MUSTACHIOED
WOMAN OF SHANGHAI

1

"Men."

"Yeah," said Marguerite as she led Louisa and Lixin into her loft. "Doesn't it sometimes just make you wanna, wash your hands of them all?"

"And I heard she had memory problems after that. Amnesia."

"From what?"

"Being punched in the face. He kept beating her, right in the café. Totally lost it."

"Wow, your place is so big. So many rugs."

"You guys have a seat down there on the bed."

"Okeydokey," said Louisa as she gingerly lowered herself on the futon.

"These rugs you sell?" Lixin was examining several pieces hanging on a wall and more stacked on the floor. "What's that? Oh, you make rug?"

"Yep."

"Really?" said Louisa. The three of them crowded over the loom. "So that's how rugs are made. I've always wanted to know. How long does it take you to make one of these?"

"About a year. This one is for my own amusement. The others are from dealers."

"It takes you a whole year to make this?"

"It could get done faster if that's all I did the whole day."

"Oh, I see. And this below is the portion you've already done."

"I recently started it."

"What this material, wool?" asked Lixin.

"Yeah."

"Where did you learn how to make them?"

"Oh, it's been years."

"When you lived in Iran?"

"And Turkey. I was kidnapped there and enslaved in a rug factory."

"What?"

"Long story. Tell you about it later. Anyway, I need to keep it up. It's very meditative and relaxing."

"You were *enslaved*? And you miss it?"

"I don't miss being enslaved. But I miss the work."

"Can we watch you?"

"Some other time. I need to get into the 'zone.' Once I start I don't want to stop."

"I thought it was in Iran you had problems."

"I was jailed there for three years."

"Why?"

"Holding an orgy in my apartment."

"You've got to be kidding. They do that there?"

"You bet."

"While wearing the hijab?"

"No, they don't wear the hijab when having sex. And what do you do, Lixin?"

"I'm graphic designer."

"That explains why you're looking at my rugs so closely."

"What's this?"

"I was going to ask you about this too," said Louisa. "You don't really..."

"Oh, my god. And that?" said Lixin, covering her face

with her hand. "Everyone use that?"

Marguerite lit a bong and passed it to Louisa. "Yep."

"I'm afraid I'm too shy!"

"I could use some of this. I haven't been able to find any in a while here. Lixin?"

"Oh, what's that? *Dama?*"

"Yeah."

"I want to try. I never tried."

"You don't really, Marguerite...in front of guests?"

"So, tell me more about this guy who beat up his girlfriend in the café. You said he's in Shanghai?"

"It happened here. But nobody knows what happened to him."

"What was his name? Just in case I may have heard of him."

"I forgot. He was an author, and she was his translator, apparently."

"And he did that to her?"

"After making her nude photos public on the internet."

"He did that to her because *he* made her nude photos public on the internet? Shouldn't it be the other way around?"

"After she confronted him."

"Trying to shut her up. You mean, like, an amateur porn site where perverts post up-skirt videos?"

"Probably. I wish I could remember his name. He published some kind of book on massage, I recall."

"Massage? You mean one of those male white trash travelogues from the Philippines or Thailand?"

"Take it all the way into your lungs and hold it in for as long as you can," said Louisa.

Lixin coughed out her toke and tried again.

"If it's your first time you may not feel anything," said Marguerite.

"Why not?"

"You sort of need to learn how to get high."

"Do you actually have guests over and they *use* this?" said

Louisa.

"Many times."

"And that?"

Marguerite walked over to the exposed toilet and pulled a hanging rug around it.

"Oh, I see. I didn't notice the track thing above. A little more civilized now!" Louisa laughed. "But you don't have the same for *this*."

"Nah. Why hide it when the whole point is to be open?"

"I'd need to be with the right people — and then maybe only after a few drinks. How many can fit in it?"

"Three, if you don't mind getting intimate," said Marguerite, stealing a glance at Lixin.

"So cool. The whole atmosphere here. And your clothes. That's quite a retro dress you've got on."

"Nineteen-thirties Shanghai."

"It's genuine?"

"Of course."

"Can I ask you a personal question? Your..." Louisa pinched the air above her lips. "You must get a lot of comments. Or stares."

"I'd get a lot of stares even if I didn't have it."

They all laughed at this.

"It does go with you. Kinda."

"I was on the subway the other day when this deaf couple were signing about me and joking about it. I signed back, inviting them over to have a bath with me. You should have seen their jaws drop."

"You *asked* them?"

"You can sign Chinese too?" said Lixin.

"I picked it up. I've picked up quite a few sign languages over the years."

"Was it hard?"

"Not that hard. Of course, I have an accent. They can recognize ASL."

"ASL?"

"American Sign Language."

"How deaf are you, if I may ask?"

"Ninety percent."

"You seem to have no problem talking with us."

"As long as I can see you speak," she said, pointing to one of her ears.

"Oh, yeah."

"And as long as you can understand my slurred speech."

"I can make you out easily. Lixin, do you have any trouble understanding her?"

"No. No problem."

"Have you always been deaf?"

"Since I was two. Meningitis."

Lixin was staring in front of her.

"Do you feel anything?" Marguerite asked her.

"Hmm, not sure. So, on subway they were talking about your...." She covered her mouth again as she laughed.

"The Frida Kahlo?"

"Frida? What's that?"

"Frida Kahlo. The female Mexican painter."

"Oh, yeah! I know. With the...." Lixin drew a line across her eyebrows.

"Unibrow. She also had a mustache."

"No, I have to say it really does suit you," said Louisa.

"I've seen Chinese women with mustaches as dark as mine. But it doesn't seem to be a matter of pride with them, with their blank, sad faces, like they've given up and don't care anymore what people think and that's why they don't shave it off. Either that or they've persuaded themselves that no one notices."

"Have you ever shaved yours off?"

"Yes. In order to make it grow back darker."

"Oh, I feel something," said Lixin.

"You're getting off?"

"What do you feel?" said Louisa.

"Did I just say 'I feel something'?"

"Yeah."

"What was I talking about?"

"You said you felt something."

"Oh, my god," she laughed. "Did I just say 'Oh, my god'?"

The three burst out laughing.

"You're learning fast," said Marguerite, who then went over to the clear-glass bathtub and turned on the tap. It sat dead center in the loft on an enormous Persian carpet.

"Did you have the pipes specially made for it?" asked Louisa.

"In fact, this was the bathroom of the previous tenants and I took out the walls. The toilet over there was another bathroom."

"Your landlord let you do all that?"

"They love my place. A young couple. They joined me in the tub once. They're interested in my antique clothes and rugs."

"They're interested in your shocking life," said Lixin. "What did I just say?"

"My shocking life."

"Sorry, I don't mean you are shocking person."

"Wait till I tell you about family," she grinned.

"What about your family?"

"No, better not. Some other time. I don't want to freak you guys out."

"You already are freaking us out," said Louisa.

Lixin laughed. Steam rose from the tub as the water level rose. The tub was illuminated underneath by LED lights. "It's so beautiful."

"Hypnotic," said Louisa.

Marguerite pointed to the tall candelabras set on the four corners of the carpet. "At nighttime I light those as well."

"No, come on. Do tell us," said Louisa.

"Well, I was orphaned at eight. To make a long story short, my mom caught my dad sexually abusing me and he shot her to shut her up, and then shot himself in the head."

"I'm sorry!" Louisa and Lixin exclaimed in one breath.

"No need to be. It's ancient history. Strangely, the

hardest thing for me to deal with at the time was that it was all over the news. A female relative took me in. She was a pretty level-headed woman and did a fair job at shielding me from the media and patching up my life."

"You seem so well adjusted. I think most people would have a hard time surviving that."

"You have no choice."

"Do you have problems relating to men?"

"No. I take each person as they come. The problem with a lot of women is they're afraid of men. I'm not afraid of men. I've never had a problem, even when I worked as a masseuse. Though it helped that Chinese men don't have the violent tendencies you see in so many American men."

"You did *what?*"

"The massage shop I worked in. Here in Shanghai when I first arrived a few years back."

"Why?"

"I needed some money till I got my rug business underway. And I wanted to see what it was like."

"What was it like?"

"I lived in a dorm with ten other girls. We worked twelve hours a day, seven days a week."

"No days off?"

"It was better than the rug factory. We had a pretty decent madam and she knew how to run the place and treat us well. If you needed to take a day off you just took it. We only had to stagger things so that there were always a certain number of girls available during peak hours."

"You were on a working visa?"

"I was on all kinds of visas back then — business visas, tourist visas — until they started tightening up. It's a lot harder to be hired under the table these days."

"How did you find that job?"

"I tried out a few places, to check out the girls and the quality of the service — the more upscale, New Agey places, not the shabby parlors. Most masseuses do breast massage and I only inquired while having my boobs done, so they knew I knew what I was getting into. They still laughed it off like I was crazy. But one place, the girl came back into the room with the madam and she grilled me. My Chinese wasn't very good then but I think she found me exotic enough to be useful."

"Did you already have experience?"

"I had picked up some basic techniques over the years. You meet guys who want it and they teach you how to do it."

"Was it safe?"

"Mostly. The drunk assholes, if they were obviously drunk, we'd kick them out as soon as they walked in. But some could hide it and would start grabbing you. I knew how to control them. You learn how to give them just the right amount of noncooperation. What they really want is attention. The male customers, that is."

"Unbelievable," said Lixin.

"You massaged both men and women?"

"Half and half. The women — Chinese women — could be just as difficult. Some would start yelling at you if a single drop of oil got on their hair. You get all kinds. I could write a book about it. Most of the Western customers were young couples getting it done together in the same room. Daring to try their very first massage and so nervous they're shaking. A lot of single Asian males too — Chinese, Japanese and Korean. A lot of Japanese females."

"Japanese females?"

"They can get it much cheaper here than in Japan. The Chinese females are the ones who usually go for boob massage."

"Why?"

"Why not? It's a health thing here, considered good for the breasts. Nobody thinks there's anything strange about it. It's also kind of erotic for them, a release, being pampered like that in the guise of therapy. Most female customers prefer to be massaged by a male, though."

"Sounds like things could quickly get out of hand."

"Masseurs aren't allowed to do breast massage. But I can

tell you it secretly goes on. They would never initiate it; that's the fast track to losing their job. But if a female customer demands it and he refuses, he'll lose her as a customer."

Lixin had a smile wrapped on her face.

"Could you go for breast massage, Lixin?" asked Louisa.

"I haven't tried. But no problem."

"Wow. That would be illegal in the States, I think."

Marguerite snickered at the mention of their country.

"How much money did you make?"

"Twenty thousand kuai in a good month. I had to quit after six months. The problem is the toll it takes on your hands. It started affecting my ability to weave. If you often go for massage, you'll notice a lot of masseuses use only one hand, or their fist or elbow to do you. It's not that they're lazy. Their hands are gone. I got out before I ruined mine. That's the biggest hazard of the job."

"Can't weaving do the same?"

"It's easier on the hands. Weaving doesn't require any strength, just technique. I had acquired good technique from the start. Anyway, you can only weave for a few hours at a time before using up your concentration."

"What about when you were enslaved?"

"You're not working the whole time. You're just kept there."

When the tub was filled with water, Marguerite stood up and pulled off her dress. "Would you guys like to join me?"

Lixin turned to Louisa.

"No, you two go ahead. I already showered this morning," said Louisa.

"Same with me. I can try next time," said Lixin.

"Come on and join me, Lixin."

"*Wo buhao yisi.*"

"How can you be embarrassed when you keep looking at the tub? I know you're dying to get in it."

"You sure this is okay?"

Marguerite opened up a bottle of red and brought out

three wine glasses. She poured a glass for Louisa and placed the other two on the floor next to the tub. One button at a time, Lixin removed her shirt and unhooked her bra. She held the bra in place in front of her.

"C'mon darling."

Marguerite pulled her up off the futon and led her to the tub. Lixin slipped off the rest of her clothes and dipped her foot in the water. "Ow! So hot."

"Sadly, I can't compete with you guys," said Louisa.

"It's not a beauty contest, girls. Everyone is welcome."

"Your tattoos are incredible."

"They're Scythian."

"Why does it go all the way up only one side of your body?"

"Asymmetry suits the body better."

"Ahh!" said Lixin as she sank back into the tub. "So luxury!"

She and Marguerite faced each other in the tub, wine glasses in hand.

"Next is massage, dear. So I can do those fabulous breasts of yours."

The steam obscured Lixin's blushing.

"Can I take a photo of you guys? It's so striking, seeing you lit up like that," said Louisa. "Don't worry, I won't post them on Moments or anything. I just want to show some girlfriends of mine."

"I'm fine with that. Lixin?"

"I can turn my face away?"

"As you like."

"Yeah, you have to be careful these days. It's so easy for compromising photos to get in the wrong hands," said Marguerite.

"Everybody sending sex pics on WeChat years ago. But recently people stop," said Lixin. "Because of scandal."

"To get back to this guy who beat up his girlfriend in the café. I'm curious about him. Why would a writer, of all people, who hired a translator, or was in an intimate relationship with her, do that to her? I mean, aren't writers a step above soccer hooligans? To write a book requires a detached and patient mind, doesn't it? A minimally civilized person."

"Alpha male rage knows no bounds."

"I hope she wasn't permanently injured. That must have been one helluva beating."

Marguerite and Lixin sat in silence for several minutes, their legs entwined, as Louisa squatted around the bathtub snapping away with her Nikon D850.

"Oh, my god," Lixin said to Marguerite. "Every time I see your glass, the wine is less. It tells the time like a clock. This marijuana is crazy. You know, I have some rugs like these in my house. I don't know if they good quality."

"Where did you buy them?"

"My American girlfriend gave them when she left China."

"She's not coming back?"

"No. I don't know where she got them. Can you tell good quality by looking?"

"Of course."

"*Tai haole.* I invite you to our place."

"Can you tell where a rug comes from? I've always been curious about that," said Louisa.

"You mean the local region where it was made? You can with Persian and Central Asian rugs but not Turkish rugs. They're no longer made in Turkey."

"Where are they made?"

"China. Henan Province."

"You mean they're all fake?"

"Depends what you mean by fake. They're made according to exact Turkish specifications."

"You can't buy a rug in Turkey that's made in Turkey anymore?"

"No. The Chinese put all the Turkish rug factories out of business. Though the dealers there will pretend to be offended if you so much as question their authenticity. Anyway, it's not really meaningful to speak of the origin of an Oriental rug. Many of the classic designs have been a shared vocabulary for hundreds of years. Even many so-called local designs were borrowed from other regions long before anyone remembered."

"Where do the designs come from? I'm totally ignorant about this."

"Where does paisley come from, for example? The pattern on shirts and scarves that was popular in the sixties."

"I have no idea."

"It's originally from Persian rugs. The main element is the boteh, you know?" Marguerite drew a teardrop with a curled tip in the air. "You see it a lot in Oriental rugs. It's one of the oldest motifs. Many rug makers don't give a damn about where their designs come from and couldn't tell you if you asked. The only thing that matters are the latest fashions, which are dictated by dealers and their customers in the U.S. and Europe. That's been the case for the past two centuries, since Oriental rugs became fashionable in the West, and even before that, since the Renaissance. We know a lot about early Oriental rug design from European Renaissance painters, who put them in their paintings."

"But where did the original rug makers get their ideas for all these amazing designs?" said Louisa, sweeping her hand across the loft.

"Good question. There's some speculation basic Persian rug design goes back to the Scythians thousands of years ago. They occupied a huge swath of territory in Central Asia, including Persia. They might have been inspired by hallucinogenic drug trances in their shamanic ceremonies."

"Oh, so that's the Scythian connection. What drugs?"

"It was referred to at the time as haoma, or soma as it was called in India. One theory is that it was cannabis. Another theory is the fly agaric mushroom."

"I remember reading about soma in Huxley's *Brave New World*."

"I just remember I have book on massage. Very weird one. I can give it to you when you visit me. But it's in

Chinese," said Lixin.

"She has such lovely eyes, doesn't she?" said Marguerite.

"You have lovely mustache," said Lixin.

"I've been waiting for that. You're the first woman who's actually complimented me on it! Ever."

"We used to not shave under arms. Then everybody stop doing that. I don't know why."

"I've had men compliment me, though. There are actually men who are into it."

"Really?"

"Oh, yeah. Some are obsessed with it. But it's very hard for a man to innocently compliment a woman on her mustache. There's no way he can come off as sincere without sounding like he's mocking her."

Louisa and Lixin laughed.

"'Oh,'" mimed Marguerite as she leaned toward Lixin, "'I just want to let you know that I'm into mustachioed women and I really, really love your mustache. Please don't misunderstand me. I truly admire your mustache. I really do.' Or, the type who's afraid to make things worse by giving excuses and just gets to the point: 'I like your mustache,'" she deadpanned.

More laughing.

"Or, because he doesn't want to sound fake, he...he..." — Marguerite was in convulsions too now — "he says with a knowing grin, 'That's a helluva mustache you got there, babe. More power to ya!'"

Lixin sprayed out the wine she had just gulped onto Marguerite. They guffawed for a minute before catching their breath.

"I'm so sorry!" she said.

"I haven't had a good laugh like that in a while," said Louisa. "Getting back to — " they laughed some more. "Oh, my goodness. Getting back to your rugs, what design did you choose for the rug you're making?"

"One of my own. I don't do traditional designs. See that scrapbook over there? Have a look."

Louisa went over to the worktable and paged through the book. "These are so amazing. Wherever did you find the ideas for these?"

Marguerite and Lixin got out of the tub and dried off. While Lixin got dressed, Marguerite walked naked over to the kitchen and retrieved a jar from a spice rack. "I'm carrying on the tradition of the Scythians, using this," she said as her swaying body ambled up to them as if bearing a votive offering.

"What is it?"

"Deems."

"What's that?"

"A sacred medicine."

"Never heard of it," said Louisa.

In her jeans and still topless, Lixin grabbed the jar from Marguerite. "What this?"

"Have you done acid or shrooms?"

"Sure," said Louisa.

"This is to acid, as acid is to cannabis. It's a technology for communicating with aliens."

"Sounds scary. It's not dangerous?"

"Can I try?" said Lixin.

"Do I look like I have problems? Lixin, how do you feel?"

"It's very interesting and funny feeling, but a kind of struggle in my head."

"Maybe you're not ready for deems, dear."

"I got really fucked up on acid once. I don't see how anything can be stronger than acid," said Louisa.

"The advantage of deems is it's really strong only for a few minutes and then wears off."

"What's it like?"

"Actually, the brain produces it naturally when you dream. And the lungs, too. You know why certain types of yoga that use breathing techniques, like Kundalini yoga, are so popular? When you do sustained, heavy breathing, you start to hallucinate from the deems that's released in your lungs. This is the concentrated form."

"Oh, is this DMT?"

"Yes. Think of it as the ultimate soma."

"Where did you get it?"

"I made it myself."

"You made it yourself? How?"

"I extracted it. And these designs," Marguerite said as she fanned through the pages of her scrapbook, "were given to me by aliens."

"Extraterrestrials?"

"Yeah. The machine elves."

"You're kidding."

"No."

"Well, I've never seen anything like this. What are these things in this one? DNA strands?"

"Yes. The universal language. The code. It's not just the chemical building block of life, but the universal internet for advanced forms of intelligence. DNA was seeded on earth for the purpose of communicating with the aliens."

"You're going to turn all of these designs into rugs?"

"If I ran a rug factory and had a bunch of slaves, I could!"

"You have these ideas when you smoke this drug?" said Lixin.

"Sacred medicine, dear."

"Which one of these is the rug you're working on? Oh, this one with the liquid shapes?" said Louisa.

"Yeah, that one."

"It looks like a Persian rug as if Salvador Dali had designed it. Really psychedelic. You know what it also reminds me of? Australian Aborigine art."

"That art is inspired by hallucinogenic medicines too."

"These drawings are works of art. You could exhibit them. And this one, with the repeated patterns. It looks more like a traditional rug pattern, but trippier, with a 3D effect."

"Psychedelic lozenges. They move and shift when you stare at them."

"Can I take photos of them?" said Louisa.

"No."

"Oh. You probably want to protect them."

"The designs are safe and sound."

"But no one can know about this work you're doing, Marguerite. You have to do something with these images." She slapped the scrapbook down on the table. "You can't just let them sit there!"

Lixin brought the bong over and set it on the table. "I want to try it."

"This is heavy stuff, honey. You have to respect it. You had three hits of my weed. You know what's going to happen if you have just one hit of this?"

"What will happen?"

"You will have a hard time finding this table to set the bong back down on. Two hits and you'll be suspended in a geometric matrix called the 'waiting room.' Three hits and you'll break through and meet the aliens. You won't return the same person."

"Should we really be giving this stuff to her?" said Louisa.

"Will I become addicted?"

"No, not at all. It doesn't work like that. For some people, once is enough."

"I want to try a little now."

"You don't give up easily. Okay, I can give you one small hit today, and then if you take to it, we'll proceed to the waiting room next time, and maybe break through after that. But don't say I didn't warn you. Sit down on the chair. In fact, we have to use this." Marguerite pulled out a small glass pipe. In its bowl she placed a pinch of the crystals.

"Maybe you shouldn't, Marguerite. She can't possibly know what she's getting into."

"Have you ever done DMT, Louisa?"

"No, but everything you're saying confirms what I've heard. Aren't you worried about having all this stuff on you, in this country?"

"I don't arrange my life around fear. I'll get you started, Lixin. Just before I give you the pipe, exhale deeply. When I give you the pipe, take it all in and hold it in as long as you can."

"Lixin, don't. You're not ready for this now."

"Why not?"

Marguerite pulled out a torch lighter.

"Marguerite, don't give it to her!"

"Louisa, I am not a child," said Lixin.

"No!" Louisa grabbed Lixin and yanked her away.

"Louisa, calm down. I'm only giving her a small amount." Marguerite turned to Lixin. "Do you really want to try it?"

Lixin sluffed off Louisa. "Yes, I want to try it."

"Now, remember to exhale and then take it in as soon as I hand you the pipe."

Marguerite held the flame over the bowl and drew in the white vapor until it filled the chamber. Lixin sucked in the vapor. After a few moments she coughed it out, her face wrinkled in disgust. "Horrible taste — oh, I feel it already." She looked around her with a dazed expression. "Oh....Oh...."

They watched her intently. She soon started to sob.

"Are you okay, Lixin?" said Louisa.

"She's fine. Don't bother her."

"She's crying."

"She's fine. She really is."

"Lixin?" Louisa went up to her behind the chair and wrapped her arms around her.

"Let her be," said Marguerite, gently removing Louise's arms from Lixin.

Lixin stood up and walked over to the futon. She lay down upon it in fetal position and closed her eyes.

"I hope she's okay."

"She's fine. If you try some, you will be able to understand what she's experiencing."

"Why did you give it to her, knowing she's vulnerable?"

"Why do you assume she's vulnerable? Why would she be any more vulnerable than you? She wanted to do it. She has intense curiosity. If I had refused to give it to her, she wouldn't stop harassing me until she got her hands on it. The urge to attain altered states of consciousness is universal. Also, she's in love with me."

"In love with you!"

"Can't you tell?"

"I think," a smiling Lixin said as she turned face up, "that was the most beautiful experience I ever have in my life."

"Glad to hear it, honey," said Marguerite.

"What did you feel?" said Louisa.

"Everything vibrating. And then everything turn into shapes like we studied in geometry class. Too difficult to describe. I still see the shapes. Oh, my god."

"I was so worried."

"Why worried? You should try this. You have to try this."

"I don't know. I'm sorry. I overreacted. I guess I'm just super sensitive about how women can be abused. I can't get that thing out of my head about the guy who beat up that woman in the café. It's probably my lawyer job. We deal with all kinds of expat cases, some of them violent."

"He sounds atrocious. But why be upset about it?" said Marguerite. "Maybe if you knew either of them. I can't get upset over something like that if I have no personal connection to the people involved. In an abstract way it's upsetting, but not emotionally."

"Anyway. The person who told me knew someone who knew her. One thing I now recall her saying is that the book the guy was writing on massage was printed in Renaissance style, of all things."

"Now that's interesting," said Marguerite. "One of my favorite topics."

"I don't know what she meant by that."

"They printed text in the margins in Renaissance books, a sort of metacommentary on the main text. It was a holdover from Medieval manuscripts, you know, with the margins exquisitely ornamented in gold leaf."

"Yet just because a man has literary abilities doesn't

mean he isn't capable of the most extreme violence."

"From what I know about amnesia, people who have it have always had it. I mean they have the tendency, a condition. Like epilepsy. It's hard to suddenly get amnesia for the first time out of the blue, unless from a head trauma. What did he do to her? Was he trying to kill her?"

"That's why I can't get it out of my head. The viciousness of it."

"Strange I never heard anything about it. Extreme incidents like this usually get into the news. Especially when a foreigner is involved. You remember that story a few years ago, the British guy in China who boasted about seducing all those women in his blog? He got run out of the country by the 'human flesh finders.' Only because he bragged. And that Russian guy on the train, the cellist, who rested his feet on top of the seat in front of him? Also run out of the country. Bam, out! Never knew what hit him."

"I know worse than that," said Louisa. "You heard about that French guy who got stabbed to death by his Chinese wife when she caught him with another woman? I guess she was from the countryside and he found someone more educated. He was a pretty good-looking guy, too, from his pictures in the news. Sad."

"Yeah, I heard about that one. That was in Shanghai too," said Marguerite. "Did you hear about that case, Lixin?"

"What? What you talking about?"

"She's still high."

"Anyway, the idea of uploading someone's nude pics on the internet without their knowledge, isn't it just the most disgusting thing imaginable?"

"That's why he beat her so badly, because he couldn't stand being confronted about it."

"And he obviously had no feelings for her."

"Do you know the café where it happened?"

"No."

"The staff there would have called the police. It must have been a real scene. If you could find that out from your friend, they would know. Just go back there and ask. We could figure out the story. Do you think it was hushed up for some reason?"

"The problem is that friend of mine and I had a falling out and we're no longer on speaking terms."

"Oh, well. You're sure it wasn't in the news?"

"I want some more of that drug," said Lixin.

"No, not today. Wait a couple days before trying it again. I'll do some with you next time."

"I do recall the café had a French name."

"That's not very helpful, with so many cafés and restaurants in Shanghai with French names. Not to mention all those faux French café chains that are actually Korean chains. But why would a litterateur, a writer if that's really what he was, do something so tacky and banal, and dangerous, as to upload someone's nude photos on the internet?"

"He was broke? Writers often are."

"But he couldn't have gotten any money out of it. Not unless she was famous. It wouldn't be worth the risk."

"Maybe she was pretty well known, by enough people that someone recognized her."

"The thing is, who actually follows those sites? If it's a famous person, there are sites devoted just to them. She wouldn't be on those. It would only be one of countless amateur sites. I think the chances of anyone she knows regularly surfing every site and just happening to encounter her pics is pretty miniscule. Plus, they're all blocked in China."

"Lots of Chinese use VPNs."

"Not that many, actually. It's too much trouble. I know a lot of Chinese, including many educated ones. They have more than enough here to keep themselves busy with and don't need the international web. There are many other ways to get porn, if that's what they want. In fact, I bet you ninety percent of porn consumption in China today is simple sexting among friends on WeChat. That's the best porn there is, because it's people you know. What probably happened was she sexted him some pics of herself and he passed them on to his friends, as men tend to do. It got back to her and things got ugly. Sexting is happening right now, millions of times a day, all over the world. Everyone who participates in this activity is to blame. I don't know. I just have a different take on it. You send someone a shot of your boobs and then blame them when they break their promise not to show them to anyone else? What hypocrisy. If you really don't want anyone to share your pics, then don't give them out in the first place."

"Unless he took nude photos of her secretly, without her knowledge?"

"We don't know that. Something doesn't sound right about this story, and now I'm curious to know what really happened. Perhaps he had a reason to beat her. I don't mean beating someone can ever be justified, but there might be a logical explanation of what led up to it."

"Sounds logical enough to me."

"Or maybe he didn't even beat her. Maybe it's all blown up out of proportion. And that's why it never got in the news. It was just a petty incident, and we got a one-sided view of it from the injured party."

"But Marguerite, he beat her severely enough to give her amnesia. I'd rather presume the worst until evidence to the contrary."

"She didn't necessarily get amnesia from being hit. It could have been just a big fight they had, and she was so upset or so angry that it was she who lost it. She may have given herself amnesia."

"Why are you saying this? Why are you defending him?"

"I'm hardly defending him. I'm just speculating based on the scanty evidence."

"Well, I've got to go. Thanks for the wine and the weed. I'll see you later, Lixin."

Louisa grabbed her things and stepped out the door.

"Louisa, wait!" Lixin threw her bra and shirt on. "Sorry, I

better go with her."

"Looks like I got her in a huff."

"I'll contact you," said Lixin, giving Marguerite a quick hug.

2

She was of conventional family background, from Jinan in Shandong Province, or more probably the surrounding countryside. Her household had not much in the way of refinement, no books but school textbooks, no music but television jingles, nothing adorning the walls but a calendar. Her father at least respected education enough to dole out regular beatings — the traditional way of ensuring a child's success at school — and Luna graduated with a bachelor's degree in English. This would have been in the mid-1990s, when China was opening up in earnest. The survivalist outlook of her parents' generation spawned by the warless war economy was giving way to a more upholstered life, seized upon by some among the younger generation. Little freedoms were blooming all around, hesitantly plucked at first, later with more abandon. Earlier in the decade it was still possible for a Chinese woman accompanying a foreigner out on the street to be apprehended by the police, charged with "hooliganism" (prostitution) and sent to a labor camp for three years; by decade's end they were striding into foreigners' hotel rooms and campus guesthouses as staff looked the other way. It was also in the nineties that curious foreigners began to arrive in the Middle Kingdom, many to work as English teachers.

Between Luna's graduation and her first encounter with Isham Cook in 2004, we can assume several developments. First, she was talented at language. She continued to hone her English skills well beyond what was required of a teaching job in the private schools where she found work, cultivating a fluent conversational English with a convincing American accent. Second, she had contact with foreign male instructors and decided that for romantic purposes they were better suited to her than her own countrymen. She additionally had a fixation on older foreign guys, in their forties or fifties. They were less aggressive and threatening, more respectful of Chinese female virtue, than their younger competitors. As we shall see, she had a daddy complex as well, and was thus in search of a father surrogate, one kinder and more patient than her own and whom she could baby in turn like a son.

A year or so before she first met Isham, something happened. Her school invited "foreign experts" from an English-language consulting firm in Shanghai on brief stints for teacher training. Luna was assigned to pick them up at the train station and attend on them. On one of these visits the consultant, an American, asked her to dinner and then to his hotel room. He plied her with wine. We don't know what transpired. She only confessed it to Isham — a few weeks after they had first met — because he was the second foreign male to get her into bed, but she couldn't bring herself to elaborate.

Isham was a university lecturer in Shanghai. He freelanced at the same consulting firm, and was the latest trainer (he preferred to be called a "technician" of English) to be sent to Luna's school. Her appearance at once enraptured him, this female full of contrasts. She had, as he described it, a primitively alluring face, a rudely attractive face, with her large mouth and sensuous lips. She used no makeup but was smartly dressed that day in a business suit and knee-length skirt. Her black hair, which she wore in a bob, was streaked with natural silver hairs. This apparent premature aging is always mortifying to a woman afflicted with it. Yet he was impressed she refrained from dying them out and told her they added to her sexiness, as did her hairy legs shining through her nylon stockings. But it was the unshaven hairs on her upper lip, dense enough at the corners of the mouth to be noticeable across the room, that really set him afire. On top of it all, she comported herself with confidence and professionalism, unlike many younger Chinese women with their gendered penchant for shyness and awkwardness. Her carrying on as if she had no idea she was sporting a mustache only enticed him the more. She sensed his attraction and approached him to exchange cellphone numbers.

Back in Shanghai a day later, he wanted to see her as soon as possible. She knew a receptionist at a hotel where he could get a favorable rate and booked a room. She used the words "we" and "our" in referring to the room she had found for them, and this also excited him. Few Chinese women would admit their intention to stay overnight with a man they had just met. As anywhere, it's impolite to expect sex on the first date. True, Isham was making the journey from another city and they would only have two nights together. They might as well be practical about it and get down to business; at least they could get started and make out a bit: thus might dating Westerners reason. That's not how things operate in China, where women's "sex face" is paramount. Sex face is the self-dignity bespeaking the gravity of the act. The herculean task might require a lengthy period of courtship (months or years) or the explicit promise of marriage, but even when expeditiously negotiated the man is required to undergo a calculated procedure of humiliation. His fumbling effort to express his desire will have his worst suspicions confirmed, that it was indeed misplaced and offensive in the extreme. Whatever gave him the idea she

could even consider doing — the word itself is taboo — *that?*
Had he no respect? Profuse apologies are of no use; he's
blown his chances and beats a hasty retreat. On condition
he reflect deeply and seriously on his moral failings, however,
she may later offer to resurrect their acquaintance — if she
likes him.

This is not to be mistaken for Victorian-style prudery. It's
another phenomenon altogether and indigenous to the
culture. To understand it, you have to adopt the Chinese
perspective for getting on in life, which differs from most
other cultures in being quantitatively based. The basic
principle is additive: whatever works, requires more of the
same. Goals are reached through sheer effort. If you fail to
achieve results, you simply aren't trying hard enough. For
example, if you want to pass an exam, you study long and
hard. It's neither a lack of training or intelligence, nor faulty
technique, but poor time management alone that explains
failure: all the valuable hours sacrificed to eating, sleeping or
otherwise procrastinating. You just didn't study enough.
Want to get promoted? Work longer hours, cut more deals
and sell more products. This requires not only that you
spend every waking minute on the job, but you are also
faster and more productive per hour than your colleagues.
The same applies to intellectual labor. Want to develop
cutting-edge software or other inventions? Get a more
muscular brain: concentrate harder and sustain that
concentration longer than anyone else.

The quantitative principle is just as important in human
relations. To get what you want from people, you insist and
you persist and you don't give up until they give in. If you
want to win a woman's heart, you don't stop until she yields
the fort. And she won't yield, not if she can help it, well
hardened as she is to the male battering ram. Taking offense
to sexual advances is woman's defense, a highly rational one
at that, against the expected attack. I have an anecdote from
a Chinese female friend. In her last semester of graduate
school, a male student approached her one day and invited

her to coffee in the library cafeteria. Out of politeness she agreed. She agreed again a few days later, but only for the purpose of informing him she had a boyfriend. This was not about to stop him, of course, as this "boyfriend" was surely fictitious, the first of her defensive moves (he had been observing her for some time and she was always alone). He made repeated attempts to take her out, all of which she rebuffed. She had to stop studying in the library to avoid him. He began waiting for her outside her dorm building. She greeted him diplomatically at first, then ignored him. Thereafter she made a point of only going about with a classmate, and when that didn't work, visited the History Department, where he was a PhD candidate, to complain to the head, but this too had no effect. Finally, the semester came to an end, she graduated and was free of the pest. Yet not for long. A lax secretary divulged her new address, and she found him outside her new residence on the other side of the city. She had to make two trips to the local police before the harassment petered out.

We seem to be dealing here, at least from a Western perspective, with a mental case, an obsessive-compulsive disorder for want of a better term; I'm not sure there's a diagnosis for those who stalk. From the Chinese perspective, though, we don't need psychology to explain the guy. His behavior was perfectly logical and there was nothing wrong with him. He knew what he wanted and was just very thorough in pursuing it. He held out the hope, not unrealistic and likely attainable through mere patience, that she would wake up one day regarding her revulsion in a new light, and give the poor lad another shot. It would make everything so much easier for herself were she to cut him some slack and humor him. The burden of being preyed upon would vanish once she realized he had positive qualities. And once the revolution was underway, it would only be a matter of time before she found herself sleeping with him. At the same time, he was clearheaded enough to know this was probably wishful thinking. But even at the risk of jeopardizing his reputation in the History Department, or the inconvenience of a few days spent in administrative detention, he would try every resource at his disposal until immovable obstacles were placed in his way. That he had tried his best to land this rare creature, possibly successfully, would be far preferable to the subsequent torture of having failed because he had *not tried hard enough*.

Seeing is believing, and having held himself in suspense until this moment, Isham was relieved to be whisked by Luna into their hotel room as if it were the most normal thing in the world. They had had a nice dinner beforehand, and he maintained the congenial mood by taking it slow. When he made his move, her lips met his and her clothes practically fell off. To his further delight, where he expected to find within her black bush the swollen gash glistening red, brown or purple, hers was the color of ivory. Never had he seen such a gorgeous vulva.

And at this point they hit the wall. Her vaginal muscles were clamped tight as a fist. He had racked up a number of deflorations over his career and fancied he knew how to go about it. Some girls are refreshingly unsentimental and once they've renounced the virginity cult wish to get the operation over with. Others need a couple sessions. For every woman it's painful, for some excruciating, but the worst is soon over. Isham tried settling her on top to allow her weight to sink onto him. He tried everything short of brute force. No matter how many positions were rotated over the sleepless night, her groin would retract and pull away even as it ground against him. She did have some raw desire for him, at least her mouth did for his cock. But when using his own mouth on her she would gasp in pain. In the morning they tried again. Her body was in complete rebellion. That's when she confessed the hotel incident with his colleague, whose name she refused to reveal.

"Well," Isham asked her, "did he rape you, or what?" She could not or would not say. "Did he force you? Did he penetrate you?" Silence. "It's *okay*. You can tell me. There's nothing shameful and it's not your fault. I'm not going to laugh at you or blame you. You'll feel better if you come out with it. What happened?" More silence. "Are you a virgin or not?"

To this all she could do was shake her head and mumble, "I don't know."

The frustrations were repeated the next night, with nary a millimeter of progress. Still, Isham was back in Jinan a week later. The second journey was important symbolically. It would reassure Luna he wasn't just after a quick fuck but respected the magnitude of the occasion, and took her seriously enough to devote this much time and effort, with moreover no reassurance of more progress.

More progress there was not. On the train back to Shanghai once again, he now reflected that a third visit, any time soon at least, would be pointless. He could see Zeno's paradox at work — the closer he was the further away he'd be. He considered everything. One factor which on the surface might have seemed decisive could be dismissed out of hand. He had informed her at the outset that he had a girlfriend, who was living with him. This was not an insurmountable obstacle; had it been, she would never have approached him in the first place. Naturally she had supposed he was married, as are almost all men in China over thirty. Because everyone is married, wedding bands aren't obligatory and there is more leeway to fool around. Everyone assumes everyone else is married. This makes it all the easier to enter into affairs.

In any case, he mused, it was only a matter of giving her some time, time to let this opportunity of putting herself on solid footing as a poised and confident woman, by which we mean no longer a virgin, sink in. If indeed she still was a virgin. Might there not be a darker reality? She had told him about her strained relationship with her parents. She had nothing good to say about them, her father in particular, and had long moved out. Isham knew not to inquire about staying at her place instead of a hotel; single Chinese women always have roommates and it's in bad form. He was just curious to know about her living circumstances. She refused to admit anything. Everything about her was a mystery. If her life was a monolithic blank, could it be something unmentionable underlay it? Had her father abused her sexually, and then the former American guy did something to compound it and seal her misery? Or maybe neither man had done anything that egregious, and Luna was dysfunctional from the start, as some people are, and if they are Chinese will always be, where there is no mental health industry to speak of despite token services. University students seldom get up the nerve to visit a campus counselor for psychological problems out of fear of being exposed and expelled, and workplaces offer nothing. No person would ever reveal their horrible secret even to their own mother. It's just something you bury deep inside.

An alternative idea occurred to him, one not necessarily involving psychosexual trauma. He recalled once reading about a disorder called vestibulitis, abnormally sensitive nerve endings at the entrance to the vagina, rendering intercourse painful. It supposedly affected up to fifteen percent of females. Though a simple operation could cure it, it wasn't well known even among Western doctors. There was no place a Chinese woman afflicted with it could turn to for help. She would have to be lucky enough to learn she even had it and find a place to perform the operation abroad. He called it up again on the internet only to find there now existed a host of related afflictions — so many he wondered if any women enjoyed pain-free sex. There was vulvodynia, which might or might not be the same as vestibulitis; a painkiller rather than an operation was advised. And there was vaginismus, the involuntary hammering of the pelvic muscles against the inner vagina, which was indeed psychosomatic and could only be cured by therapy. Isham sent Luna a text message asking if she might not have one of these conditions, knowing full well a response to the bizarre question, in a culture where women are not taught to take responsibility for their sexuality, would not be forthcoming.

With that, he set about forgetting her.

A month later, she contacted him to announce she was moving to Shanghai where she had found a teaching job. She asked to stay with him for a few days while she arranged her own accommodation. Bonnie, his live-in Chinese girlfriend, reluctantly agreed, knowing him well enough; Isham wasn't the sort to shack up with a woman who wasn't openminded about things like this. They made space for her on the living-room couch. This was disheartening to Luna, as was the sound of their lovemaking at night. She then did her best to create tension in the air, by refusing to speak to Bonnie. When Bonnie was out, Isham made a couple more attempts with her in bed. It didn't help he was growing impatient, curtailing things to a mere half hour, if that long, before getting dressed and dismissing her. At last, giving up trying to explain things face to face, he informed her in an email:

> Out of China's 700 million women, congratulations on having the imagination to join the majority, almost all of whom are conventional and mired in relationship jealousy. Here I am offering you the opportunity to liberate yourself and rise above the swamp of pettiness, and you all the more stubbornly insist on being just like everyone else. Are you proud of your ordinariness? Are you proud of being sexually self-centered?
>
> This is a polyamorous household. That means whatever group of adults, and of whatever sex, happen to be thrown together, it is their duty to accommodate. It could be two men and a woman. It could be five men and five women. It could be ten men and no women. Whatever the combination, they all adjust to one another. We are presently two women and a man. Now Bonnie, you may have suspected, is not women-oriented. She's heterosexual. Nonetheless, she tries. Because experimenting with women is part of her sexual development, and enlarging her conceptions is the philosophical thing to do. But it only works with friendliness and camaraderie on all sides. In response to

our hospitality, we thought you'd provide some generosity of your own, say chipping in for food, or cooking a meal, or helping to clean up a bit, or if these are all too much of a challenge, at the very least you'd offer your body, on your own initiative and not guiltily in secret to me alone, to both of us.

Bonnie had a different take on the matter: "Isham, look at the way she dresses. She wears that stupid T-shirt with the cartoon characters over a long-sleeved dress! And those shoes and white socks and the pink ribbons in her hair — she's like a six-year-old. Did you see what she eats every day? Spam sausage in instant noodles for breakfast, lunch and dinner. And when you're not here she sits there on the couch and she rocks, back and forth, staring into space. She obviously has mental problems. Why do you waste your time on this rural trash? I thought you had better taste in women."

Luna soon left and was out of the way. They expected they would not be hearing from her again. Failure to turn her into a woman was too bad, after all the effort that went into it, an increasingly ridiculous and degrading business, one that should have been halted earlier. It was not a question of dignity but of common sense. The idea of a woman on the verge of thirty stuck in sexual infancy was, quite frankly, disgusting. Isham assumed Luna would be too mortified to contact him again, and he wasn't planning on contacting her.

Nevertheless, he underestimated and misunderstood her capacity for kindness. Pure kindness is infinitely patient and immune to doubt. The email started rolling in. She acknowledged in somewhat cryptic fashion the logic of his arguments:

> You hit on the point in your email. Beat up and collapsed, I dare no longer look you in the eye while facts jump out of your mouth. Thanks for that hit-and-run which was like a morning call. The harder you hit, the stronger I am transformed. Fine. A form of a prayer, the

morning call serves to help you tune into a frequency. It wakes up or activates the awareness. The frequency shapes the life of people and needs to be heard. Otherwise, one is lost and gets nowhere. The frequency is equal to the total population of people and things. Abundant. And I ended up being seriously overdosed on endorphins and dopamine. With that, I fought against the sleepless night, and epinephrine won. On the other hand, no people are upset or uncomfortable about sex. No one. Naturally! How could all the planet's species come into being if there was no sex? It's a holy godly given gift.

Then again, she could be clear and straightforward:

> Little Isham, today is a brand-new day and a brand-new week and a brand-new month. To begin the brand new with the end in mind, I'm listening to what your lines are saying. Excuse me, may I get carried away a bit and try to whisper something? May I, as a silver-haired friend, remind you that togetherness means more than marriage. And time means love. You are in. Cherish it before it's too late or you'll lose it. A more appropriate way is to express a sense of care. It's a good feeling to know someone cares about you. And you might want to be listened to as well. If so, I'm all ears (and eyes since all we have now is email), when you feel you want to tell me how you have been doing, even if you don't feel like telling me anything.

Her letters continued to arrive on a daily basis, many about his estranged relationship with his mother. Luna found it incomprehensible he neglected to make any effort to amend things and at least keep the lines of communication open with the person who gave him his life. There were also frequent emails about his health and diet:

> I'm not a physically strong person but I can't remember when I last caught a cold. I happened to evolve into a state like this by using cold water to wash my face every winter morning. I take a hot shower before going to

bed in evenings. I just don't shower on winter mornings. Challenge yourself to use cold water to wash your face every winter morning. Dude, it's really tough. But if I can manage it, you can, too. And I bet you'll never catch a cold again.

In her capacity for kindness Luna could be quite creative. Imagine having spent your life in failed relationships, and then being confined to an environment where opportunities for meeting people were diminished, isolated from society in a remote rural area, a strange country, a penal colony, or which is equivalent, by middle age itself, when you become repellant to those younger than you, no matter how handsome you were in your prime. Imagine musing, all alone in your shack, cabin or trailer, on the most poignant of those long-lost loves, perhaps one in particular, the woman you blew off most cruelly precisely because she was the most loving and attentive of them all, and how wrong you had been in doing so, a truth realized too late, after the severing of all lines of communication, her email address long forgotten or inactive. Now imagine one day, just when you are thinking about this very woman, you see for a split second her apparition appear and disappear in your window. A hallucination. No, it can't be. And the face pops into view again, less hesitant now, a smiling angel, a miracle!

Isham wasn't in such dire straits, still hale and hearty enough to enjoy the attention of more than a few "robust female specimens," as he liked to refer to them, including one now living with him, that old warhorse who stuck with him after all the others had fallen by the wayside, Bonnie. But as her emails were no longer returned and she had not been invited back, Luna felt she needed to reach out with a bit of playful drama. She had been observing what time Bonnie left for work and the days Isham wasn't in class. One morning she went round to his side of the foreign experts' guesthouse and peeked through a gap in the curtains of his bedroom window. The morning, while one is still in bed, is the most erotic time of the day — he'd likely be having an erection that very moment — and the circumstances most propitious. She felt herself to be ready, readier than she had ever been. He'd surely find the spontaneity of her arrival arousing in its own right. She wasn't intending to be noticed when poking her face in the window, just wanted to confirm he was there, yet she hoped to be noticed, as it meant he lay in expectation of her.

Well, he did notice her. Throwing on some clothes and dashing outside, he grabbed her by the arm and yanked her in the direction of the school gate. He wanted to smack her in the face but kicked her on the shin instead. "Fuck you!" he yelled.

"Isham, what — " She was at a loss for words and tears came to her eyes. "Why?"

"Oh, I'm getting a reaction out of you. You're beginning to get it. You have just made a tremendous leap in understanding. You see that I am angry. Yet I fear you're only halfway there, and we're not going to get anywhere until you understand *why* I am angry."

"Isham, I only wanted to — "

"*Why* am I angry?"

"I don't know."

"I'll tell you why. You are *stalking* me. Do you know what stalking is?"

"I...I..."

"Did I ask you to visit me?"

"No, but I just — "

"Did it not occur to you I might be with someone?"

Marching her to the school gate, he told the guard he was being harassed and not to allow the woman back on campus again. Guards at Chinese universities tend not to involve themselves in petty disputes. Luna returned over the next few weeks, waiting for Isham to emerge from the guesthouse as she stood forlorn at a distance, wishing he would melt and speak to her. She knew he was about to make a long-awaited trip back to the U.S. for the remainder of the summer, and was waiting for him again when the taxi to the airport arrived. She ran after his taxi as it drove away.

Two months later he was back in Shanghai. He had blocked her cellphone number but not her emails: he wanted to monitor them in case the harassment took a more threatening turn. But she appeared to have gotten the message and was no longer to be seen, and her email became more sporadic until it stopped.

Isham had a longtime friend, Jim Spear, from northern Wisconsin. Jim's two decades of travel to distant ports while serving in the navy had left him with a taste for the East, and upon retirement he launched into Chinese-language study at the Shanghai university where Isham was teaching at the time. They met in the foreigner cafeteria and hit it off. Though from deer country, redneck territory, Jim was a Democrat and into the blues, while Isham, a leftist Chicagoan with a PhD in rhetoric, was into early classical music. Jim was from a hunting family: a Ruger 22 semi-auto pistol, a Smith & Wesson police 38, a Springfield 22 rifle, and an AK-47 (an effective hunting gun which would also come in handy against hostile foragers when the U.S. economy collapsed) were the only firearms he needed; Isham was afraid to look at a gun. But they had a few things in common. Both were atheists, down-to-earth in temperament, straight talkers, with a fondness for craft ales and voluptuous Asian bodies.

They returned to the U.S. for a spell around the same time, and Isham drove up from Chicago to visit Jim in his rented flat in Green Bay, on the second floor of a house overlooking Lake Michigan. Jim was one for hospitality. He cooked venison steak from a deer bagged by him and his father on their annual November hunt, and insisted Isham have his bed while he slept on the couch. Isham brought his Kodak projector and carousels of hundreds of nude photos he had taken of Chinese and Japanese women over the years. Jim's white curtains, stretched taut, were perfect for projecting the images on. Halfway through the slideshow a horrifying thought occurred to them. Jim dashed outside and to their relief found the street deserted: the porn show — erotic photography, Isham corrected — had been brightly projected to any passersby. They had a good laugh over this.

Isham had introduced Luna to Jim, and the two became friendly. When Isham cut her off, she turned to Jim for solace, and he began receiving her email. Jim was as keenly attracted to her as Isham had been (hirsute women being another of their shared interests).

"Please, please, take her, she's all yours," Isham told him. "I wish you better luck than me."

On a return trip to Shanghai, Jim managed to get her over to his place, but she was preoccupied with Isham and sat stiffly the whole time. They fell out of touch after he returned to the U.S.

On his next trip to Shanghai ten years later, Jim looked her up and she was amenable to a date. She seemed to have matured; more contemplative, as if having undergone some psychological trial, while she gave no suggestion of being hooked up with a man. "She's put on weight. She was wearing a tight skirt and you shoulda seen how round that ass of hers is now," Jim told him.

Isham perked up at this. Could it be that time had turned her into a worthier creature? Had she mellowed over the years and acquired some wisdom, some character, some inner peace, on top of a ripening figure? He was one of those rare birds, a man drawn to women in their forties and fifties. She wasn't quite forty, but Jim's news changed things. He contacted her. She played coy at first, and it took a few exchanges before she agreed to see him.

He booked a room and they met in a seafood restaurant next to the hotel. But despite having accepted his dinner invitation, she refused to eat any of the food he ordered. For the sake of digestive health and weight loss, she explained, a full meal should be eaten only at lunch, and a snack in the evening. He wanted to know how she had been getting on over the years. She said she volunteered for an animal rescue organization.

"Yes, you've always been doing that. And you've always taken in stray cats. That's good of you. But what's your job? Your day job?"

She was watching him eat. "Isham, you need to adopt my suggestions if you want to lose weight."

"I agree, I could lose a little weight. Can't we all? I know the midday meal is more important than supper. I used to live in Europe, where it's the custom. But you're not answering my question. I want to know what your job is. Is that too much to ask?"

"I worry about your health. At your age — "

"I'm trying to have a conversation with you, and you're talking to yourself. Are you aware of that?"

" — the metabolism slows down and exercise isn't — "

He slammed down his chopsticks. "Why can't you answer my question? What's your fucking job?" He got up, paid the bill and walked out.

Luna followed him outside. "Isham, I'm sorry."

He took her up to the hotel room and did his best to calm down. After getting out of their clothes, he opened her legs. She seemed to be even hairier than he recalled. The trend of trimming the pubic bush down to a thin vertical strip, sparked by American porn of the nineties, had evolved further. These days only baby-smooth genitalia were considered civilized, with Japan and China the last redoubts, though it couldn't be long before they too succumbed (the sad shaving of the erotic underarm hair was a fait accompli in China by this time). Isham respected this sexual naïf for one thing at least, simply allowing her body to be. He dug his face into her with a moaning hunger that's difficult to explain to those without the need. I suppose a meth addict's fix might be the best analogy, or a closeted gay man's desperation to get his mouth around his first cock. He took his time cunnilinguing her. Then when he placed himself at her entrance he lingered there, massaging the labia with his glans before pushing in ever so slightly. She gasped in pain and retracted. Once again, that was as far as they got.

He later reflected that the best solution would have been rape — benevolent rape. Force was not something he was inclined to use, but it would have taken care of the problem. For millennia that's how it was done. It's still done that way in less developed societies, places like rural Romania or Bulgaria, where women are kidnapped, literally carried away kicking and screaming by the pursuer and his male relatives. Was Luna of primitive provenance as well? Could her difficulties opening up be an unconscious expectation that only a real man, a warrior, was worthy of taking her virginity? He was confident she would not have regarded it as rape. On the other hand, he suspected she would be fully capable of threatening a rape charge in order to hold onto him.

With these uneasy thoughts it took a few months before Isham was ready to see her again. On this occasion he chose a different hotel, and he instructed her to meet him in the outdoor restaurant patio next door for dinner.

The evening culminated in a tub of margarine splattering against the hotel room wall.

3

They sat up on the bed. Lixin caressed Marguerite's mustache, pulling at the hairs. "Why it gets darker on the sides? I wish I could grow a mustache. Look, I'm growing hair back." She lifted up her armpits.

"But you can do *this*," said Marguerite, pointing between them.

"Still so wet. So sorry."

They burst out laughing.

"I said don't worry about it. Really. I'll buy one of those plastic waterproof things. I wish I could do that. You've got the gift."

"I can't control myself. I couldn't control myself for past five days. After what you did to me in bathtub."

"What do you mean?"

"You know what I mean. You were bad. Putting your toes between my legs."

"You put yours in me first."

"You did."

"No, you did."

"Did Louisa notice?"

"No."

"She noticed."

"No, she didn't."

"She did notice."

"She did not notice."

Marguerite took Lixin's nearest breast in her fingers and twisted it.

"Ow!"

"You don't need to WeChat me so much."

"I can't control myself."

"Yes, you can. One or two messages is enough. Not fifty."

"Fifty! No, it was that many?"

"About ten a day. You know, the fewer the messages, the more important each of them will be."

"You will get 100 every day I can't see you. I want to live with you. I'm tired of living with Louisa."

"Why?"

"She always complain. She's not happy."

"What about?"

"Everything. She says I'm brainwashed like all Chinese women. Says we're childish, always laughing at nothing and have no knowledge. If she's so smart why she in debt $90,000?"

"For what?"

"Student loan. She knows nothing about financial planning."

"That's what American universities cost. They don't have any choice."

"Chinese parents can pay for their children to study in U.S. They save money, no loans. Why can't American parents?"

"They're in debt too. But I agree. I've long believed there should be no such thing as math class. The class should be called Money and teach students how to save and invest. By the time they're in high school they're already investment gurus. There's no other practical use for mathematics."

"And she wants to sleep with me."

"Why don't you?"

"I just don't want to. I refused her."

"Sounds indeed like she's on the way out."

"What?"

"You want to move out?"

"I think I will."

"You could stay here. But you might find me more difficult to live with than you imagine."

"Why?"

"You'll see."

"Marguerite, really? That makes me so happy. I won't get in your way. I know your work is important. I can read when you're working — oh, just remembered."

Lixin got up and fetched a book out of her bag.

"What's this?"

"The book I told you about last time. On massage."

"My Chinese reading ability isn't that great. It'll take me a while to get through this. How is it?"

"Weird. I don't really like it. Maybe you will like it. Louisa thinks the author is same person who beat that woman in café."

Marguerite pointed to the dedication page. "This I can read: 'To everyone in my life who has praised my massage.' What an odd thing to say. I wonder if she praised the brutal face massage he gave her in the café." She flipped through the book. "Yep, this has that Renaissance-style text on the margins. What does the text say?"

"Just philosophy sayings, about sex freedom, things like that."

"She was the translator? Is that her name?"

"Yeah. Lu Na. I remember something in the book. He was in massage school in America. He got in trouble for going naked."

"Massage *school?*"

"And he spent years trying to visit every massage shop in China. He calls himself obsessive-compulsive massage neurotic."

"He admitted that too? That's funny. Here's a photo of

him on the back. A middle-aged guy."

Lixin jumped onto Marguerite and straddled her. "I want more of that drug."

"Deems? Hey, I got something else you might want to try. The toad."

"Toad? You mean frog?"

"Five-Meo. Also known as the void. Well, no, maybe that's not such a good idea now. You didn't have enough deems last time. The toad will be too much. Oh, I have an even better idea. Have you ever dropped acid?"

"What?"

"LSD."

"I heard of. It's not dangerous drug?"

"Not as strong as deems but stronger than that little dose you had. And it lasts the whole day. You've got today free, right? This will be your training session for the void. Next time we do it together we can hit the deems or the toad when the acid peaks."

"I don't understand — when acid peaks? Do what?"

"That's for next time."

"You will do it with me today?"

"Of course."

"Yes, I want to."

"You sure you're ready for this? It lasts the whole day."

"It's fun?"

"More than fun. We need to get into the mindset, though. We'll play hippies. Let me dress you. Then we'll go get some lunch and I'll explain more about what to expect."

Marguerite picked out a black V-neck halter top and Indian batik wrap skirt for Lixin; for herself, a bright orange robe and flaming pink bandana. "Put these on. We're going braless and pantyless."

"No bra and panties!"

"Acid teaches your mind how to breathe. Your body needs to breathe as well."

"Everybody will stare at us."

"So what? They'll stare anyway, trying to figure out what

the hot babe is doing with the strange foreign woman with a mustache. It's an honor to be stared at. You can exercise your freedom for one day, can't you? You're not going to the office, after all."

"You look like Buddhist nun in that," said Lixin as she maneuvered into the top and stretched it over her breasts. "This is offensive. People will think I'm a *liumang*. Hooligan."

"You're willing to drop acid without knowing anything about it but you're afraid to go braless! Your country needs more female hooligans. Well, suit yourself. Your black bra will go well with the top."

Lixin adjusted the top over her bra. "Still shows too much."

"It's your big tits. C'mon, you can show them off for one day after hiding them for the other 364 days of the year. Now, for the crowning touch." Marguerite gave her a long kiss on the mouth. Lixin tried to pull her back down on the futon. "No, let's go."

As she ordered them shawarma wraps and Brooklyn IPAs at Brothers Kebab in the South Shaanxi Road area, Marguerite responded to a question she had heard countless times before. "Of course I like Chinese food. I just need my Middle-Eastern fix. I'll take you to my favorite dumpling soup restaurant tonight, huge succulent mushroom pork dumplings."

"The *hundun* place next to Ximo Bieshu?"

"Yeah, the old Seymour House. With the crazy façade and the 'Juliet balcony.'"

"Another Middle-Eastern shop like this next to Lao Shanghai Hundun Pu. And the Rooster bar on Shaanxi Beilu where the American men go."

"How do you know all this?"

"I know where foreigners go. That soup is not dumplings. It's *hundun*."

"Yes, wonton soup. But they're so big they're like dumplings."

"When will you give me the LSD?"

"I already gave it to you."

"When? When we kissed?"

"There was a lot of stardust in that saliva I passed to you."

"Oh, no. What did I do? What will I feel?"

"It starts off a bit like weed, a happy, goofy feeling. As the feeling deepens, a sensation of awe comes over you. It's the mind's way of coming to terms with the scale of the experience you're about to have."

"Weed?"

"Marijuana. Then the show begins. Okay, imagine you got high on marijuana and went to an amusement park. You know the rush of sensations when you're strapped in a roller coaster and flying straight down, straight up, upside down and around in circles? Well, on weed, you could imagine, it would be a lot more intense. Now, a good strong hit of acid is something else altogether. You don't have to go to an amusement park because it turns your head into an amusement park."

"What do you mean? It's stronger than marijuana?"

"Oh, yeah. You experience *time* as a roller coaster. It speeds up and slows down. Or you're entirely detached from time, like it's a toy you can pick up and play with." Marguerite held up each hand. "You have five fingers because five minutes have passed, and it's hilarious because you have five fingers on your other hand and you don't know which came first and whether those five minutes have come or gone. Meanwhile, the idea of an 'hour' is so sad and alien it might as well be the moon."

"You're frightening me."

"Oh, but it's marvelous, even when it's scary." Marguerite paused for emphasis. "*Learn* to be scared. Drink that fear like it's the most expensive wine you've ever had. Acid is the greatest teacher."

They walked over to the city's main expat haunt, Aspidistra Books.

"Feeling anything yet?" said Marguerite as they sat down with their gelatos and coffee.

"No."

"I am. Oh, I forgot to bring that massage book. I wanted to have a closer look at it. Do you think they might have the English version?"

"I can ask."

Lixin returned a few minutes later with the book in hand. "They have it. I found it in health section."

"*Massage and the Writer.* Isham Cook. Here's that dedication again, 'To everyone in my life who has agreed to a massage.' Here the English makes a bit more sense. Do you think the translation is good overall?"

"It's okay, I think. Maybe too formal and proper. Oh, I feel something."

"I'm getting off too."

"I feel good. More sensitive. Everything looks sharper. I like it."

"I just thought of something," said Marguerite, dipping into the book. "Let's ask if they have this guy's contact information."

They went up to the cashier. He looked in their computer and seemed perplexed. "*Deng yihuir.*" He went upstairs to a back office and returned with the manager, who examined the book curiously.

"No record of this," said the cashier.

"What do you mean?"

"We never sold this book."

"Then why is it here?"

"*Wo ye bu zhidao.*"

"It's not officially listed," the manager explained to Marguerite. "Not on the government-approved list. That means we can't sell it. It looks like the kind of book that won't be approved."

"The author himself must have planted it here. Can I buy this? It doesn't have a price."

"You can just take it."

"Great, thanks."

"I'm really feeling it now," said Lixin as they sat back

down. "Your skin is glowing. Everything duplicated on you. Every hair is two hairs. You have two pairs of eyes, one below the other. Not like drunk on alcohol but very sharp and clear. The air is thick, like jelly."

"I'm going to see how much more of this I can read before I start getting restless myself."

Lixin got up and wandered around the store, peering at book covers as if she were an alien anthropologist.

"His writing actually isn't that bad," Marguerite said when Lixin returned. "How *are* you?"

Lixin typed into her cellphone. Marguerite's chimed and she picked hers up. "'How is the English translation?' It was originally written in English!"

"When you speak I can see your words fly out into the air," said Lixin. She typed another message.

"Why are you sending me messages? You can talk to me right here." Marguerite went back to her book.

Lixin was staring in front of her. "Oh, my god."

"Listen to this: 'A massage business could vastly increase its clientele if a bondage option were offered, where the customer is fastened to the massage table with shackles.'"

"I don't understand."

"It says massage shops should offer an S&M service, tying customers down to the table."

On the massage table, Lixin was silently crying.

"*Ni mei shi ma?*" asked Lingling.

Marguerite reassured her Lixin was fine and to continue. The two masseuses synchronized their strokes. As Ailing pushed her palms downward over Lixin's breasts, belly and pubic mound, Lingling glided her hands up each leg and into the vagina.

"Whoa! And listen to this: 'The normal person on the massage table expects oil, the madman the hatchet, the artist menstrual blood.'"

When they arrived, a masseuse was waiting for them in the lobby. "*Nihao*, Lingling!" Marguerite said as they embraced.

"*Haojiu meijian!*"

Marguerite introduced Lixin and they headed up to their room, joined by three more masseuses. The Thai-themed room was outfitted with Lotus figurines, wide massage tables draped with silk sashes, and soft flute music. The deluxe tables had indentations in the sides for resting one's arms on shelves underneath. They drew a curtain between the tables, separating them for privacy. The girls showered.

"I still don't understand."

"I mean time is bendable, flexible. Like Dali's melting clocks." Marguerite finished her IPA. "I need some coffee. You know Aspidistra Books?"

"Yes, I love that store."

"Later we can go to this massage shop that specializes in four-hands massage. I'm friends with the masseuses there. I used to work with one of them at the old place." Marguerite leaned forward. "They'll do you erotically if you want. Four hands on you at the same time. Totally mindblowing on acid."

"Are you sure I'll be okay?"

"The one thing you have to remember is no matter how scary it gets, it will pass. It can turn from funny to scary and back to funny again in minutes. Go with the flow. Don't run away from it. You can't. You can't run away from yourself."

"Sometimes I think I'm a savage inside."

"I just thought of another place nearby I can show you later, an art gallery slash teahouse and women artists' collective. I know the owner. She and her friends once staged a performance piece where they served the customers naked."

"That's illegal."

"It wasn't advertised. Only friends had advance warning. Shocked the hell out of the customers but they seemed to be in no hurry to leave. But I'm not sure if anything's going on there today."

Lixin was toying with her gelato.

"You aren't eating your gelato. There's something about

the sight of melting ice cream that is intolerable. Can I finish it for you?"

Lixin typed a message.

"Thank you. Now stop texting me and speak to me directly."

"It's so quiet here. Like an abandoned store in a movie."

"I like the quiet. Some cafés put the same music on repeat the whole day. Sometimes the same *song* on repeat. They don't understand playlists in this country. Drives me insane and I wouldn't be able to deal with that now. That's why I like this place."

"I want to leave."

"Let's go for massage. But I have to let them know we're coming in case they're busy now."

They sat down on a bench in Xiangyang Park. Marguerite put her arm around Lixin. "You okay, dear?"

"I feel gloomy."

"Tell me what you're thinking."

"Look at my hands. They're sweating. The trees are twisting. I can smell them."

"The park has a powerful smell."

"People's faces look like masks. Peking Opera masks. They're staring at us."

"Stare back at them."

Lixin burst out laughing. "You have Peking Opera mask on your face." She ran her hand over Marguerite's cheeks. "Your mask is white, the color of death."

"Your face looks darker than usual. I thought it was a rich yellow but it's more like butterscotch."

"I'm too dark. People think I'm a peasant. What's butterscotch?"

"A candy. I love dark-skinned Asians. Are you ready for the massage now? You still look kind of grim."

"I want to sit here for a while."

"It will help you relax."

"They will give me sex massage? I'm afraid."

"Only if you want it."

"They will give you the same massage?"

"I'm not sure. I only know two of them who will do it and I'm having them do you. It doesn't matter how they do me."

Marguerite got off her massage table to check on Lixin. "You okay, lovely? Oh, you're crying!"

"I am okay. Leave me alone."

Later she heard Lixin's breathing speed up behind the curtain. Marguerite asked her masseuses if they recalled a regular customer, a middle-aged American male named Aishamu.

"*Haoduo waiguo keren lai zheli.*"

"Yes, there are a lot of them in this area, but he would be a massage connoisseur."

When her masseuses had left and Lixin was getting dressed, she showed Lingling and Ailing the photo of Isham Cook on the back of the massage book.

"*A! Renchulai ta.*"

They both recognized him. Lingling had even done house calls at his home. The last time she saw him was around a year ago, though, and she hadn't seen him since. She still had his address in her cellphone and would WeChat it to Marguerite later.

"How was he as a customer?"

Friendly and courteous, she said, not pushy or rude. Enjoyed erotic massage but never demanded it and was content with a little genital teasing. Eventually she brought him off one day out of pity. He tipped her. Oddly, he never came back and that was the last she saw of him.

"*Wo ye fashengle!*" said Ailing. She had had the same experience with him and his sudden disappearance.

"They won't be embarrassed if I get on the table naked?" asked Lixin.

"They'll give you these disposable panties. Just remove them when you're ready to be massaged there. But keep quiet if you feel like cumming. My masseuses might be embarrassed if they're not supposed to know."

"How will I relax if they have Peking Opera faces?"

"Close your eyes. Try closing your eyes now."

"I can still see the trees."

Lixin leaned back into Marguerite and the fear-fueled fragrance of her thick hair enveloped her. They sat there in silence for some time before leaving the park.

"When we entered the massage shop, I had that same feeling like in the bookstore," said Lixin. "Old museum with nobody in it. Strange tinkling sounds like broken toys. I thought the woman in the lobby was statue. When she started speaking I was terrified. But felt better that you knew her."

Lixin's hands were shaking with nervousness as she took off her clothes.

"No, not here. Change in the shower room they showed us down the hallway. Unless you're comfortable bumping into male customers with just a towel wrapped around you."

"So awkward."

"Are you starting to feel better now?"

"I think so. Finally, I could relax and then I got excited when her fingers were inside me. Oh, god, I'm so embarrassed." She blushed and covered her face with one hand. "I caused a mess on massage table. But I had such rush of feeling from it and the gloominess went out of me."

"Is the acid under control?"

"It's still strong, but better. I'm not so confused now. It was hell in that park."

"I've already peaked. Actually, I think you got more than me. I chewed it pretty thoroughly in my mouth but you swallowed most of my saliva."

They were sitting outside at Peet's Coffee on Donghu Road. The dog-day haze had dissipated and the late afternoon sun was bringing out the colors.

"That's quite the robe you have on. Very striking," said a foreign male with an American accent at the table next to them.

"Thank you. Authentic Hare Krishna robe from 1960s

Berkeley."

"You from California?"

"Afghanistan."

"Wow."

Marguerite received a message on her cellphone. "Isn't this address close to the Conservatory of Music?" she asked Lixin.

"Yes. Fuxing Zhonglu. You will try to visit him?"

"Yeah. I'll go myself. You don't have to be involved. I think it will be easier to explain my purpose that way. If he's still there."

"What do you want to find out?"

"What his story is. If it's anything like Louisa described it could be more interesting than any book he wrote. I have no idea what I'll find out."

Several days later, Marguerite helped Lixin carry two taxi loads of her belongings up the stairs to her loft.

"Louisa was okay about you leaving?"

"No."

"Don't tell me she threw a fit."

"I paid her three more months my half of rent payment."

"I got a very inquisitive phone call from her. She's jealous. How are you feeling? Ready for some more acid?" grinned Marguerite.

Lixin was silent for a moment. "I need some time to turn it into philosophy."

"Why don't you use that philosophy to consider why you need to keep sending me so many WeChat messages. It's starting to annoy me."

"I'm sorry."

"But you felt fine the next day."

"Yeah. It was very powerful. You said DMT is a lot stronger? How could that be?"

"It's different. When you're ready we'll try some more of it, a blastoff dose, unlike the kiddie dose you had last time."

"How about that author? You visited him?"

"I visited his apartment. His girlfriend was living there."

"She's Chinese?"

"Yeah. She was sort of suspicious and reserved but she invited me in. She wasn't willing to divulge his whereabouts. I didn't want to pry, so I asked her about this Lu Na or Luna, the translator. I made it seem like I was interested in her for other reasons and didn't mention the rumors about him beating her. She said she knew very little about her and had never met her. In fact, she seemed strangely relieved that I wanted to know more about Luna. Maybe she thought I could find out things she didn't already know. Yet she didn't ask me to get back in touch with her. She gave me the email address of an American male friend of his named Jim who lives in the U.S. He was apparently friendly with both of them. I mean Isham and Luna."

"How was his apartment?"

"Comfortable. Lots of books. Anyway, I emailed the friend and he replied right away. He was also rather suspicious of my intentions, but when I asked if I could visit him to talk about it in person he agreed. That should break the ice. He lives way up in the Wisconsin north woods and is probably lonely."

"Visit him? You will go all the way to America to see the friend of a violent man?"

"It's called investigative reporting," Marguerite winked. "No, actually I've been needing to make a trip back to the States. I have business in Chicago that I've been putting off and this is a good excuse to get the trip out of the way."

Lixin was crestfallen. "When are you leaving?"

"I think next week. I still have to arrange everything. You'll be fine here. I'll only be gone a week."

"You will stay with him?"

"Not unless he invites me."

"You will sleep with him?"

"I have no idea. The path to sex with someone is often a tangled forest. But it sure helps things along if you're trying to get information out of them."

*

Marguerite's rental car pulled off the country road and into a driveway which curled around to the back of a small red cottage. She was greeted by a yelping dachshund that jumped on her lap as soon as she opened the car door.

"Xiaolong! Don't worry. He won't bite. He loves women."

"Jim Spear, I presume?"

"That's me all right. Marguerite? Nice to meet you."

"Nice to meet you, too. You were right about the deer. Thanks for warning me. They appear on the road right out of nowhere. Must have passed about thirty of them on the final stretch up here."

"How long was the drive?"

"About four hours. I drove up from Chicago yesterday and took a detour to the House on the Rock and Mazo Beach."

"Oh, yes. I'm ashamed to say I've never been to either place."

"I got here earlier than expected because Mazo Beach has been shut down. For good, it seems."

"Yeah, I seen reports in the news about the police harassing people there."

"It was the Midwest's greatest nude beach in its heyday. Utter tragedy. Is this your garden? Lovely tomatoes. You've got a whole cornucopia growing here."

"Zucchini, cucumbers, leeks, green beans, peas, and asparagus."

"And grapes!"

"These vines here are Marquettes. Those are Briannas."

"You make wine?"

"Got fifteen gallons currently fermenting and another ten left from last year. As well as crab apple and cranberry wine."

"I'm impressed. As I am with *these*. You aren't worried about law enforcement?"

"I'll be harvesting these babies before they get tall

enough to be seen. The winds are blowing in favor of legalization anyway. May be just be a year or two down the road."

"Oh, is that a little sauna?"

"A two-seater."

"It's rock heated?"

"You bet."

"You know what the ancient Scythians did — they would crowd into communal sauna tents and throw cannabis on the rocks and inhale the fumes." Marguerite opened the car's trunk and hauled out a suitcase. "I've got something here for you."

"Let me help you with that. I hope you don't find my bachelor pad too ramshackle. I'm on a Navy pension and not exactly living in luxury."

"Well, you seem self-sufficient food and booze-wise."

"That much is true."

"No, your place is cozy!" she said as they entered.

"Have you made arrangements to stay anywhere, by the way?"

"No. Not yet. Can you recommend a place in Minocqua?"

"I could. You're also welcome to stay here. You can have my bedroom. I'm perfectly fine sleeping on the couch."

"Hmm."

"It's up to you."

She opened the suitcase. "Let me show you what I have here."

"Are those Oriental rugs?"

"I brought different sizes since I didn't know how big your place would be."

"Beautiful. But I'm sure I can't afford any of them."

"This three-by-four meter should do it. You want to have enough floor space around it to frame it."

"It's gorgeous. But I really can't — "

"I'm in the rug business. This costs me nothing. It's yours. End of discussion."

"I don't know what to say. Thank you."

"In case you're wondering if there's some kind of a catch, don't worry. My only agenda is what I mentioned in my email — to learn a bit more about the massage book. It's causing quite a buzz in the Shanghai grapevine, but no one knows anything about the author or the translator. They both seem to have disappeared off the face of the earth. And you're one of the few people who personally knew them."

"What's all the buzz about?"

"One thing at a time. I'm actually kind of hungry. Is there a restaurant around here?"

"Let me slap something together. It's the least I owe you. You're in good hands. I'm a part-time chef."

"Fantastic. I'd love to try some of your wine."

"What would you like to start with?"

"All of the wines you mentioned. You play guitar, I see. And what kind of a guitar is *that*?"

"The other one?" Jim said from the kitchen. "That's a three-string cigar box guitar. It allows you to play blues with a slide because the action is set higher."

"And you paint! Nudes."

"Another one of my amateur hobbies." He handed her a dark liquor in a port glass. "This is some chokecherry wine I still have left."

"Oh, Jim, is this marvelous. Oh, my goodness. I've only been here ten minutes and I'm drowning in rustic luxury. That means, of course, I have to stay."

"Here's something else I created. A brandy oatmeal cookie — hold on a second — made with marijuana butter. You don't want to eat more than one of these."

She snatched it from him and took a bite out of it. Xiaolong came up and dropped a rubber ball out of its mouth. Marguerite bounced it around the room for him to fetch while Jim cooked. She examined his CDs and books. He emerged with different samples of wine and finally, steaming dishes. "Homemade hand-stretched noodles with hickory-smoked bacon and baby ramp pesto. Corn on the cob stir-fried with butter and Sichuan peppercorn."

They set to eating.

"Your cooking is worth the price of this rug. If I were selling it, that is. So you used to live in China?"

"After retiring I enrolled in a Chinese program for foreigners at a university in Shanghai. That's where I met Isham. He was teaching in the English Department. I wanted to stay in China longer but couldn't get a job there without a degree. So I came back to the U.S. and picked up a B.A. in journalism. Went back to Shanghai and found a job as an English radio announcer."

"You did all that after you retired? How old are you?"

"Fifty-five. I retired when I was forty, after twenty years of service."

"You look great for your age."

"I came back here for good in 2010. Traveling was my life. I've been to many of the world's ports on my tour of duty, including all over East and Southeast Asia. But my roots are here and my father is getting old. I sort of need to be around."

"You're from Minocqua?"

"That's where I grew up. My dad lives out on Blue Lake. I was living in Green Bay for a few years, with a window facing Lake Michigan, and it was actually cheaper than Minocqua since the tourist boom up here. Then I found this cottage."

"How did you meet Luna?"

"Long story. She was one of Isham's many women. A sad case, though. Really crazy and fucked up."

"What do you mean?"

"I was attracted to her too. Sexy as hell, her appearance anyway. Not her personality."

"Is that painting of her?"

"It's of Bonnie, his longtime girlfriend. They go way back."

"The one who gave me your email address?"

"Yeah. He once lined up about ten women for me to photograph in the nude and paint their nudes from. She was one of them."

"What was the problem with Luna, exactly?"

"As sweet as an angel, with a seriously major case of OCD. And borderline paranoid schizophrenia. She'd clamp onto an idea like a pit bull and wouldn't let go of it, no matter how wrongheaded it was. She had some kind of virgin complex and they couldn't have sex. Couldn't get his one-eyed snake inside her. I suppose it was pretty clear why. She just couldn't let go, with all the other women he was juggling. But at the same time, she couldn't let go of him. That was the problem. Constant emails and phone calls — and stalking him. It got to the point where he had to cut off all contact. That's when she started calling me. Every day. And an endless stream of bizarre, incoherent emails."

"All the while she was helping him translate his massage book?"

"That was much later. He had cut her off for years. And then hooked up with her again around five years ago, I think. The book came out just a few years ago, didn't it?"

"The original was published in 2015. The Chinese translation in 2016."

"You cannot believe all the frantic, fucked-up emails and phone calls I had to deal with from her. Until I had to cut her off too."

"Oh, tell me about it. I may be dealing with the same problem myself. I recently got involved with a Chinese woman, a real beauty, who also has an OCD tendency."

"A woman?"

"I'm bi. I invited her to live with me after she had a falling out with an American woman she was living with. Now I'm wondering if I made a mistake."

"She's obsessed with you?"

"You could put it that way. I've told her repeatedly not to send me so many cellphone texts but she keeps doing it. About a hundred messages over the past four days since I left Shanghai. She's going to hear about this when I get back. Any advice on how to handle it?"

"Are they threatening messages?"

"No. She's in love and doesn't have any sense of limits. Just a pure, unadulterated outpouring of all the feelings she's accumulated in her life. Like a faucet on full blast."

"Well, I suppose it matters how much you like her yourself."

"If I can influence her and bring things under control there's hope. But what do you do — be gentle and persuasive or a strict taskmaster?"

"I can tell you I would *never* be able to live with a woman like Luna for one minute. No matter how much I'm attracted to her, and I was attracted to her."

"Anyway. I like your painting style. A fresh cross between Matisse and folk art. I love that one with the squatting nude holding a wine glass."

"I haven't painted anything in a while. I have so many other projects going on that I get sidetracked."

"What if I posed for you?"

"Now that's an interesting proposition."

"Your wines are so orgasmic I could even take my clothes off right now. Sorry, only kidding. I have a natural inclination to boldness."

"If you dressed in a gorilla suit with a strap-on dildo and wanted to roger me to death, now that would be bold."

"You're funny. No, really? You sure you could handle it?" She undid several of her shirt buttons.

"I love artist types, the free-minded. Totally my thing. Yes, by all means make yourself comfortable."

"You get your easel ready first."

"Oh, that's a bit of trouble. How about tomorrow? You might find me weird in saying this, but I find your mustache a turn-on."

"Quite a few people do. The ones who dare admit it."

"And I would love to see those breasts of yours."

"Watch out. I get horny on weed. The cookie is hitting me. How much did you say you put in it?"

"I see you ate half. That will get you nicely stoned. A

whole cookie is more than enough for most people."

"You'd better keep me distracted. Tell me more about Luna."

"She also had a mustache, almost as dark as yours."

"Really. Do you think there was anything to trigger her behavior?"

"Let me give you an example. He wrote a story in one of his books — I don't think it was the massage book — about sex robots run amok and a male character somewhat resembling Isham who was raped by one of them. Luna somehow got the idea into her head he had written her into the story. Or maybe she was another robot, not the one who raped him. Something like that. He couldn't get it across to her that the story had nothing remotely to do with her. She just pulled the idea out of thin air, out of her paranoid fantasy world, and once lodged there it wouldn't budge. She was calling me about it in tears."

"Did anything come of it?"

"As soon as she got hold of a new obsession, she dropped it. Like it had never come up at all. But what about you? I want to hear about *you*. Where are you from?"

"I was born in Afghanistan."

"Afghanistan!"

"We fled after the Soviet invasion and made it to the U.S. as refugees. I don't have much memory of that time. I went back by myself after the war ended, as a teenager. It was horrible and I escaped into Iran and got ensnared in the carpet-weaving business. Later in Turkey as well."

"So you're Muslim?"

"No. Not at all. My parents were secular and that's why we got the hell out."

Marguerite burst out laughing and went to the bathroom. When she returned, she tucked her legs under her on the couch. Her bra was gone.

"What was so funny just now?"

"I can't get that place out of my head. The House on the Rock. It's a total riot."

"I've heard it's interesting."

"This madman named Alex Jordan created it back in the 1950s. It started off as a Frank Lloyd Wright-type house on the top of a big rock. He kept adding to it over the decades and turned it into a massive museum filled with mechanical music boxes and circus orchestras performed by life-sized dolls. There's this gigantic carousel. The naked mannequins riding the horses have realistic nipples. The climax is this huge hall surrounded by church organs set on different levels with twisting walkways going up and around them, like a drug-induced amusement park ride. The only problem is the organs don't play. Many of the museum's machines are broken. They should repair them. The place has an abandoned feel. Can I use your shower in a bit?"

"Of course."

"After one more glass of that white wine."

4

To understand how a tub of margarine got splattered on a hotel room wall, we need to backtrack to a more important question, why a private galleon of such intricate construction kept crashing into rocks on its journey through China. The galleon was Isham Cook's philosophy of polyamory. Polyamory's pejorative connotations present something of a challenge when trying to explain the term to the Chinese, or to almost anyone for that matter. The concept is universally dismissed out of hand by civilized people as at best a naïve and flaky hippie pipe dream and at worst a ruse of irresponsible males for acting out their lust on as many women as possible. It would help, however, if we were to make a decent effort to understand it, and with it the wreckage of a hapless navigator in hostile territory.

Some contemporary English-Chinese dictionaries have the word but mistranslate it as polygamy or polygyny: *yifu duoqi*, "one husband, many wives." Polygamy has a specific historical meaning in China, where up through 1949 any man of means could have multiple wives (i.e. concubines). Today it's viewed as a sorry, feudalistic legacy of the past, a few ethnic minority groups notwithstanding – harmless curios such as the Mosuo in Yunnan Province still practice a form of matriarchal polyandry – whereas polyamory, from the Greek *poly* and Latin *amor*, meaning "many loves" (an awkward compound in the view of etymology purists) only entered English a few decades ago as an Americanism. A Shanghai friend suggested a literal gloss in Chinese of "many loves," *duo ai*, would short-circuit the reflexive associations with polygamy and work well enough.

Polyamory is a consensual intimate relationship involving more than two people. The core polyamorous unit is the triad: three people sharing each other lovingly and sexually. It's not a one-off or occasional threesome; there is a mutual effort to cultivate the relationship, indeed stabilize it through "the logic of the tripod," as Cook called it. Polyamorous "throuples" need not confine themselves to the triad. There is no limit to the number of partners, of whatever sex or gender, that can be added to the group and "interlace the varied fragrances of their nakedness." Any partner is free to leave and join another group. Living together is not a requirement but is the logical outcome: the communal family. There are as many types of polyamorous relationships as there are people practicing them. This variety is upheld as vital to the definition of the term.

To repeat: polyamory is distinct from and incompatible with polygamy, the sexual domination or coercion of more than one woman by the male head of a household. Once monogamists acknowledge that polyamorists are not polygamists, we can get to the real issue at hand – monogamy itself, that deeply entrenched ur-faith. Polyamorists have no desire to take anyone away from their partner. They only seek to be legally allowed to practice among themselves something better and thus sway by example. Monogamy is rigid; it is limited to the dyad and prohibits intimate or sexual relations with people outside of the dyad. Polyamory is open, fluid and democratic; it enables and encourages the natural desire to enter into new relationships while being loyal to existing ones. It affirms that the quality of sex life withers when a couple is confined to each other alone and blooms with the infusion of fresh blood. It affirms the lifelong need to love — and fall in love with — more than one.

Another respect in which polyamory is superior to monogamy is the salubrious upbringing it provides to children. The monogamous household is a mini totalitarian state. As demagogues whip up hysteria and brainwash and bully the populace, the tyrant parent likewise has free reign to terrorize the child. The polyamorist communal household preempts tyrannical parenting and reduces the likelihood of psychological, physical and sexual abuse. But even well-intentioned monogamous parents may instill personality distortions in the child given the absence of alternative perspectives. When the number of parents and siblings increases, the biased and irrational influences of the few are counterbalanced and kept in check by the wisdom of the majority. At the same time, the multiparent household need not preclude the child's being cared for and raised primarily by his or her biological parents.

When "privacy" is put in its proper place as an outmoded nineteenth-century construct and the veil of familial secrecy is lifted, honesty, accountability and responsibility come to the fore.

The danger of infection and disease among the sexually "promiscuous" is not a valid argument against polyamory. The incidence of sexually transmitted disease is already high everywhere, not least in conservative societies where sex is hushed up and STDs circulate silently. This is due to a societal failure, the lack of effective, shame-free, universally available sex education. Most cultures still languish under repressive, puritanical morality. In no country is there anything approaching a positive and comprehensive sex education for adolescents, created for them. There is no reason why teenagers couldn't be as knowledgeable about STDs as doctors. Sex education should also be fun and engaging and include, for example, live demonstrations in class by specialists and the option of student-on-student participation.

Absent a corrective sex education, repressive morality is left to rage with devastating psychological consequences, perpetuated from generation to generation. The first figure to explicate this in all its dreary clarity was Austrian psychoanalyst Wilhelm Reich, in such books as *The Invasion of Compulsory Sex-Morality* (1932) and *The Sexual Revolution* (1936). On this vital topic the polyamorous household has an important role to play in educating its children. Of course, sexual contact between children and adults is prohibited, in accordance with existing laws and mores (while noting that the age of consent has varied widely over time and across cultures). But open discussion in appropriate contexts should be encouraged and parents' own healthy, polyamorous relations held up as a model. Family nudity is encouraged as well (long practiced in many European countries).

Among the growing library of articulate advocates for the polyamory movement, Ryan and Jetha's *Sex at Dawn* (2010) is the best known and most eloquent. But long before the term was invented two books spelled it all out. In *The Origin of the Family, Private Property and the State* (1884), Friedrich Engels enumerated in cogent detail the many alternatives to bourgeois marriage which the tribal or communal unit had at its disposal for arranging itself, as evidenced in non-Western cultures throughout the ages. And there was German psychoanalyst Erich Fromm's stunningly simple insight in *The Art of Loving* (1956), that contrary to the conventional notion of love (and its destructive obverse, jealousy) as a commodity of limited quantity easily squandered unless saved up for the exclusive chosen one, love is an infinite resource with no inherent limit to the number of people it can be showered on not only over the course of one's life but at one and the same time.

So self-evident are these truths that any clearheaded

teenager can grasp them. As Cook saw it, it's not polyamory but its universal absence that's shocking. That so many sex lives are attenuated and cut short, lost to confusion and self-deception, to the miserly hoarding of the body, cruel recognition achieved in old age when it's too late, was perplexing and tragic enough. Most frustrating of all were the many highly educated, progressive friends, leftists who should have known better, so-called intellectuals, who seemed even more enslaved to bourgeois morality than conservatives he knew. With Chinese friends he made a bit more progress in conveying the concept, perhaps due to a notorious yet quite sensible precedent, the polyamorous-like setup among some households in rural China, where a wife agrees to share her bed with her husband's brother in exchange for another hand on the farm.

Isham was plainly honest with every woman he got into bed. Without trying to spoil the romantic mood, he told them at the earliest opportunity that though he was capable of loving a woman with passion and devotion, sexual ownership and fidelity was a different matter altogether: contrary to nature, repugnant and wrong, something he was both constitutionally incapable of and opposed to in principle. If the woman he was explaining this to refused to have any more contact with him, if all women refused to have any contact with him, fine. He'd confront that with the same serene fortitude of a life sentence in prison or the loss of his groin in a car accident. He could not, and would not, compromise his beliefs; the very idea was philosophically nauseating. Ironically, his blunt pronouncements worked just as often as not. Chinese women expected men to lie their way into their pants. This guy's refreshing, disarming honesty had the opposite effect and earned their wary respect.

If you're attracted enough to a person, it doesn't much matter what they say, what ink cloud they spew at you to throw you off or warn you of what you're getting into. You will still latch onto them if given the chance. Isham was exactly the man Luna was looking for — he was the only man she was looking for — and had heard him out calmly and with little change in her demeanor on their first dinner date in Jinan. It's not clear how well she absorbed his ideas or whether she understood them at all. It wasn't a language problem, but rather the great cultural and conceptual gulf between them. The only important thing at the time was they were spending their first night together. She proceeded to fail in bed and was deeply upset. She would continue to be upset with herself on their subsequent attempts. Now, ten years later, she was more pained than happy to hear from him, having put that past behind her. But seeing him again was a forgone conclusion.

He was impatient and angry over dinner in the seafood restaurant and things had concluded badly. She was afraid of him and this fear was lodged in her vagina. It foreclosed the possibility that night of any sexual progress. For his part, it wasn't so much the virtual certainty of no progress which made him impatient; it was the pointlessness of all their interactions. He told her about another woman he was now seeing named Kitty. He hadn't planned to do so but felt a pointed comparison might get through to her, because the two had more than a few things in common. Kitty was employed at an investment firm and quite the financial whiz, yet like Luna she was kindhearted and also had a keen interest in animal protection. Like Luna, Kitty had a mustache (a darker one yet) but kept it out of the way with depilatory cream, it being, alas, unacceptable at her workplace. Unlike Luna, Kitty enjoyed a nice meal and could converse on a range of topics.

This wasn't the first time Luna found herself in the competition, having of course endured a spell living with Isham and Bonnie. This revelation of yet another enemy on the horizon was bad news, but she managed to maintain perspective. She and Isham had been apart for a decade and it was hardly surprising he had acquired another mistress, one he could even make love to, which was more than she could say. Stoically, she considered the really important mystery and matter at hand: why Isham insisted on lying, on claiming he wasn't married to Bonnie when they were surely married. Assuming for the sake of argument they weren't, could this new mistress be the reason? Was Isham torn between the two and struggling with the prospect of leaving Bonnie for her? Luna asked him more about Kitty. What was it that made her outshine Bonnie? "You're missing the point," he said. "I'm polyamorous, remember? It's not a competition between them. Unfortunately, they don't seem to like each other and have no intention of ever meeting, but they complement each other. I intend to hold on to both of them. I could hold on to you too if you solved your sexual problem."

To Luna, there was no more misguided idea than this polyamory. She regarded Isham as confused, lonely and deluded. By forcing the issue, she hoped to bring out the truth of what he had sought all along. As hard as it was to encourage him to choose between Bonnie and Kitty while leaving herself out of the picture, she might very well triumph in the end. If Isham was torn between the two women, that meant he truly loved neither. With patience, Luna might guide him back to herself. And despite his loss of confidence in her sexuality, she was ready and eager to open up. She was ready to tell him why he hadn't succeeded but would still be able to, but that too required patience, a patience he had not yet attained. All was immobilized in a morass of misunderstanding. She would be the catalyst, the one to break through the logjam, resolving things in one direction or another. She only wished he could see her selflessness and altruism in this regard.

After that night, Luna continued to press Isham about Kitty in frequent emails. He ignored them, until he succumbed one day in a more sympathetic mood and agreed to give her a final shot. *On condition you not bring up Bonnie and Kitty.* As he waited for her to join him in the restaurant next to the hotel, she texted him that she was on her way and bringing his dinner, which she had already prepared.

"My dinner? I thought we're eating together in the restaurant outside. Wasn't that the plan? It's a budget hotel with a tiny room. It's not set up for food. I don't want you to bring anything."

"I've already checked in and the food is getting cold," she said upon arriving at the restaurant. She was wearing a frilly polyester dress over track pants and over that a Goose Island T-shirt from Chicago he had given her on their last meeting.

"Things are not getting off to a good start."

The tiny room was built around a queen bed, with only enough space for a small desk. Luna laid out the items she had brought: a bowl of spaghetti, sliced bread, plastic cheese, and a tub of margarine. He occupied the sole chair while she sat on the edge of the bed. He gestured at the food.

"I already ate," she said.

"First of all, I again tried to invite you to a nice dinner at a restaurant. Last time you joined me but refused to eat anything. This time you refused to even join me. Second, you are staring at me while I'm trying to eat. Third, you had no idea what I'd like to eat but brought these horrible processed foods, and you claim to know about healthy eating."

"I researched how to make spaghetti on the internet because it's Western food."

"Why do you presume I need to eat Western food? Have I ever given you any indication I can't eat Chinese food? What's this meat in the sauce? Oh, it's spam! You don't make spaghetti sauce with spam. And you made the sauce using ketchup!" He dropped his head in his hands.

"Isham, I want to talk about Bonnie."

"Hold on. Didn't we agree not to talk about her?"

"I want to know when you married her."

"What? We're not married. Whatever gave you that idea?"

"You are married to her. You need to admit the truth."

"Why do you assume I'm lying? We are not married. You

are rapidly spoiling the mood with this nonsense."

"Isham, she wants to have a child and start a family. Have you told your mother yet?"

"Told her what?"

"About your marriage to Bonnie?"

"I told you I am not married."

"You are married and I'm waiting for you to admit it."

"Fuck, this is annoying. I don't like to be accused of lying when I'm not."

"I hope you didn't hide your marriage from your mother. How can you improve your relationship with her if you don't — "

He threw the tub of margarine at the wall. "Get out! Get out of here, now! I'm through with you!"

"No, Isham! I'm sorry!"

"Get out!"

"No! Please."

She blocked the door as he tried to open it. He caught himself.

"Okay, okay. You can stay. I don't want a hallway scene. I have work to do. I will stay here, you stay there. You will not speak to me for the rest of the night. You stay on your side of the bed and shut up."

She collapsed onto the bed in tears. For the rest of the night she lay sleepless in her clothes, her back to him, silently crying. She left early in the morning.

Sometimes it takes a crisis to clear the fog. Luna recognized what went wrong. If her previous emails to Isham had been frequent, she now redoubled her efforts and sent him five, ten emails a day, long emails, starting off with this, the first of them:

> My goodness, I need to catch my breath. I need some air. This is Luna live from her sanctuary. I'll update you on her mental situation — if she could manage to survive Papa Isham's enlightening, informative, liberal, artistic, lovely sex bomb. I'm exploded. You got me, sir. Holy cow! And happy Thanksgiving Day, a day for people to fill up

their hearts and minds with gratefulness instead of grumpiness, warmth and friendliness instead of coldness and hostility. On this day, constructive attitudes will substitute for destructive negativities. Show me the broadmindedness you've acquired through being a writer.

Dear Isham, if you have pressure to release, I can help you to release it in whatever way you prefer. I just hope it's not violent like throwing things, as happened the other night. I understand at that very moment your heated temper just skyrocketed and it was out of control. Please don't do that again, my love. It's a lose-lose situation. Next time, harness your negative feelings to positive passion first, then fold me in your arms and kiss me deeply. What do you think? Come on, handsome. I'm imagining crawling on top of you this very moment and taking that big thing of yours inside me.

I'll tell you a secret. If I could draw you away from your work for a few minutes the next time we're together, if you spent just a little more time gently kissing my body all over, I would open up. I get very excited when my breasts are kissed and caressed. But it seems that your computer has a vagina which greedily sucks up your dick instead. I am eager to know more about you. My mind hungers for new perspectives, orgasms from innovative ideas. I hate small talk. I want to talk about atoms, death, aliens, sex, magic. I like a person with a serpentine mind.

PS. Are you disappointed that we talked about your relationship with B and K in the hotel room? Is this what you were angry about? Look dear Isham, what if I pretend not knowing your feelings toward B and K, and you pretend not knowing that I know your feelings toward B and K, which I think is exactly what happened between you and B about you and K. My love, I don't want to be the next B. And I'm not K. I am your friend and your woman.

In other emails, she took a more creative approach:

Papa Isham,
    I finally figured out what you were trying to tell me when you came up with your Chinese name, Aishamu.

I'm not sure if you know the meaning behind the
characters, but 艾 is mugwort, a traditional Chinese
medicine plant used in *aijiu*, moxibustion. There is a kind
of *aijiu* treatment for older men's penis to restore virility.
They place the burning *ai* in a chamber over your genitals.
It symbolizes Bonnie trying to help your sex life with her,
because you've been together for so long. The middle
character, 沙, means sand. It has the water radical on the
left (three strokes) and the *shao* radical on the right, which
means something tiny, like little rocks, or sand on the
beach. But *shao* also means very little of something, or
lacking something. It symbolizes Isham lost and lonely on
the beach, looking for his mother. The third character, 姆,
means female, or wet nurse. It has the woman radical on
the left, and the mother radical, *mu*, on the right. The
mother radical shows a woman's breasts, lying on her side
(the two dots). This symbolizes Kitty, who is nourishing
Isham with her fresh milk. Bonnie and Kitty have got
Isham trapped between them. "Aishamu" is your cry of
help. You chose it as your Chinese name because your
books are your only way of communicating honestly with
me. It's why you asked me to translate *Massage and the
Writer*.

    Yours,
    Luna

As Isham had by now blocked Luna on WeChat for
good, she was relegated to viewing his Twitter posts, along
with Kitty's Weibo posts (China's Twitter), another valuable
source of information, and ferreting out their veiled
messages. As she told him in one of a hundred unanswered
emails that followed over the next few months, she was
wrong about his supposed marriage to Bonnie and hoped he
wasn't offended by her mentioning it: "It's good that you
indicated your marriage to Mrs. Kitty Cook, which I read
from your Twitter and her Weibo. I admire your marriage.
You did the right thing, especially after how much you've
hurt her emotionally." He was a proud man, she continued,
and understood how difficult it was for him to admit his

love. But monogamy works. Polyamory is just a way of killing time until you find the right person. The reason she hadn't been invited to their wedding, she surmised, was he had likely denied Kitty one, given his aversion to ceremonies (he had once mentioned his former marriage to a Chinese woman in the 1990s, a low-key affair at a government office and a simple dinner with her family). This was indeed a shame, yet she still had much useful advice she was hoping he could forward to his new wife.

The more Luna learned about Kitty, the more she realized Kitty was everything she was not. If the two bore some superficial physical resemblance — fine-boned yet shapely figure, intense eyes, a mustache (or the capability of one) — they were worlds apart in character, temperament, accomplishments. Kitty came from educated stock, a good family, with a Masters in Finance from Fudan University, one of China's best. In a culture which discouraged female excellence, she had passions and hobbies and the nerve to barrel her way forward with them. She could walk into a nightclub, persuade her way up on stage and belt out stunning renditions of Chinese songs to a wowed audience. She painted. She was quite talented at photography, practicing on her attractive colleagues and subordinates who eagerly posed nude for her, once they saw her formidable array of camera gear and lenses. One of the benefits for a Party cadre of secure managerial position was abundant annual leave. Whenever traveling solo to a new country, she would rent a car and head to a remote setting where no Chinese had ever ventured and post photos on her Weibo blog, along with smartly penned, historically informed essays contextualizing the photos, some of which won awards in photography magazines.

Her female friends envied and idolized this free and independent spirit. Luna too was impressed and became a devoted fan of Kitty's blog, perhaps more than anyone else, judging by her interpretative acuity. For his part, Isham read all of Luna's emails, thenceforth his sole source of information about her. He needed to track her evolving state in case things took a turn for the worse, signs of which her more recent missives hinted at: "Oh, God, Isham. You're revealing what I wrote to you to Kitty. You're pulling my leg and making fun of me. You are laughing at me and ignoring my good intentions. I can't believe you're doing this to me. Please stop asking Kitty to communicate with me through her Weibo."

This prompted a response from Isham, demanding that she provide evidence Kitty was doing what she claimed she was. Then the interminable stream of email was followed by silence — a permanent, not an ominous silence, he hoped. But a few months later Luna started up again, with an altered tone:

Hi Isham,
    How have you been doing? I haven't written to you for a while. I'm not sure if it's safe to contact you through this email box. After you read this message, please delete it. Also, make sure you're reading this alone by yourself and not with someone else, if you can. I will delete it right after I send it to you. I'll check this email box during breaks between some business I have to do today. I probably won't be able to reply to your response until later.
    Cheers,
    Luna

Subsequent emails were more worrisome:

    Please delete my WeChat account from your phone, otherwise Kitty will not stop her lunacy. She will interpret it as you're still interested in me, which is not the case. This behavior of yours is hurting me. Do you know how much of my personal information Kitty has stolen from me? I saved my account names and passwords for social media, emails, banking, etc., all in one email. She attacked my computer and she has everything! And she watches me whenever I'm online. Whatever I do on the Internet, she

will pop up a window to show what I'm doing. If you were
me, would you go to the police for this crime? Your advice
is appreciated.

This was all baffling to Isham, for Kitty knew nothing of
Luna's existence. He would never have dared mention being
acquainted with such a person. What the hell are you doing
with this pathetic woman? — would have been her response,
as had been Bonnie's. She would also have asked him how
much Luna already knew about her. If he had been pressed
to explain why he had revealed her Weibo to Luna in the
first place, I'm sure he'd deny it was to humiliate Luna but
to educate her, to point the way by positive example to what
she herself could be. Anyway, there was no harm in it.
Kitty's blog, which was after all a public profile, was visible
to anyone.

Whatever could have deposited these seeds of delusion
in Luna's head? A primal rage against the enemy
unconsciously projected onto Kitty so that Luna became the
object of her own rage? A cognitive dissonance so intolerable
it caused a psychologically crippling rupture? Or more simply,
her despair at succumbing to the truth that she really was cut
off and once again wouldn't be seeing Isham for another
decade? One decade was manageable; a repetition of it was
not. In other words, was Isham making her mad? Or if not
madness, instead of fading away like last time, was Luna now
contemplating taking things into her own hands?

She threatened to contact the police. Go ahead, he told
her. Unless she could produce any evidence, she'll be
laughed right out of the station — or kept there for causing
trouble. However, when he had first told Luna about Kitty,
he mentioned in passing the name of her investment firm, a
prestigious company. He wasn't sure why he mentioned it
other than to embellish her with a few colorful details, and
likewise revealed her full name. This had been a mistake, a
serious one, for she now threatened to contact Kitty's
workplace.

"I strongly advise you not to do that. Do you have any idea what you're getting into? Kitty is well connected in the Party hierarchy. She's a tough, no-nonsense woman and has no patience for petty people and their narcissistic fantasies. She could destroy you. I am telling you, you do not want to cause her trouble."

Luna's threat nonetheless put Isham in an awkward position, because he now had to spill all Kitty. "It shouldn't be a problem if she contacts your workplace, right? She has absolutely no evidence you've ever harassed her. She's just a crazy woman I regret being involved with who can be dismissed out of hand."

"The thing is my superiors will see me as having moral issues and a messy life," said Kitty.

"I feel really bad about this."

"I know she has problems and you would never intentionally have set her against me."

It's hard to imagine that the life of someone idolized by all those around her could have flaws. But this aspirational female patriot had gotten tripped up at work by several mishaps prior to the entrance of Luna onto the scene, and the timing couldn't have been worse. Before she met Isham, Kitty had been engaged to a Chinese man whom she caught in bed with another woman shortly before their wedding date. She dumped him but maintained contact and they stayed on cordial terms. Years later, not long before Luna's harassment campaign began, her ex's girlfriend developed her own inexplicable obsession with her. The woman made several calls to Kitty's superiors accusing her of harassing her. She flatly denied it. While Isham was inclined to believe her when she later told him about it, who knows what went on between the two women. But though Kitty was capable of enormous anger, harassment wasn't her style; she had worthier hobbies. To compound things, her new boss happened to be harassing her himself. Nothing more blatant than a few insistent dinner invitations of unclear purpose, which she provoked by virtue of being attractive and unmarried, and which she found excuses to turn down. He took the occasion to warn her about the alleged and ongoing harassment of her ex's girlfriend.

Around the same time, Kitty had taken an unauthorized trip with Isham to the U.S. Party members couldn't just travel anywhere on a lark. International travel was more tightly controlled for them than it was for ordinary citizens, and they had a special company-issued passport requiring permission for each trip. There were furtive ways of working around this, magic hats a private passport could be pulled out of, thus enabling Kitty to troll the globe as much as she had. The hitch was that a subordinate on her team spilled the beans during a meeting where her boss was present. Kitty was disciplined and an ungainly chunk of money taken out of her annual bonus, a common punishment in the Chinese workplace.

It wasn't long after this that Human Resources passed on the present allegations to Kitty's boss: her involvement in a love triangle and her hacking into the electronic devices of her accuser, with whom she was evidently engaging in an unaccountable campaign of warfare. The revelation wasn't quite as sexy as it seemed, for no evidence was provided by the victim. Still, a pattern had formed and management had had enough. Kitty was demoted in rank and divested not only of her remaining bonus but also her team of subordinates.

And this wasn't the end of her worries. Had it turned out that Kitty really had hacked into Luna's electronics, had Kitty really been caught up in some mental affliction or temporary insanity driving her to go after another woman in jealousy bloodlust, a severe reprimand might have come as a godsend. Though harassment could be grounds for gross misconduct and termination, mitigating factors would be considered. The Party office in Kitty's firm wouldn't allow one of its members to be dismissed without conducting its own investigation. So far things had not become quite serious enough for that. They would give her the chance to snap out of it and get back on track, and that would be the end of it.

But what if, as we are presuming, Kitty was innocent, and Luna's attack proceeded from a state of full-blown paranoid delusion? This was more perilous, since Luna would continue to rage no matter what Kitty did. True, Luna still wasn't providing any evidence. Yet why, if it was all a hallucination or a fabrication, was she going out of her way to call Kitty's company in tears a second and even a third time, to complain that the harassment was not only not going away, it was getting worse? Kitty was monitoring her twenty-four hours a day and watching her every movement through her cellphone and computer cameras, Luna claimed. These allegations weren't just coming out of the mouth of an angry or vindictive person; they seemed to be a call of distress, enough to give her superiors pause. Whereas they wanted to believe, and still believed, Kitty to be incapable of engineering such destruction behind the scenes, they couldn't dismiss the suspicion she might be a very good actor.

"Oh, I'm anxious, anxious, and anxious," she told Isham. "If the Party launches an investigation, do you know how bad that could be for me? I'm meeting with her next week to see if I can get to the bottom of it and find a solution."

"You're meeting with Luna? How in the world did you ever get in touch with her?"

"She contacted me through my blog. You don't need to be involved. I can deal with it."

A week later, the day after the encounter with Luna, Kitty asked Isham to come up and see her at once, as she needed to discuss what happened. She picked him up at a subway station and they drove around looking for a café. She was cold and tense and distracted, as if not knowing her way around her own neighborhood. They circled through the underground parking of a shopping center in vain trying to find a parking spot. It was a sweltering Saturday and the crowds were seeking refuge in the air-conditioned malls.

They gave up and found a coffeehouse on a nearby street.

"I'm grateful you agreed to make it here from across the city on such short notice."

"What happened?"

Kitty showed him her bruised wrist. "We met at a restaurant for lunch. I tried talking to her about animal protection and other things I thought she could relate to. She just stared at me and hardly spoke. When I got up to pay the bill, she stood up and shoved me and I fell down and hurt my hand."

"Oh, Jesus."

"I took her to a computer shop to prove I never hacked her. They examined her cellphone and my cellphone and showed conclusively that I was innocent. She wouldn't believe it. She accused the staff of secretly colluding with me and hiding the truth. Nothing came out of it. The whole meeting was pointless."

And the calls and the threats from Luna continued.

5

"What a great day trip this is, and we haven't even gotten to Lake Superior yet. This date bread from that monastery bakery is heavenly. What's the place called again, for future reference?"

"The Jampot. You'll need to keep to the speed limit up here, Marguerite. Michigan police have nothing better to do than issue tickets," said Jim as he caressed her thigh. "They're worse than Wisconsin police."

"And what a scenic town with that dramatic view of the river back there."

"Houghton. Copper Harbor is coming up soon and we'll be able to get out onto the lake there."

"Who would ever think to head all the way up here? And that waterfall."

"Bond Falls."

"Did you ever take Isham here?"

"Yes, I did in fact. When he was last here, with Kitty. The same trip we're taking, all the same spots."

"Who's Kitty?"

"Another one of his girlfriends. Talk about another crazy case."

"I wanted to ask you something. It's said that Isham beat Luna in a café and injured her. You know anything about that?"

"He did? No, I didn't know about that. That's odd. He would have told me. Or maybe not. Luna never mentioned anything to me. If it did happen it must have been after I cut off contact with her. But I'd be surprised. He wasn't the violent type. That would be a first."

"Yeah, I guess he gave her amnesia."

"Amnesia?"

"From beating her. She forgot who she was and disappeared."

"Oh. You're talking about Kitty."

"Kitty?"

"Not Luna. Kitty. What you heard about is what happened to Kitty. But he didn't beat her. She exploded at him in a café and they struggled over his iPad. What a story that was. I was going to tell you about it last night but didn't want to exhaust you. We would need the rest of today to go through it from start to finish."

"The rumor going around is it happened with his translator."

"No, no, no. Unless I've been kept completely in the dark. It was Kitty. Uh oh, slow down. That cop who just passed us is turning around."

"Oh, shit. His lights are flashing."

"Yep. I knew he was after us as soon as I seen him hit those brake lights."

They pulled over. Marguerite rolled down her window as the cop came up and fixed him with her slate-blue eyes.

"You know how fast you were going just now?"

"Sorry, officer, I can't recall."

"I clocked you at seven miles per hour over the limit. Can I see your driver's license, proof of insurance and vehicle registration?"

He returned a few minutes later. "I'd advise you to button up your shirt the next time you get stopped. Your breast is exposed. You could be searched for suspicious appearance if another officer is unhappy about it," he quipped, handing her a ticket.

She smiled back. "Yes, sir. Understood."

They got back on the road.

"Looks like he knocked you down to five above the limit."

"Is female toplessness allowed in Michigan? No, of course not. What am I thinking. This ain't New York."

"Not up here, unless you belong to the biker crowd. Then you have to do a titty drop as part of your initiation."

"It's legal in Canada. How far away are we from the border?"

"If you could take a boat across it's right on the other side of the lake. To drive to Canada though you'd have to head east for a good six hours to Sault Ste. Marie."

On a deserted shoreline at the tip of the Keweenaw Peninsula, a bed of polished pebbles lay below the limpid lake surface like some Ice Age currency. They skipped them on the water.

"I'm trying to process what you told me. So nothing happened with his translator?"

"Luna? No. But she abandoned the translation before it was finished. Or I should say he dumped her before it was finished."

"Why?"

"Because of all the problems I told you about last night."

"But the translation was published."

"With lots of errors, he told me. He couldn't take her craziness any longer. And then with Kitty he went from the frying pan into the fire. Things all went downhill with Kitty's jacuzzi photo."

"What happened?"

"They were fine when they came up here. After they left, they spent a night in Madison after visiting that nude beach you mentioned."

"Mazo Beach."

"He took a photo of Kitty sitting in their motel room jacuzzi. She was naked from the waist up."

"He shared it on the internet?"

"No, just with me. But without asking her permission. She went ballistic when she found out. It was a gorgeous photo, with those big puppy-dog eyes of hers and her body shrouded in the hot steam. She always had this saucer-eyed look like she was seeing a man's pecker for the first time. Isham looks at everything in an artistic way and never meant any harm by it. But she just lost it."

"Yeah, I guess his translator also lost it when she found out he had shared her nude photos on the web."

"What, Luna? I never saw any nudes of her. I asked her many times to show me something revealing but she was pretty shy about that. Kitty was different. She was an artist, and a photographer. She posted all kinds of nude photos and paintings of herself on Facebook. We warned her that her account could get shut down but she somehow got away with it. That's how I met her."

"On Facebook?"

"Isham introduced her to me on Facebook. We had some things in common, like painting, she being a free spirit and all that. I normally don't make friends on Facebook with people I don't know in person, but I made an exception with her. We hit it off and were soon chatting like old friends, and she started confiding in me how hard it was dealing with Isham."

"Why?"

"They were always at loggerheads. Incredible screaming matches."

"Over what?"

"Everything."

"Why didn't they just break up?"

"She loved him. She really loved him."

"And he didn't love her?"

"I don't think Isham ever loved anyone in his life. Even

if he did, how can you love someone you're fighting with all the time? And also, you know, he was always split between different women."

"Something must have been keeping them together. Why do you suppose she got so upset over your seeing her nude photo when you already saw nudes she had posted of herself?"

"That's exactly what Isham couldn't understand. Probably because her face was visible. She was careful not to expose her face in her own nudes. The main problem though was he didn't ask her permission. She couldn't trust him after that. She assumed he shared the photo with all of his friends."

"Did he?"

"He claims he didn't. But that's what tends to happen with nude photos on the internet these days."

"Yeah, you can't even go to a nude beach anymore, with cellphones secretly snapping you and uploading you and databases putting all the pieces together. Her photo didn't get out anywhere?"

"No, but it caused a big mess."

"I'm curious to see the photo. You still have it?"

"I deleted her and everything connected with her when she turned on me."

"Turned on you?"

"Just as she turned on Isham. Because I didn't immediately tell her that he sent me the photo. She thought I was in cahoots with him and planning on sharing it with my friends too."

"How did she find out Isham gave you the photo?"

"Because when she asked him about it, he assumed she had asked me. So he had to tell her. He's not the lying type. When he confessed to it, she confronted me. I seen that photo for all of about two minutes and had no idea what was going on. How about you? Would you let nude photos with your face in them circulate? You seem pretty liberated."

"Quality erotic photography? I have no problem with the

idea, or even homemade porn. But I have to be careful living in China and the nature of what I do."

"How could it affect your rug business?"

"Oh, that? Not at all. It's my other activities."

"What, are you a spy or something?"

"I'll tell you later. One thing at a time. Anyway, painting is perfectly safe. I have no problem with you painting me any way you like."

"Can't wait to. We should start heading back now if we want to get back in time to cook us up some dinner."

Over oxtail soup at Jim's place two remaining exotic wines were sampled, an elderberry and a dandelion wine. "I was saving the last of these for just the right occasion. Elderberries are really hard to come by and I don't know if I'll be able to find enough to make it again."

"Just divine. I like it when the wine isn't too sweet but is at that exact midpoint between sweet and sour so they fuse into a kind of neutral sensation."

"So, what is this mysterious activity of yours that you're reluctant to tell me about? You've gotten me curious. Whatever you say won't go any further than this house."

"I make psychedelics."

"Wow. In Shanghai?"

"It's a lot safer than smuggling, though I do that too."

"What kind?"

"Mostly by extracting from plants. DMT, things like that. I only smuggle stuff that's almost impossible to get caught with, like acid. You want some? I have a whole shitload of it with me."

"No, thanks. I'm not into hallucinating drugs. You mean you bought it here and are carrying it back to China? What if you get searched?"

"They won't find it."

"How can you be so sure?"

"An industry secret. Weed — no. Edibles, no. Chinese Customs has been wising up to edibles. I have a reliable weed supplier in Shanghai anyway."

"It grows wild in Xinjiang."

"It grows wild all over the world. Back to that jacuzzi photo, which I'm now obsessed with. How did Isham share it with you? By email? Messenger?"

"Messenger."

"If you have him on Facebook the photo should still be there in his Messenger feed."

"No. He deleted everything related to her too when the police got involved."

"How did they get involved?"

"She accused him of practically every crime in the book."

"He got arrested?"

"Yeah, but was only held temporarily at first. I don't know what's happened since."

"You don't know where he is now?"

"No idea. A few months after the café incident he just dropped out of the picture. Even Bonnie his girlfriend doesn't know. Unless she's keeping mum about it. He was threatened with deportation, and that's the last I heard. We don't even know if he's still in China or another country."

"What happened in the café, exactly?"

"Again, I have no idea. He said she tried to steal his iPad. She said he assaulted her. Oh, I remember something. He sent me several long accounts of what happened before he disappeared. It was distressing for all of us at the time and too much material to go through, and I never got around to reading it. That I still have. I can forward them to your email, and maybe you can work it all out."

"That would be great."

"I'm really kind of overwhelmed by you. This has been a whirlwind over the past twenty-four hours. Do you really have to go back tomorrow?"

"Yeah. I will definitely arrange to stay longer the next time I visit. I like it here."

"I can't do a decent job painting you if you have no time to sit for me."

"We can get started now. I can hang around till noon

tomorrow."

Jim went up behind her, slipped his hands around her shirt and pulled it apart. "I may be falling in love with you."

*

She jumped on her before she even had time to set down her luggage, clamping her legs around her waist. Marguerite carried her over to the futon, Lixin's mouth glued to hers, and plopped her down. She proceeded to strip Lixin of her clothes and tie her up with a spool of warp yarn, passing it under her knees and pulling them up flush against her chest and binding her hands behind her back.

"What are you doing to me?"

Marguerite slapped her across the face. "Shut up!" She wrapped more yarn around her mouth. "I'm going to leave you here for a while to think over how *fucking* annoying you were while I was gone. Why? Because you only look at the world out of the tiny little window in your head. You have *no* idea what's going on outside of yourself. Everything you see is a projection of your infantile desires. You treat me as a fantasy and know nothing about me. You're spoiled. You have OCD. In the Middle Ages they threw people like you naked in a dark room and whipped their senses back into them. That's what I need to do with you. Maybe a few years in a rug factory would teach you something about life."

Lixin mumbled in protest.

"You know *exactly* what I'm talking about. Oh, and did you pick up the bread I asked you to get from the Lost Bakery this morning? No, I can see you didn't. I'm expecting a male contact over here. He's on his way now and will be here shortly. I'm going to tell him you get off on being tied up and exposed to strangers. I bet this actually excites you. Let me see. Oh, yes, indeed. You're wet!" Marguerite flicked Lixin's vulva with her finger and it squirted. "No kidding! Boy, is this going to be fun."

Tears streaming, Lixin lay tied up on her side as

Marguerite unpacked her belongings and put them away. The buzzer rang. She let in an African man of muscular build in neat white slacks and striped nylon T-shirt. "Good to see you, Gabriel. How've you been?"

"Hello, Marguerite," he said, shaking her hand. "I'm doing well. And you?"

"Very well myself, thanks."

She invited him to her kitchen table and popped open a couple Chimay Ales. "How's business these days?"

"Ah," he said, sipping his ale. "You always know how to treat your guests. Business, you say? Well, it comes and goes. Visa situation is tighter. Before we had space. Now you don't arrange yourself, trouble they call you. I got gist they going apartment to apartment checking papers."

"Yep, I was visited not long ago. They were polite about it, though. You can soften them up if you speak Chinese. But you'd better be legal."

"Nobody works for me who speaks no Chinese. You really sell all these rugs? How you take sell so many?"

"Mostly wholesale to shops."

"And that one you're working on now?" Gabriel walked over to the loom. "It's nice."

"That's just for my own amusement."

"I would like to buy it," he smiled.

"A lot of people want to buy it."

"Eh — what's this?" he said, pointing to Lixin. "Who is she?"

"That's Lixin. She's being punished."

"Because why?"

"It's our own little affair."

"You let her lie there all day with her bobbi sticking out?"

"Yes, and tomorrow, too."

"You gave her a dirty slap. And how can she go to toilet?"

"She can't. She won't dare soil anything."

Lixin was sobbing quietly.

"For goodness sake, Marguerite. Why are you doing like this now, when you have guest?"

"Don't worry about her."

"I bring my boys here, they no dey take eye see woman."

"What?"

"They can't see without touching. I am looking at things my eyes are not supposed to see. Let's return to business. What have you brought for me?"

"Now listen. I couldn't risk blotter."

"The dogs, you mean? China dogs are not trained to sniff blotter. No way. They don't look for that."

"I'm not going to be the first to find out."

"What do you have, then, microdots? Pyramids?"

"I can sell you a gram for 100,000 kuai."

"A *gram*? What's the catch?"

"My chemist is experimenting with new materials. You'll probably want to convert it back into liquid and then distribute into whatever medium you want."

"What material?"

She pulled out of her handbag a package containing ten rolled objects sealed in plastic wrap. "Hold on. I need some latex gloves."

"What's this?"

Her hands sheathed, she unrolled one of them. "This contains a hundred milligrams. These are the other nine."

"Woman's *pata*! What am I going to do with these?" he said, exasperated. "Why don't you put one on *her*?"

Marguerite leaned forward. "Do you know how many hits are contained in a gram of LSD? There are two things you can do. If you're in a hurry, you can buy an industrial paper cutter, the kind with the metal base and gridlines, lay them flush like paper and cut them up into 10,000 tabs or as many tabs as you want. How much are tabs going for these days?"

"Single tabs? People will pay anything for acid when it's scarce. One hundred. Even more. But people they expect normal blotter with artwork, not little scraps of tissue."

"People expect quality acid, and once they try this they'll come back for more. Trust me. Now the other thing you can do is to turn it back into liquid by diluting it in distilled water or ethanol. That's better for long-term storage. Then you can convert back again to blotter or something else."

"With all this trouble, why not just give me liquid LSD?"

"Too dangerous. What would I disguise it as, a bottle of eyedrops? And a Customs officer asks me to put a drop in my eye? I'd soon be throwing up and completely incapacitated for the next forty-eight hours."

"Marguerite. I'm acting big man, but I'm not the boss. I was not expecting this. This deal no get head at all."

"Think it over for a few days. You can test it out. I promise you, you won't be disappointed. Let me cut out a small sample for you." She grabbed a scissors and a tape measure. "This is one square centimeter, which I'll cut into four. Take a quarter yourself and give the rest to three more people you know."

"How strong is it?"

"Put it this way. You won't care a hoot they don't have fancy cartoon characters on them because you'll be hallucinating cartoon characters all over the place."

When Gabriel had left, Marguerite frowned sternly as she untied Lixin.

"What you two talking about?"

"Why am I angry?"

"You carried LSD in your panties?"

"I'm talking about *why* I am angry. Tell me why I am angry."

Lixin wrapped her arms around Marguerite's waist. "I know I sent you too many messages. It was only because you don't understand my passion."

"Your passion is out of control. Why do you do something you know I don't like?"

"I'm really sorry and I won't do it again."

"Well, at least you seem to be aware of the problem. But it's going to take a massive DMT session or two to fix your obsessive-compulsive disorder."

Lixin walked over to the kitchen table.

"Don't touch that." said Marguerite. "You need to wear gloves."

"One-time use panties?"

"Disposable panties. They've been soaked in LSD."

"The same drug you gave me?"

"Yes, but that pair of panties contains enough for a 1,000 people."

"*Wode tian.* If I wear it, I will get high?" she laughed.

"You don't want to do that. We're trying to figure out how to get it out of the panties into more consumable form."

"Can you cut out little pieces with scissors?"

"That's not very accurate. They'll be different sizes and shapes and thickness. And the elastic bands have a lot more in them than the rest."

"You can mix in water?"

"Yes, we need to dilute it. Then we need to figure out what to put it on, because we don't have blotter paper."

"What paper?"

"Paper to soak up the diluted LSD."

"Why not dilute into many small bottles and just drink?"

"You have 10,000 bottles?"

"You dilute into ten bottles and sell them. Next person dilute into ten more bottles, and next person like that."

"It has to be done very precisely and carefully, and most people don't have the patience or knowhow."

"Why not just do one bottle at a time and store the rest?"

"I may have to do that. The question is what to dilute it in that's safe and discreet. I've heard of people using vodka but it will degrade in the bottle if it's exposed to light."

"Any alcohol okay? Why not Chinese *baijiu*? Many *baijiu* brands don't have clear glass bottles."

"Now that's an idea. You may be of some use after all."

"Buy one hundred different brands *baijiu* and start collection. Expensive brands have attractive bottles, each very different. You can put them on shelves like a museum."

"Yes! A hundred bottles would make for a much more manageable hundred hits per bottle. And I could sell each bottle for 10,000 and make a lot more than getting rid of it all at once."

"You already try this LSD in Chicago?"

"Yeah, it's good."

"I have question. You're not afraid to bring all these drugs into China? What if you get caught?"

"The kind of stuff I bring in is way over their heads."

"How about the DMT?"

Marguerite took out four jars of colorful powder she had brought back from her trip. "You know what these are? Indigo. Cochineal. Syrian rue. And mimosa bark. They're some of the natural dyes I use for my rugs. If anyone at customs questions me, that's what I tell them." She picked up the mimosa powder. "This makes that." She pointed to a deep red hue in the unfinished carpet in the loom. "This also happens to make deems."

"The same stuff? How?"

"Don't worry about how. Just take my word for it."

"But why you need to bring LSD panties?"

"Acid's too difficult for me to make, dear."

"And you visit that man named Jim?"

"Yes."

"What happened?"

"I'll take you there next time and leave you with him."

"You know I'm not into men."

"It's not a question of whether you're into men. It's whether you're into helping out your friends."

"Have sex with them?"

"Perhaps, since it follows from friendship. Fucking is a duty among friends. Regardless of who they are or what they look like or what gender they are. It's the most honest form of communication."

"Your ideas are so weird. You find out more about the author?"

"Yeah, all kinds of stuff. And some ideas of his I happen to agree with. Like his concept of sexual generosity: sleeping with someone not because you want to but because they want to."

"I can't sleep with someone I don't love."

Marguerite covered her ears. "Please, oh please, spare me the clichés!"

"We are not animals. We can't sleep with everyone."

"Most people live lives of sexual misery because they're not sleeping with *anyone*. Some people can't find a partner. But most could if they weren't held back by their own sexual selfishness."

"How come he beat Luna?"

"Maybe he didn't beat Luna. I'm still going through all the material. It seems he got into a fight in a café with another woman he was involved with, named Kitty."

"What material?"

"Jim gave me a bunch of stuff Isham sent him about what happened."

"Why there are rumors he beat his translator?"

"Rumors can twist things around. What I gather happened is that he photographed this woman Kitty in a jacuzzi and sent the photo to Jim. He didn't think it was such a big deal because Jim had already seen Kitty's nudes. They were in a café. She made him show her his Facebook conversation with Jim about the nude. Or maybe she just wanted him to delete the photo and prove he deleted it. Anyway, she grabbed his iPad and he tried to grab it back. They fought and something happened. Maybe he hit her."

"Did those two women know each other? Maybe it was about jealousy?"

"All I know is they were always fighting. Isham and Kitty. Jim emailed me several long accounts of what happened that Isham mailed him before he disappeared, plus hundreds of screenshots of WeChat conversations. I need to read through the stuff to put it all together."

"You mean you have Isham's own writing?"

"Tons of it. Enough for a book. I just got started on it on the plane and it's pretty wild. Not long after he met Kitty, another woman got involved with them."

"How he met Kitty?"

"Several years ago, around the time he got back in touch with Luna, after cutting her off for years. Shortly before he took Kitty with him to visit Jim in the States, a woman named Abby somehow befriended them. Her sister had thyroid cancer and she wanted to know if Isham could pick up a certain Western medicine for her on their trip. Kitty knew a doctor who was a cancer specialist and helped Abby get her sister transferred to his hospital. The two seemed to hit it off and became friendly. In fact, Abby became obsessed with Kitty, with her beauty and talents. She started enticing both of them with increasingly explicit erotic photos of herself. She told them she wanted to have a threesome and watch Isham *rape* Kitty. She told Kitty this. Kitty was a bit annoyed. I mean Abby was sexting them pics of herself masturbating. But Kitty did agree to let Isham massage Abby while she photographed them."

"Was she a normal person? What was her job?"

"Yeah, married with a kid and had some successful business. She was well off. But here's the weird thing. They arranged again and again to meet at a hotel for the massage photo session, but Abby never made it. She always had some bizarre excuse and you almost had to believe her because each excuse was better than the last. First, she was on the way to the hotel when the hospital called and said her sister had a relapse and was in a coma. The next time, she was on the way to the hotel and was rear-ended and had a whiplash. The time after that, her husband noticed her exchanging messages with Kitty about the hotel and demanded she tell him what was going on. She showed him Kitty's profile showing it was a woman. Why the hell was she arranging a hotel tryst with a woman? Abby was honest and said she was super attracted to Kitty, who had agreed to being massaged by her. This got him all worked up and he wanted to participate. Kitty didn't like men, she told him. Fine, in that case, he said, he wouldn't let her out of the house. Something hilarious always came up at the last minute to abort things, and always after Kitty and Isham had checked in at the hotel. But by now the two were already becoming good friends. Kitty frequently met Abby at the hospital during visits with her sister. Isham never got to meet Abby."

"I think the woman never wanted to meet for sex but just had fantasies."

"Exactly. She couldn't deal with the reality of it. But she kept on arranging to meet them again, as if stuck in an obsessive loop. I think she was trying to work through her own contradictions and just wasn't able to. There's more. Around this time Kitty and Isham had one of their tempestuous fights. Abby sided with Kitty and turned on Isham. It had something to do with Bonnie — his live-in girlfriend — hacking into Kitty's WeChat account and falsely posting lewd information about her which caused her account to get temporarily shut down. And somehow Abby's sister herself got involved with this and it was a huge mess."

"Her *sister*? In the hospital?"

"Yes."

"I like this story."

"It gets even more complicated, but I have to get caught up on sleep before I can finish telling it. The jet lag is starting to hit me and I need to rest for a while. Later we can go out to dinner."

Marguerite took a shower in the glass tub with its handheld nozzle, lay down and fell instantly asleep. Lixin kissed her lightly on the lips and pulled out her cellphone.

The next day a delivery of several boxes arrived.

"*Baijiu*," said a smiling Lixin, as she began pulling out the bottles and arraying them on the floor. "Each a different brand. I couldn't get all same-size bottles, but no any of them are transparent glass. Some are 500 milliliters, some 475 milliliters. Alcohol degree is also different, some fifty-three percent, some fifty-six percent, some fifty-nine percent. I guess you want strong alcohol type."

"When did you order these?"

"Yesterday when you were sleeping."

"Aren't you amazing. I hope they weren't too expensive."

"A little. You just add price of the *baijiu* to them and pay me for that when you sell them."

"It doesn't work like that. I have to sell them for an even 10,000 per bottle. Just keep a record of what you paid."

Many of the hundred oddly shaped bottles were decked out in shiny primary colors with gold-ornamented caps like garish religious paraphernalia, while others were tricked out like clay-fired ceramics suggesting ambrosias of ancient origin. They got right to work. Marguerite partially unrolled the first of the ten panties into a flat rectangle and divided it into ten sections with a scissors. She measured them out on a precision digital scale, adding snippets here and there to equalize their weight down to a tenth of a milligram. They opened the bottles and with Korean steel chopsticks inserted the potent pieces of tissue, plunging them deep inside and stirring them around before re-sealing. The floral aromas of the premium sorghum liquor, the most pungent of alcohols, shot through the loft and lingered for hours after they had arrayed them on the floor along one of the walls, until shelves could be installed.

"How much should you drink to get high?"

"A teaspoon is five milliliters and it's about what you had. You don't want to take more than that unless you know what you're doing. Each bottle will contain a hundred teaspoons. We will make sure anyone buying a bottle knows this. Anyone willing to spend 10,000 kuai on a bottle will know it."

"That man who came here yesterday will buy them?"

"I don't know. I've already decided to change the terms. I have a feeling he isn't interested."

"He won't come back?"

"Why? You like him? I thought you didn't like men."

"It was exciting when he looked at me."

"Oh, so you really do have an exhibitionist streak. Hmm, we're going to have to do something about that. But he's not the right person. He has a family and he's on the conservative side. That's why I wanted to dump the stuff on him right away and get rid of it. We need to be careful. People talk. My place is a showcase apartment, you know, and I'm a bit notorious. It's my weakness."

There was a knocking at the door. A woman and two men announced they were from the building management office and wanted to confirm the loft's residency. One of the men was in a *chengguan* uniform, a sort of intermediate role between security guard and police officer. Marguerite invited them inside. They wandered a few steps into the loft and glanced around while she fetched her apartment lease and passport. She told them Lixin was a friend. They thanked her and were gone.

"Thank god we got that over with," said Marguerite, as the they stared at each other with relief at the close call. "They only come round once in a blue moon and shouldn't be back any time soon."

6

I t wasn't an online dating site that had thrown them together, the usual method of hooking up with a new partner, but a former student of Isham's from a decade back who had been her high school classmate. Kitty was seeking an educated foreigner for help with her English. There was no suggestion of anything on the burner besides business. But the moment he set eyes on her in the Italian restaurant in Shanghai's Jing'an District, he knew the language practice would give way to a more consequential intercourse. She made him distinctly uneasy. Then again he was drawn to women who made him uneasy, and he was powerless to stop it.

She later told him she could make him out through the restaurant's window at a distance. He didn't see her enter, indeed had no idea what she looked like. Then there she was standing by his side, understated in appearance, in a loose sky-blue summer dress, hair in a simple pony tail, a delicate makeup job on a still youthful face. The open stare she greeted him with was unlike any he had witnessed when meeting a person for the first time. It was as if she was shocked, although there was nothing in the least out of the ordinary about him. It was the look of a nervous Chinese woman in a backwater city being thrust before a foreign man for the first time, though Kitty was not from a backwater city and was a seasoned global traveler.

The Chinese don't like to overwhelm or display much personality on first encounter, and the conversation was reassuringly boring. "I hate my job," she said. "I need advice on my English in my application to emigrate to Canada."

"Your English is already quite good."

A month later she asked Isham for more language help. He invited her to a talk he was giving on one of his books in a teahouse run by a Chinese artist and his American wife. They arrived early and he went over another writing sample she had brought. When the event was over, he handed Kitty two books of his in translation.

"This is the first time an author himself gave me his books," she said, flattered.

She texted him now almost daily. "I don't like your writing," she announced.

"Why not?"

"It's vulgar."

"That means I'm on the right track."

"Do you have time to meet tonight?"

"Sure. I know a nice place."

They met in a 1930s-themed restaurant lined with candelabra, framed paintings and gilded mirrors in Xujiahui, formerly Siccawei, Shanghai Puxi's main business district at the French Concession's western end, close to where Kitty worked. After dinner he took her to a café with private rooms. She sucked his cock. The relationship was on.

The next time they met, he asked her to explain an aspect of Chinese psychology that had long perplexed him: *mianzi*, or "face."

"'Face' is supposedly about self-esteem yet you have no control over it. One's 'face' is entirely dependent on others. You fail to compliment me, I lose face. You have more money than me, I lose face. You're promoted at work, I lose face. You have a nicer car, I lose face. You didn't do anything to me, yet I make damn well sure it's *your* fault. It's *you* who's to blame," said Isham. "How childish and pathetic. What's really going on, if you ask me, is face is a weapon people use to get leverage over others. The slightest advantage someone has, exploit it, attack it with the accusation, *you* are making me lose face. Therefore, *you* owe me something. Keep piling it on, gaslight them with so much guilt they start to have doubts and take you seriously."

"I know what you mean. It's a kind of psychological warfare. Or you can just call it vanity. *Mianzi* is the abuse of self-esteem."

"The worst is with families. You can always blame a family member for losing your face, because they're at the center of your relationships. Their shortcomings make you come off badly next to other families."

"I can give you an example of that," said Kitty. "Once I forgot my house key. I called my ex-fiancé to go home and get it, but he was playing golf with clients and let me go to a café or a beauty salon to wait for him. I didn't listen to him and went to the golf course to fetch the key. He was very angry because his friends laughed at him. They said I went there just to make sure he was with men and not women, and he's a henpecked man. I made him lose face. From then on, whenever we bickered he would bring it up, which made me feel I owed him something."

"Likewise," said Isham, "a female student of mine once got a job at a bank. Her family was from Sichuan but her father was staying with her in her Shanghai apartment. He was constantly complaining about her reluctance to find a husband. He became so depressed over it she had to take him to a psychiatrist to put him on anti-depressants. The medication didn't help. Why? Because it was all *her* fault. It was she who made him lose face among his friends back home because she didn't have a nice family and a baby. It was she who made him ill, and the only thing preventing him from committing suicide was for her to find a husband.

She was the source of the problem. *She* was a 'leftover' woman. What a loser he was."

"So what happened?"

"She bought him off with face money — gave him a big sum of cash, kicked him out and sent him back home. That's what the problem was at bottom. She made him lose face because she was a successful career woman earning a lot more than her parents on their meager state pensions, and he felt humiliated by that."

"She's also an investment banker."

"How do you know that?"

"You can't hide anything from me. You used an example to compare your lover with me."

"My *lover*? What are you talking about?"

"When did this happen? Her problem with her father."

"Not long ago. What does that have to do with anything?"

"Of course, you know what's happening in her life because you're still in contact with her."

"Yeah, we're friends. What's wrong with that?"

"You had sex with her, right?"

"Years ago. So what? She has a boyfriend and hasn't the slightest interest in me anymore except as a friend."

She covered her ears. "I don't want to hear about your lover. You could have chosen other examples but you had to choose her. I've lost my appetite and I can't eat anything," she said, as the waitress brought their dishes.

"She's *not* my lover. What's wrong with you?"

"You deliberately mentioned your lover to upset me."

"This is unbelievable. How can you be like this?"

Kitty gathered up her things and walked out.

Now, to regard Kitty as the intolerant shrew she might appear would be premature. As we shall see, it was a woman grappling with an unprecedented sort of man, one who would seem to be defying her expectations by the day, and it took her some time to understand the complicated foreigner. Let's adopt a more nuanced view of things, set her actions in context. She wasn't the only one he gave copies of his

translations to at the book talk. Another woman came up to
him. He gave her his card. She was intrigued by a title listed
on the card not yet published in Chinese, *Massage and the
Writer*. It took Abby months to get up the courage to contact
him, and when she did, he couldn't recall her, even after she
showed him her photos, first of her face and then of her
body. She began expressing massage fantasies. Yet she was
reluctant to meet alone with him. By this point, she had
become interested as well in Kitty and her Weibo posts
showcasing her extensive travels and photography. We don't
know if Abby was attracted to Isham, or merely to the idea
of him. If she only agreed to meet with him in Kitty's
presence, he was fine with that. He stood a better chance
riding along than trying to arrange things without her. Kitty,
as we have seen, was even open to the idea of photographing
him massaging Abby, for a book they planned to create
together, an illustrated guide to sexual massage, replete with
artfully explicit photos and poetical flights of prose, a book
devoted to the art like no other, one with the potential to
become a cult classic.

It bears highlighting that Kitty was cooperating with
Isham on a book so daring and disarming they could never
hope to find a publisher on the Mainland. Isham was
knowledgeable about book design and confident he could
produce it independently to a high standard, registered and
printed in the U.S. There was no shortage of massage books,
not a few describing techniques of "sensual" excitation and
some even displaying nudity, but they were predictably,
unforgivably bland and inoffensive and purchased by no one.
What could not be found was a book bringing sharp-edged
talent to bear and working up the concept to its logical
outcome: oiled fingers arousing and engorging the genitals
and captured in photographs so compelling, layered over
and illuminated by textual exegesis so lucid, as to hypnotize
and incite the reader to demand to massage the first stranger
at hand.

If Kitty went along with all of this, it was not just to

please her "boyfriend" (the quotes would be removed once she succeeded in severing him from that concubine of his, Bonnie). The groundwork had already been laid, with her keenly developed interest, well established before she met him, in nude photography. She was so good at it her female colleagues invited themselves over to be immortalized while still young. After several failed attempts at finding a soul mate, Kitty herself was approaching forty. And then came along just the right man, a foreigner she found physically attractive and intellectually challenging, with keen artistic interests of his own. If anything, too much so. He spouted the most disturbing of ideas, ideas she had no choice but to reject and cast right back in his face even as she grasped them intuitively, a few of which, she had to admit, validated her own.

Isham's philosophy grew out of a major misunderstanding, held by just about everyone since time immemorial, that to be good, and to be cultured, required taming the sex drive; only after putting sex in its proper place does space open up for art, spirituality and philosophy. All of this was backwards. It wasn't that sex was more important than cultural pursuits, he claimed; it was, rather, inseparable from them. Not only that, sex drives not just culture but intelligence itself; sex *is* a form of intelligence. As he patiently explained, it's well known, at least among an enlightened minority, that smart people, really creative people, tend to have a lot of erotic interests.

The reason for this is simple enough, but more clichés need to be cleared away to understand it. Intelligence is not a quantity people are born with in differing amounts, a myth propagated by capitalism's mechanistic ideology which requires a convenient way to slot people into respective socio-economic classes. This myth convinces you that a number assigned to you from a single primary school test, which you happened to perform badly on because your parents were fighting at the time or shouting at you, is an accurate and indelible measure of your mental capacity, your

"IQ." What can be said is if you believe intelligence is a number, you betray an astonishing lack of it. Intelligence develops in a conducive and nurturing environment where it is already present. Intelligence grows and expands as it feeds on new information. It's dynamic, autonomous and manifold, and it's powered by a strong sex drive.

How can anyone with a love of life, a zest for life, a passion for new experiences, a profound curiosity for all things, not also be fascinated with all things sexual? How is it possible that a searching intelligence could allow itself to be tripped up by prudish discomfort and flee the most mysterious thing of all, sexual energy, while embracing everything else? We don't mean the brute sex instinct but more crucially, the *erotic* – the enlivening and elaborating of sex in the mind: erotic intelligence. Intelligence is the capacity to *see*, to take in everything, not just figuratively, in the mind's eye, but literally, the capacity to notice the world around you. The erotic eye differs from the ordinary eye in being shamelessly, promiscuously open. Although it takes a mental leap to grasp it, in its sheer tactility sight itself is sexual.

More mundanely, the mere sight of sex taps deep into the well of creativity. Isham was fond of relating, without embarrassment, how an X-rated cinema in downtown Chicago had once helped him to work out problems in his college literature papers. He would head there every Friday for the new double feature. This was not out of sexual frustration, though he had his share of that. In fact, he found many of the films palling. But he discovered that the sight of writhing bodies acted on his brain like a designer drug, warming over the unconscious and freeing ideas to bubble up with surprising fecundity. This perhaps gets at Picasso's quip that "Sex and art are the same thing."

Isham's ideas could not but strike Kitty as outlandish and extreme. Nevertheless, she was cooperating with him on a book that embodied and exemplified these very ideas. Moreover, she was putting words to action and enlisting a friend whose flashy body would be, they hoped, the first of a series of attractive models to grace its pages. A string of mishaps, however, was preventing Abby from joining them for the inaugural photo session. Her husband got wind of her chatter with Kitty and wouldn't let her out of his sight unless she took him along. By this point, Isham was so curious to know what Abby looked like in person he was willing to forego the encounter just to confirm she actually existed. He proposed that Kitty should go ahead and invite Abby and her husband to dinner at a certain restaurant in Xintiandi. Isham would be sitting at a nearby table, allowing him to get a good glimpse of her. The three of them could then proceed to the hotel — a five-star hotel for the occasion — and enjoy themselves, while Isham would wait patiently for the next opportunity.

Kitty and Isham arrived at the restaurant early, to hash out a few particulars regarding their upcoming trip to the U.S. "How much time do we have?" he asked.

"I think they're going to be late. She is not sure her husband is really coming."

"Oh, so we'll have the hotel tonight after all?"

"I don't know yet."

"Anyway, I'm unhappy you're now telling me you want to go to Niagara Falls. We don't have time."

"I can take a side trip there if you don't want to go with me. I can drop you off at Chicago on the way back from visiting Jim. We'll have four nights left."

"I thought you were spending the whole trip with me."

"You arrange everything around what *you* want to do. I'm not your slave. I have never been to the U.S. before."

"We already discussed this. Of course, if you were going there alone you could plan out a nice itinerary for yourself. But this is my home. I have a better idea how to use our limited time. Look, if I were traveling to your hometown, I would let you take care of everything. I would be honored to be your guest and in the hands of a local. I have things to do in Chicago, business to take care of, friends to visit. I need all the time we have. I would like you to be with me. I know you're not comfortable meeting strangers but you need to trust me you'll have a good time. I've organized everything. Violet and Bob are eager to meet you."

"I don't want to meet them."

"But you said you would. We fixed the date with them. Now you're changing your mind?"

"I don't want to see your lover."

"Here we go again. She's *not* my lover. The last time we slept together was fifteen years ago. She has a boyfriend. That means the four of us will be together. Anyway, I told you we don't have to have sex with them, just a nice dinner at a restaurant. They're fine with that. Violet doesn't have a chance to meet a lot of Chinese friends, after so many years away from home."

"She invited you to have sex with her. Of course you will."

"*They* invited *us* to have sex. I explained this to you. They're swingers. Since you're going with me, obviously I hope you could join us. Why would I want to sneak off and see them alone when it would be more fun with the four of us? They were thrilled to hear I would be bringing a beautiful woman with me. It's not about her. It's about two couples sharing each other in a more intimate way. It's about friendliness and open-mindedness. What's so hard to understand?"

"Are you friendly with *me*? Letting me watch you have sex with her?"

"As I said, we do not have to meet them for sex. You're willing to watch me massage Abby. How do you explain that?"

"She's not your lover."

"Neither is Violet. So, what you're saying is it's okay if *you* know the woman but not okay if *I* know the woman? You're not being rational."

"Just go to your country yourself and see your lover! Be honest with me. You don't want me there."

"Why are you so stubborn about this? Okay, fine. Go ahead and cancel your plane ticket. I'll go myself."

Kitty grabbed her cellphone and tapped at it. "There. I just did."

Isham stormed out of the restaurant and headed home through the leafy French Concession, canopied in white-barked plane trees and winding streets that swerved you around in fresh directions, reinventing the day. It made Shanghai one of the best walking cities in the world. Even in the evening the lingering suffused light of the plane trees cast an enchanting green glow. Other cities like Wuhan and Zhengzhou had their own old plane-tree neighborhoods, but beyond the usual run of grimy noodle and cigarette stands, dowdy women's apparel and lottery shops what they lacked was surprise — the artisanal bakeries, library-themed cafés, specialist boutiques (one devoted to Japanese sake!), snazzy wine bars. Shanghai provided the perfect space for random situationist excursions and was the only city Isham ever needed. Tonight, however, he walked all the way home to the Jing'an Temple area in a decidedly unmeditative mood, without once looking around.

When he finally glanced at his phone, he found a score of messages from Abby. "Where the hell are you?" she yelled. She had escaped from her husband and was consoling a sobbing Kitty in the hotel room. By the time he saw the messages, Abby had gone home.

To her credit, Kitty was apologetic and did her best to repair things. She rebooked the flight. She reiterated her willingness to meet Violet and her boyfriend for dinner and promised not to let her jealousy flare up on the trip.

The détente didn't last long. Only days later, Kitty texted Isham a message with a confusing pair of screenshots. To help him promote his books to Chinese readers she had created a public WeChat account for him, visible to anyone who followed it, using her own identifiers. She posted catchy quotes, accompanied by suggestive photos. One screenshot was of one such post, with a quotation attributed to the photographer Helmut Newton, known for his loathing of "good taste" but worked up in Kitty's enigmatic Chinese into: "In my vocabulary, art is a dirty word. Massage is more art than skill." The image attached to the quote might at first glance have been a Newton nude but was in fact of Kitty herself, cropped to show only the shoulder and side of her breast, minus the nipple. The other screenshot was of someone's profile, showing her private WeChat ID. It was Bonnie's.

"This is how you respect me? So disgusting and unpleasant."

"What's the matter?"

"*That* woman reported me to WeChat for being obscene and my account was shut down for seven days. They gave me a warning. If I do it again it could be shut down for good."

Isham showed Bonnie the screenshots. She too was at a loss. The photo barely qualified as erotic and could hardly have been in violation of community standards. "Look, I was the first person to comment on her post," she exclaimed. "The time shows ten minutes after she posted it. See what I wrote: 'This is a great post, just to my liking.'"

Isham got back to Kitty. "Bonnie would never do something like that," he protested. "I've known her for over ten years. She has never caused the slightest trouble with any of the women I was involved with. It's not her style. She's above that kind of pettiness. You can see from her comment that she praised your post. Why would she turn around and report you for it?"

"I even found out her location when she reported it and her cellphone make."

"It's impossible. Somebody must have hacked into her account. Wait a minute. How did you find out that information?"

"Abby's sister works for Tencent in the WeChat security department. I asked her to check who made the report. I cancelled my ticket. Go to the U.S. yourself!"

Isham contacted Abby. "I heard your sister helped Kitty find out who reported her to WeChat for that post, and she told her. That is certainly illegally obtained information and a violation of privacy. We could report your sister for that."

"Listen to me, Isham Cook. You can make whatever threats you want. Go ahead and try to report my sister. You won't get anywhere. How dare you allow your live-in girlfriend to insult Kitty like that! Don't you ever contact me again either, or I'll report *you* for harassment!"

*

Kitty recovered from the unresolved WeChat flap to once again book the flight in time for the trip. They were off. The first week went smoothly. They were staying in the guest bedroom of his longtime Indian friend, Robi, who invited them along to a sitar raga concert the very day of their arrival. With his eclectic musical tastes, Isham was thrilled to see live Indian classical for the first time, in Chicago of all places, though he and Kitty were brought low by jetlag and had to make an early exit. The next night he took to her a concert version of Debussy's opera *Pelléas et Mélisande* at the Chicago Symphony, a work that, despite its towering status is difficult fare even for regular classical fans, yet Kitty sat still through it all. "Listen to the orchestra, which tells the story in dark orgasmic rumblings and spurting fountains of pathos," he had instructed.

She loved to drive but handed him the wheel from time to time in their car she insisted on renting and choosing herself.

"Why are the roads in America white?" she asked as they proceeded north through Wisconsin on bleached asphalt.

Jim at last got to meet Kitty after months of Facebook exchanges. This was one thing he and Isham both agreed on, above all in the Internet age: there could be no true friendship if it's not grounded in the physical presence of a person.

They headed back to Chicago via Madison and Mazomanie. Kitty was at the wheel. Isham was fiddling on his iPad with maps of the obscure country roads that led to

Mazo beach when a nude image slid into view.

"Who is that picture of?"

"What picture?"

"The naked woman."

"It's just a friend."

"Don't lie to me. It's your lover."

"Okay, it's Violet. But she's *not* my lover."

"Why did she send it to you? Tell me!"

Kitty liked to drive fast and she now hit the accelerator.

"Slow down! Jesus Christ, your silk scarf is tangled around your foot and your thermos is lodged under the brake pedal!"

"Don't tell me how to drive!" she squealed as the car swerved and then recovered.

Isham had oft frequented Mazo beach via both car and canoe on the Wisconsin River. You used to be able to drive down the gravel road and park on the side close to the beach. But the guardians of morality had been gaining the upper hand and the beach's days were numbered. The road was now blocked off to vehicles and the final mile had to be traversed on foot. "Inappropriate behavior will not be tolerated!" warned a sign, aimed at those considering having a little fun at the beach's once notorious gay section.

"I don't believe you." Kitty had never been to a nudist beach.

"I'm telling you it's not just men there. You'll see women too."

"There is nobody there. You arranged for all your male friends to be there so they can rape me."

"Yep, let's go get you raped."

"You'd better be telling the truth."

It was late May and too early in the season for more than a modest crowd, a good hundred people. With nothing but a towel draped around her neck, Kitty cautiously wandered the length of the novel environment, as if only by covering every square inch of it could she confirm for the first time the existence of authentic nudists of both sexes.

When they checked in at the motel Kitty had booked in Madison, she discovered their reservation had been changed to a smaller room. She was not one to allow them to get away with this. The receptionist, an attractive Latina, was apologetic and upgraded them to a jacuzzi room at no cost. Kitty was still not satisfied because the listed price of the jacuzzi room was less than the undiscounted price of the room she had booked. She was getting impatient with the receptionist. Isham pressured her to accept it.

"Damn you!" he yelled when they were in their room. "I'm tired of your stubbornness! She was cooperative. This is a nice room. What's the matter with you!"

"They cheated me! You support them or you support me?"

He sat down on the bed and took a deep breath. "Okay. Let's calm down and try to have a nice evening."

"I *am* calm."

"Let's try out the jacuzzi, and then we'll go to that blues bar nearby I told you about."

He filled up the tub and they got in. Kitty lay back in it with her sad doll eyes. Isham couldn't resist snapping a picture of her. And later in the evening during the live blues gig, after a couple ales, he couldn't resist passing it on to Jim.

It was a good thing Robi was spending the night at his girlfriend's when they returned to Chicago the next day, for he would have been caught in the crossfire.

"Did you show Jim the photo you took of me yesterday?" she blurted out without warning.

"Yeah, I did. It's a beautiful photo. He thought so too."

"But you didn't ask me."

"All right, I'm sorry. I should have asked you. But he's seen nudes of you before. You know that. It was an artistic photo. What are you afraid of?"

"How can I trust you if you do that? You're not honest. Just like you weren't honest about that naked photo yesterday in the car."

"Okay, I'm sorry. Why are you making such a big deal of

this?"

"Fuck you and die!" She started packing her suitcases. "I can't trust you. I want to go home. Where are the keys to the car? I'm going to the airport."

"You can't go there now. It's almost midnight."

She collapsed on the bed in tears. "I want to see my mama."

"Would you please calm down? Go to sleep. If you still feel like leaving in the morning, I will help you get to the airport."

She slept on the living-room couch. Isham awoke early. Kitty was packed and about to leave. She refused his help. He had to tug the larger of her two suitcases out of her hands to carry it down the three flights to the building entrance. He was halfway down when he heard her trip and tumble down the flight above. He helped her the rest of the way down. The car was parked right out in front but she was limping. He walked her to the driver's seat.

"I can drive to the airport myself," she said.

"Which leg did you hurt?"

"The right one."

"How can you drive if your leg is hurting?"

"I think I will be okay after a few minutes. You can go now."

"You're in no shape to drive. I'll drive you there."

"I don't want you with me."

"You can't drive, Kitty."

"Leave me alone."

He got out and slammed the door. Okay, that's it. Now that they had washed their hands of each other, he was free of her at last. He headed for the elevated train station and his favorite café in the Lakeview area. He got only as far as one stop when Kitty texted him. "I need your help. My ankle is too sore. I want to go back up to the apartment and rest."

He returned to find Kitty slumped over the steering wheel. The car doors were locked. He banged on the window and she didn't respond. Fearing she might have had a heart attack or a head injury, he asked a Mexican man in a neighboring front yard to call an ambulance. He banged on the car window again. He was about to ask the man to grab him something to break it with when Kitty sat up startled. Soon the ambulance arrived. Two strapping paramedics in T-shirts with medical logos lifted her out of the car. "We'll take care of her," they said, and gave Isham the hospital's address.

He arrived minutes later. She was staring vacantly as they hooked her up to an IV and put a brace around her sprained ankle.

"Her blood pressure is low from not eating. She was weak and that's why she fainted," said a doctor. "We'll keep her here for an hour before releasing her. She'll be fine."

Once discharged, he drove her to a Walgreens to pick up some medicine and drawing materials before dropping her off at a café, where she wanted to be alone and sketch. She was cold to him over the next few days. She perked up a bit when he took her to an outlet mall for some shopping. On their last day, he intended to show her one of Chicago's sights, the ghetto, but decided on a better idea, the ghost city of nearby Gary, Indiana, with its burned-out apartment buildings, jungle-like vacant lots, and trees emerging from abandoned houses. Kitty was walking better now and snapped away at America's most picturesque ruined city.

"I'm willing to go to your friend's place tonight. I don't know if I can participate but I can watch," she said.

"Fantastic. I'll tell them."

They were late getting back into the city. They had to forego dinner with the couple and headed straight for Bob's place. Violet had been Isham's student in his first teaching gig in China in the nineties when she was a college senior. While not a great beauty, she was nice enough looking and unashamed of showing off her ample cleavage, at a time when her more hidebound classmates wore frilly dresses reminiscent of children's apparel from the 1950s. Isham was mesmerized by her breasts, their beautiful hang unmistakable even in a bra. As if in compensation, she told him after class one day that her boyfriend was a painter and invited him over to meet him. He painted nudes of her in the traditional Chinese ink-style mounted on silk scrolls. Violet would break up with him a few years later, but by that time Isham and the painter had become chummy. The two conspired to persuade a series of Isham's female grad students to pose nude for the guy in exchange for a free painting; he would dash off two more paintings, one for him and one for Isham. Violet eventually made it over and slept with Isham, but only once, having the usual misgivings about sex outside a committed relationship.

They stayed on friendly terms. He helped get her admitted to the accounting MA program at his alma mater in Chicago, and he introduced her to a jazz saxophonist he knew there. They got married, had a baby and divorced. By the time she had set up shop with Bob, a municipal environmental inspector, it had been fifteen years since Isham had last seen her. The right combination of encounters and experiences had transformed Violet into an openminded woman, and he was practically stunned when she proposed, out of the blue, "Do you want to have sex with us?" That was a first – being invited to a couple's bed.

Isham and Bob shared beers while the ladies chatted in Mandarin.

"Well, I'm going to make myself a bit more comfortable," said Violet, breaking the ice by pulling off her top. Her assets were as glorious as ever but riper now, more banana-shaped, with areolae the size of cookies.

She and Bob started making out. Kitty sat stiffly on the sofa. Isham was reluctant to act, worried she might bristle at the slightest pressure.

"You guys wanna join us?" said Violet as she and Bob headed for the bedroom.

Isham got up to follow them. "Come in," he said to Kitty, nodding toward the bedroom.

Kitty stayed glued to the sofa. Bob went back out and

spoke with her. He then returned, and soon Kitty herself was peering in the doorway, watching with petrified, open-mouthed fascination. Isham, however, couldn't get it up. The primary reason was a keen, peculiar letdown he felt at the sight of a pussy in the unnatural state, shorn of its hair. Violet had succumbed to the unfortunate fashion that had gripped the world since the turn of the twenty-first century of shaving the pubic hair. He was not able to get aroused and that was all there was to it.

There was no delicate way of explaining it. It wasn't a mere matter of taste, as in preferring red wine to white, or brunettes to blondes. The hygiene and cosmetics industries employed an ever-expanding array of skin products to convince females (and males through the tacit collusion of the porn industry) to become far more finicky about their body, all for the absurd purpose of coaxing it to a pre-adolescent ideal of hairlessness. More to the point: women who shaved their pubes could be described as enablers of male pedophilia. Isham found it incomprehensible so many women fell for the ruse and basked in their own brainwashing. He had the deepest respect and admiration for those who saw through it all. The rare sight of tufts of hair sprouting from a liberated woman's armpits had the same fiery impact on his brain as if the same woman exposed her groin to him. He denied it was a sexual fetish, or that it was only a sexual fetish. It was a matter of the intellect: one's ability to recognize ideological indoctrination for what it was and reject it. It was symbolic.

This realization became amplified and distilled into a more exotic conception: a defiance of all sexual conventions, a dissolution of all artificial distinctions and tropes. The ultimate sexual fantasy for Isham was a woman with breasts and fully functioning penis, and beneath the scrotum, a fully functioning vagina. And of course, a mustache.

A savvy couple they were, this free Chinese woman and her engaging boyfriend with whom Isham could converse on any subject. But they fell short of the mark on the final criterion, and that gave Isham the perfect excuse for his evident impotence: Kitty's contagious nervousness, and the late hour. They still hadn't packed and had an early flight. He apologized to Violet and Bob, and they cut the visit short.

Kitty was tense and silent on the drive back. In spite of her own best efforts, Isham feared the experiment may have traumatized her; she might possibly be suicidal. They hadn't eaten anything since lunch. After depositing her at Robi's, he went in search of some takeout food. When he returned, he found her curled up in fetal position on the bed. But then she came to and joined Isham and Robi for pizza and wine. For the first time in days, she was in good spirits.

7

Low-heeled dress shoe, calf gripped by tight white slacks, other foot following gingerly, heavy camera, and those shocked eyes of hers locking on his as she descended into the Macau bookstore where he was preparing his talk. It was Isham's most memorable image of Kitty. She had flown down separately to photograph both the event and the wavy mosaic-tiled pavements spiraling out of the Ruins of St. Paul, that subtle signature of the city she instantly grasped. As usual she hadn't eaten and left the talk early to check in and gobble down a bowl of congee in a stall across from their hotel. When he arrived, they went for Portuguese cuisine – grilled octopus and a bottle of Douro red.

Macau's historic center is connected by long-span bridge to the island of Taipa, the bustling nightlife enclave with its decidedly more Cantonese feel. Taipa is joined to the next island, Coloane Village, whose quaint egg-tart cafés return us to old Europe, by the strange contrivance of Cotai, a Vegas-imitation strip built on reclaimed land and with all the charm of an airport runway. To draw business, the Cotai Strip casinos offered steep discounts on their hotels, and that's where Kitty stayed on her frequent gambling outings.

Gambling had about as much appeal to Isham as a methamphetamine addiction; the casino atmosphere was as menacing as a mental hospital. He had grown up in a family ignorant of the simplest notions of budgeting and saving, and his knowledge of money management was haphazardly acquired. Online banking frightened him. He hesitated to open a retirement account for fear of being locked out for good by a mistyped password or security question, as happened with one of his credit cards. He wasn't as bad as a college friend with a similar affliction who had kept all his money in his desk drawer, but that was the extent of Isham's financial prowess.

China happened to be at the global forefront of e-banking (that's right, ahead of the U.S.), and Shanghai was where it was happening. Kitty had a degree in finance and years of experience on the job and off. Money was sport to her, playing the stock market as easy as playing cards. She played real cards too, in the casinos, where she was every bit as much at home as in her investment firm office. After all, wasn't it all the same shell game, whether employing corporate shares, roulette wheels, or cups and balls? You only needed an encyclopedic knowledge of the myriad rules, and that she had.

"I'm curious, but isn't there a contradiction between your gambling and being a Communist Party member?" he asked her.

"They don't know. Of course, Party members aren't allowed to gamble. They don't even know about my trip to the U.S. with you. I'd be in trouble if they found out."

"Why?"

"We have to get our company's approval to travel anywhere abroad. Most of my personal trips, I use my other passport."

"Other passport?"

"I pretended to lose my company-issued passport and applied for new one."

"You can get away with that? You're living a double life."

This trip to Macau, however, was for a riskier gambling proposition, that of promoting an independently published book. Despite the odd nature of the book, one Kitty herself was uneasy with, this was new territory she could learn from, and she threw her best effort and considerable intelligence into it.

The book had a central problem. Massage is a physical technique, the explication of which requires graphics. The only published books on the subject were straightforward guides, unless they were a collector's item for the connoisseur, such as the erotic massage photo extravaganza they were planning. At least that was going to have pictures. A book on massage without illustrations was like a book on origami, birdwatching or midwifing without illustrations. Isham's earlier publication lacked illustrations but it was not a guide. It was something else altogether, an essay collection and a travelogue, but above all an exegesis, with *massage* the master metaphor for the indelible relationship of all things therapeutic and all things sexual. No other vocation encompassed so many incongruous activities and domains — the hospital, the sports venue, the New Age retreat, the red-light district. Indeed, the contradictory meanings of "massage" had deeper implications, requiring a book-length treatment in itself. *Massage and the Writer* was only ostensibly about massage. What it was really about was the violence of categories — and the need to counter such categories. This in turn made the book impossible to categorize, and difficult if not impossible to sell.

A friend in the book world secured Isham's gig at the Macau bookstore, and the owner generously bought up a bunch of copies and invited a decent-sized crowd to the talk, including a couple magazine reporters. At other bookstores, the person in charge either rejected the book outright or paged through it quizzically before offering to get back to them later. Soon Kitty went on a business trip to Hong Kong and took along more copies of both the original and the Chinese. The owner of one bookstore seemed intrigued. He wanted to look at the book more closely. Stanley claimed to have contacts in the Mainland publishing industry and gave Kitty his card. He also suggested talking to a friend of his named Nathan. Nathan was cultured and literary and happened to be a massage aficionado. Even more intriguing, he ran a string of exclusive massage parlors in Hong Kong. Kitty contacted him and they met for coffee.

"He bought all of the copies," she told Isham when she was back. "He said he knew some friends who might be interested in the book."

"The English and the translation?"

"Mostly the translation, I think. But his English is good and he knows lots of people."

"You spoke English with him?"

"I spoke Mandarin and he spoke Cantonese. We could understand each other."

"So, what next? Will he get back to you if he has any leads?"

"Yeah. I'll let him contact you. I don't want to talk to him anymore."

"What's the matter? He wanted to massage you?"

"You can guess."

"Oh, so he bought my books just to please you?"

"Maybe. Maybe not. Just don't let him talk about me. I despise his type."

"What does he look like?"

"Handsome. And those women working at his massage parlor are hot."

"He took you there?"

"It's luxurious. More than you can afford. He wants to open one in Shanghai too."

"I don't need to go there. The quality of massage in expensive shops is seldom any better than ordinary shops. I have long experience in this."

"He said he has special services for favored customers."

"All the luxury shops do."

"This is different. You can talk to him."

She gave him the man's WeChat contact. He was quick to respond and they started messaging. He expressed what seemed to be genuine interest in Isham's book, which he said he was already halfway through reading.

Nathan's successful massage business allowed for a leisurely jet-set life and frequent flying between Hong Kong and Shanghai, the Mainland's only claim to a cosmopolitan city and thus the perfect place to expand his chain. He showed him photos of one of his Shanghai flings named Bunny, a former flight attendant, now retired in her late thirties and embarked on online business with her husband. She was as attractive as they get and boasted substantial, unattainable breasts.

"How did you ever meet her?" Isham asked.

"On a flight to Shanghai a few years ago."

"You can get them into bed?"

"No problem."

"I thought that only happened in the 1970s, and then only in the movies."

"Nope."

"You're still involved with her?"

"Sure. I have to juggle my Shanghai girlfriends on my trips there and can only see a few at a time. I told her about you and Kitty. She's interested in being massaged and photographed. This is her WeChat contact. She's waiting for you to add her."

"She knows I'm viewing these pics of her?"

"Yeah. As long as the nude shots don't have her face in them."

"The one with her legs wide open is intense. Wow. I thought Chinese stewardesses were all from the countryside and so pure they're shocked by their own vagina."

"They're people just like you and me. Mainland girls are even bolder than Hong Kong girls. They get it on with the pilots. Sometimes while flying."

"You're kidding."

"The competition for the job ensures a steady supply of beauties. Most Chinese pilots are young guys. How can they resist?"

Isham contacted Bunny. She replied right away and got to the point. His book's translation was riddled with typos but that didn't stop it from making her horny. She wanted to invite a female friend of hers to join them for the massage session, if he didn't mind, a former colleague still working as a flight attendant. For a teaser she showed him a shot of the airline's magazine. The gorgeous model on the cover was, like Bunny, in her late thirties, with a slight matronly slackness to her neck and cheeks. Apparently, she was the company's promotional senior flight attendant. "That's Candy. Here's her WeChat."

It would be hazardous not to keep Kitty in the loop every step of the way. Yet she unexpectedly agreed to the engagement, but only if Nathan wasn't present. He was gentlemanly enough to accede. It's unclear what then transpired to muddle things, but technology may be partly to blame. In WeChat you can create group chats. Isham and Kitty started arguing over something trivial, and the viciousness escalated and spilled over into the group. Candy got weirded out and quit the group. Then Isham quit. To lure him back, Bunny texted him more frank pics of the parts of her body she said were in desperate need of massage. The meeting again was on, though without Candy. Isham was only minutes away from the hotel when Kitty accused him of coming only for the purpose of having sex with Bunny. He turned around and headed home. Bunny was left to console Kitty in the hotel room.

"Hey, I heard what happened," messaged Nathan. "You need to cultivate more patience, man. Don't take her outbursts so seriously. Go along with her, play her game. Make up to her. Apologize. Show a little affection and she'll melt and do anything you want."

"She attacked me in the group with an unfair accusation. Of course, I was eager to massage both of your friends. And

I would have been happy to massage Kitty too. In fact, I would have gotten so excited I would have happily fucked her right in front of them. She was rude to all of us, implying it was only about me, when Bunny and Candy were also looking forward to it, and Kitty agreed to it in the first place."

"She's nervous and needs comfort and reassurance. You should anticipate that and guide her into it. Then she'll grow more relaxed and confident each time. You need to talk softly to her. That's the only thing that works with women. I speak from long experience."

"She accused me of being insincere. I can't whisper sentimental platitudes without her again accusing me of being insincere. Don't you see the trap I'm in? I'm just being myself. I like straightforwardness. Nothing turns me on more than a woman I can speak directly to like a man: Would you like a massage? Are you interested in getting sexual? If not, fine. No problem. If she's unhappy about something she can just level with me instead of blowing up. I can't censor myself and pretend to be someone else. I'm not an actor. Kitty can't deal with that. Thanks for making me understand this more clearly. It's over between us. I've already forgotten about her."

The next day Nathan conveyed these words to Kitty while she was driving. They were so upsetting they caused an accident. Nathan quickly reassured Isham he needn't make the trip to Kitty's hospital as he was already with her.

"Is she hurt?"

"Just a little scrape-up. She'll be out today."

"You flew in just for her?"

"I was coming to Shanghai anyway. Her hot coworker, Daisy, is here too. I've already got her on WeChat."

Kitty was back to normal the next day. She was embarrassed by Nathan's seduction of her subordinate. "I could see they were attracted to each other at the hospital. She didn't tell me she's flying to Hong Kong this weekend to see him. Nathan told me," she said. "She's supposed to get my approval. She's married, you know. I don't care that she's married but if my boss finds out it's a problem."

The following week Nathan showed Isham shots of his latest conquest, with her evident approval. Early thirties, impossibly pretty, voluptuous. He said Daisy was keenly interested in being massaged. Kitty too was amenable but would not be present. "You know how awkward it would be for me to do that with someone on my team at work. You and Nathan can massage her."

"She also told Nathan she wouldn't do it unless he was present. I'm fine with that. I haven't yet had a chance to meet Nathan in person."

Isham hooked up with Daisy on WeChat. She poured on the nude shots. "I'm mortified by my thick thighs. I look like a whale," she wrote in surprisingly good English. "The black-and-white ones are better since they were taken a couple years ago before I gained weight. My boss took them."

"Not in the least. You have what is known as a woman's body. A great body."

"Nathan told me he saw pics of my boss sucking your cock. How did he get to see them?"

"I asked her and she let him see them."

"Show them to me."

"I have to ask her again. Some other time. I don't want to press her now. She'll think I'm hitting on you."

"Show me your own pics then."

He pulled out his erection and sexted it to her.

"You got me wet. Why do you two always fight?"

"I don't intend to fight but we always set each other off."

"You don't understand women. You should use sweet words with her instead of always losing your temper."

"So it's only me who needs to control myself? She has some responsibility too. It got so bad on our trip to the U.S. in May that I decided to leave — "

"She went to the U.S. with you?"

"Yeah. Didn't she tell you?"

"No."

"Oh. Maybe you weren't supposed to know. I shouldn't have said anything."

"She didn't even clearly explain to me you are her boyfriend. It's a sensitive issue at work because she's single and almost forty. She's terrified of gossip."

Kitty's worst fear came true. At a team meeting a few days later with the big boss present, Daisy mentioned her trip to the U.S. in front of everyone. She tried to make it come out spontaneously, as if she was only envious. Kitty was reprimanded. She was angry with Isham but acknowledged he didn't cause the trouble intentionally.

"I should have warned you Daisy has a big mouth. She's very outspoken and says whatever is on her mind. This is not the first time she's embarrassed me."

"I find it unbelievable she would blab about it in front of your coworkers and boss. Why?"

"I have to keep on good terms with her."

"You mean she's a loose cannon?"

"What's that?"

"She's out to destroy you? Is she your enemy?"

"No. Usually we have a good relationship. It's too complicated to explain. You need to understand Chinese office politics. Don't blame her either."

"I already confronted her about it. I told her I can't trust her after this. I quit the massage session with her and Nathan."

The cannon was looser than expected. Isham had been hosting a soirée at his apartment attended by Chinese and foreign friends interested in classical music, about which he was fairly knowledgeable. Since leaving teaching he missed the steady supply of new faces, and the monthly get-together brought the classroom into his home. Some guests were former students, others colleagues from work; they brought their friends, and many became regulars. Each soirée had a theme — say, the Arab-Andalusian connection in medieval music, the dulcimer family of instruments, classical-influenced rock music — and selections from Isham's vast

CD collection were played on a high-end audio system, interspersed with his commentary, in his spacious living room which could accommodate twenty, even thirty people on floor cushions, with snacks and wine. Sometimes he invited performers – a Japanese shamisen player, a Dutch composer of electronic music, a madrigal troupe, a ravishing Chinese professional cellist dividing her time between Shanghai and New York City. Over the years he had expanded his email list of invitees and cultivated a WeChat group devoted to the soirée, which numbered close to a hundred. One day they all had the pleasure of viewing an erect penis, courtesy of Daisy, whom he had invited to the group so that he might get to meet her in person. Isham's penis, she pointed out to everyone. The offending screenshot included their dialogue when he had exposed his member to her.

He could do no more than apologize and hope everyone would forgive the rude and degrading intrusion.

"That was really inappropriate," the cellist retorted to Daisy. Several others chimed in.

Isham forthwith deleted Daisy from the group and from his WeChat contacts. But the damage was done. A few members dropped out. His subsequent soirées saw dwindling attendance and he had to end them altogether.

"Why did she do it?" he asked Kitty.

"She said you weren't respecting her."

"*Respecting* her? What does that have to do with anything? There must be something else going on."

"She already feels bad about it. She said she wanted to apologize but you deleted her and then blocked her WeChat."

"Oh, she feels bad about it. That's it? How is an apology going to help things? What's she going to do the next time she's upset, send my cock to my workplace?"

Kitty too felt bad about it and threw renewed vigor into seeking out a publisher for Isham's book and their massage photo album. She contacted the Hong Kong bookstore owner who had introduced her to Nathan and made a proposal. Stanley was not only quick to see the potential, he was a step ahead of Kitty. He had been following her WeChat Moments (like Facebook's News Feed) and recognized her talent with the camera. He proposed serving as their agent for the Chinese translation of *Massage and the Writer* and a volume of photo essays devoted to Kitty's travels. Moreover, he would promote the two as a hip interracial couple and launch them on a China-wide book tour. What an exotic draw that would be — an American man and a Chinese woman jointly representing the arts of massage, photography and literature. As for their planned X-rated massage photobook, that could hardly be publicly promoted, but they would slyly allude to it and create a mystique around it, and fans would hunt it down. Stanley couldn't wait to cobble up a contract, though he underestimated Kitty's business acumen, who wrung him through numerous revisions. Plenty more details and deadlines needed hammering out. The Chinese translation of *Massage and the Writer* called for expert revision, Kitty had more globe-trotting to do to flesh out her photobook, and they had yet to pull off a single massage photo session.

Nathan was willing to invest money in Stanley's venture. To get the ball rolling he showed Isham some startling black-and-white photographs of him straddling a series of women on massage tables.

"Where did you get these?"

"I had a professional photographer shoot them at one of my massage locations."

"These are exactly the kind of photos I want Kitty to take for our book."

"You can use them."

"Who are the women?"

"Customers. I ask the attractive ones if they'd agree to model. Most say no but a few go for it. They get a free massage and exclusive access to my club."

"They don't mind their face being visible?"

"They're still mostly anonymous since their eyes are closed and the lighting as you can see is subdued."

"They also agreed to have sex?"

"Yeah, sure. Most of them have exhibitionist tendencies anyway and completely open up on the table."

How in the hell did Nathan do it? Now, Isham had been a decent enough-looking guy in his prime, more than most. He was tall, broad-shouldered and handsome, having what one woman once described as "distinctive eyes" and according to another, a "classic face." Yet he experienced the universal torture all males undergo in their shy and awkward teens and early twenties, the arid sex life, long stretches of lonely desperation lasting months, years, willing girls few and far between. In the midst of PhD study in his twenty-eighth year, something changed. He had grown slightly more assured, more manly, and women all of a sudden made themselves available. The prime lasted for two decades before female interest began to fall off and he saw the gradual return to the former desert of his youth, not a precipitous drop but a graceful arc. He had grown a bit overweight over the years, nothing too drastic; his body was still holding up and not about to collapse. Certainly, he could have prolonged his prime by working out. But as he had already accumulated a rich store of relationships and memories over the decades, it was time to focus his attention on fewer women and more on his writing.

Isham in his prime, however, was no match for the likes of Nathan. Nathan wasn't so much the proverbial lady's man as a lady's genius. He was not only wealthy, intelligent, cultured and charming; with his sculpted physique, his muscular (not muscle-bound) biceps and thighs, and his friendly eyes, he was irresistible. He trampled over the proudest of married women. He was a perfect male specimen. It had to be considered he was actually an android, or if not, a procreationally fortuitous genetic accident. He showed Isham images of the many women he'd gotten into bed, not just Hong Kong and Chinese natives but foreign women, white women, more accustomed to their robuster male counterparts than the stereotypically spindly Chinese. He even had a Japanese AV star bedmate and showed Isham her pics to prove it. Before the fiasco with Daisy, he had already cut a devastating swath through the soirée attendees after taking up Isham's invitation to join it, chatting up every attractive face in the WeChat group, women Isham was quick to admit being attracted to, and frustratingly so.

There was short but curvy Hongling with rare tawny eyes. There was big-hipped Belinda, less pretty than Hongling but oddly more enticing. There was Ling, a Shanghai agent for visiting foreign classical performers, too slim for his tastes but whose bold black eyebrows promised a hirsute groin, which he was able to confirm from Nathan's cellphone pic. And there was resplendent Peipei and her shock of wavy hair, who ran an art gallery and had once invited Isham over to massage her, only to discover she had forgotten her laptop in the restaurant and they had to rush back; it disrupted the moment and she never made it up to him. Some simply weren't into him, while others held back because he was living with a woman. None of this was an obstacle for Nathan, who could afford to be picky. Belinda and Hongling didn't make the cut, though he teased and tormented them and extracted the most revealing pics out of them as well, readily passed on to Isham, the guilty voyeur. Nathan even toyed with Bonnie, Isham's rock. She too didn't make the cut, but the flirting was fun. Once she understood he had no interest in her, he made the revealing admission to her that "all men are lying including me no matter how frank they seem to be."

Things finally seemed to be working out. Stanley was eager to come to Shanghai for the contract signing and to meet Isham. Kitty suggested a luxury resort in Qingdao, recently opened by a former college classmate of hers where they could all stay for free. Nathan had been planning to take his parents on a trip to Shanghai around the same time. Qingdao was a bit of a hike by fast train but only an hour by plane, and they agreed to make the detour.

Nathan showed Isham a cellphone shot of luscious, pink-nippled breasts dangling out of an open shirt. "Meet Etty."

"Who is she?"

"Stanley's bookstore manager."

"Don't tell me you slept with her too."

"Yep. She'll be contacting you soon about arranging a book talk here in Hong Kong. Stanley has space in his bookstore. We need to order copies of your massage book, the English and the Chinese, and you can give her the details about that."

"I thought we were going to wait till the polished Chinese translation comes out."

"The existing translation is good enough for the time being. It's an opportunity to start generating buzz about the Mainland book promotion. And while you're in Hong Kong I'm thinking of arranging a massage party, where you can meet some of the hotties I've shown you pics of. I asked Etty and she's willing to come and let you massage her."

"She knows I'm seeing her boobs?"

"Yes."

"Does Stanley know?"

"No."

"It's funny I have to go to Hong Kong to meet you guys, since I haven't had any luck in Shanghai. Not one person I've met on WeChat through Kitty have I succeeded in meeting in person. The women won't see me unless Kitty is present. But as soon as a date is set, she finds a reason to blow up and abort things. Abby claims to have met me at my Shanghai book talk last year but I don't remember her. She and Daisy are finished now anyways. Bunny and Candy – I tried inviting them out for coffee just to get acquainted. That's important to me. If you've never met someone face-to-face, it's a fake friendship. Misunderstandings easily arise and you can be dropped in an instant. Yet while they demand to be massaged, they can't manage a simple coffee date."

"You would have met them all a long time ago if you could only work things out with Kitty. It's not hard, man. The contract signing this weekend will take care of that. You'll also get to meet Fanny, her college friend who runs the resort. She told me Fanny is another stunner, and she's reading your book."

"I hope so. I was discussing this problem with my American friend Jim. He said to me, 'Isham, the reason you never meet any of these people and these massages never materialize is *they don't exist*. They're figments of Kitty's twisted imagination, her bizarre alternative reality, and she's convinced you otherwise.' Now, I don't believe that of course, or else I wouldn't be chatting with you now on WeChat. And I don't think he really does either. But it did get me wondering if there isn't some advanced software out there that can do this. I mean, let's say she had that software and concocted all these profiles of hot women and a few men to create the illusion of a whole community of friends, out of some perverse need to control me, some cyberweb of hers to entangle me in. With a few tweaks the software takes care of the rest, generating convincing conversations with each of the avatars based on my input, learning as it goes along, as AI is able to do these days, and keeping me deluded that they're real people."

Nathan might have appreciated that the conspiracy theory was conveyed in jest, but Kitty did not. She responded almost as soon as he finished chatting with Nathan. It wasn't so much the silliness of the idea that outraged her; it was the flippant manner in which he appeared to be regarding her friends — friends who were trying to help him get established in the Chinese publishing world, as well as fulfill his sexual proclivities.

"And Nathan told me something else, about that ugly dog you live with. He said other people who come to your music parties said she's a boorish peasant who pencils in her eyebrows and yells and curses like a fish-market seller. How can you call yourself an intellectual if you associate with someone like that?"

"How dare you insult her. She doesn't curse or pencil in her eyebrows. You know nothing about her. I don't know who said those things to Nathan but if I hear you mention her again, I'm cutting off contact with you for good!"

"No need to. I'm cancelling the contract signing."

Before Isham could reply to this, Kitty had blocked him on WeChat.

"So dramatic," said a bewildered Stanley. "What kind of hot-tempered couple are you two? Please try to calm her down and reason with her. I even prepared a 20,000 kuai advance to give you on your book. It's a win-win situation for everybody and we're all counting on you both."

"She can't control her temper. I'm used to that. But I draw the line when she insults my girlfriend."

"Come on, it's natural for her to feel that way when *she* considers herself your girlfriend. I'm sure your live-in must be a lovely woman and it's just Kitty's way of expressing her envy and jealousy. You need to see beyond that and react calmly. By the way, Etty is also quite confused by all the fighting and asks me to tell you to straighten things out with Kitty or she'll have to cancel the Hong Kong talk."

"Why? Did Kitty say something to Etty?"

"Nathan told her about the massage party he's planning in Hong Kong and that Etty would be attending. At first Kitty was willing to participate but then changed her mind. She thinks you're only interested in having sex with Etty. She was courteous with Etty but said she no longer wanted to come to the party or the book talk. She got Nathan to admit he showed you Etty's naked pics. She told Etty you can't be trusted with women's photos and will show them to all of your friends."

"Where did she ever get that idea?"

"I don't know."

"As for Etty, I've yet to exchange a single word with her. The first time I even heard about her was earlier today when Nathan showed me her pics. I have no idea what's going on."

An irate Isham tried to dig out the source of the rumor from Nathan. Nathan turned out to be surprisingly knowledgeable about Isham and Kitty's entire relationship history. He had also become obsessed with the now famous jacuzzi photo and wanted to see it.

"If I were to show it to you Kitty would have me thrown in jail. You know what happened on our U.S. trip over that photo?"

"I know all about it. She told me your friend Jim told her that you sent the photo to all of your friends."

"I never did that. He was the only person I showed it to."

Nathan showed him the screenshot Kitty took of her final Messenger conversation with Jim, in which he had told her, "He takes nude photos of you and gives them to everyone."

During that uproar Jim had admitted to Isham saying as much to Kitty; he then added that he had meant to say "me" instead of "everyone." As Jim was capable of the occasional sloppy use of language, as we all are, Isham didn't think much of it at the time and forgot about the conversation.

"When Jim said 'everyone,'" Isham explained to Nathan, "he didn't literally mean everyone. It's simply his way with words, exaggerated talk, hyperbole, common enough in everyday conversation. It's like when I just said 'Kitty would have me thrown in jail.' I didn't mean she'd actually do that but only that she'd get very angry. The point is I never sent it to everyone. Jim was the only one who saw it. Why is she bringing it up again now? If she really believes I sent it to everyone, then it's all the same whether I did or not. The problem is her paranoia, not the photo. If I were a woman, I'd be proud of that photo. You'd hardly object to me showing it to you. I know she's worried about people at her job seeing it, but who's going to leak it there? The person doing so would be in more trouble than Kitty. By the way, I found out you told Kitty I have Etty's boobs shot and she told Etty I can't be trusted with it. Now I fear Etty won't want to have anything to do with me."

"The difference is Etty's face isn't in it. She agreed to show it to you. She's impressed with your book and already respects you enough to let you massage her. I know her. She's her own person and smart enough to take what anyone says with a grain of salt."

Etty emailed Isham later that day.

Hello Mr. Cook,

I'm glad to be working with you on your book talk. You need to tell me how to order your books. We may need to express deliver them to make sure they arrive in time. We're thinking sometime later next month. But I just found out you and Kitty had a fight and cancelled your book promotion contract.

Stanley and Nathan both tell me Kitty is a shrewd businesswoman and is working extremely hard on your behalf. I recommend you stay on good terms with her and apologize if necessary, since I don't see the point of your Hong Kong talk if everything else is cancelled. Once we decide on the date it can't be changed, for obvious reasons. If we cancel because you have another fight, it's for good.

Etty

Nathan tried to get Kitty to relent on the contract signing but she stonewalled. As his parents were already enthused about the Qingdao resort, he had no choice but to take them there anyway. They were impressed with Kitty. Nathan was impressed with her college friend and host.

"We arrived yesterday," he messaged Isham. "Fanny is absolutely first-class. A rare beauty, with taste. Maybe too slim for you but shapely. Sophisticated and depraved. In a good way, if you know what I mean."

"Not sure what you mean."

"She's bi."

"So am I. That's not exactly depraved."

"She's open to any combination of men and women doing it together."

"Now you're getting my attention. She told you that? I

presume you'll be able to make progress with her."

"I already did."

"How?"

"Her husband is away. She snuck into my bedroom after my parents went to sleep."

"Does Kitty know?"

"Yeah. She could tell something would happen. Oh, and I gave Fanny your book. She's expecting to be massaged by you soon."

8

Fanny applied her considerable hospitality skills to bringing Kitty and Isham back together. She invited them again to her resort. She also began sending Isham enticing photos of herself — Nathan had of course preempted her — and pointed out quite plainly that her massage fantasies were in a painfully swollen state and needed immediate relief. Kitty agreed to let Isham massage Fanny. An opportune date was coming up: Isham's birthday.

Isham had been involved with a Japanese woman in Shanghai several years back named Kikuko, whose birthday happened to be the day after his. She wanted to celebrate their respective birthdays with a single cake to be cut just before the stroke of midnight. He would have been delighted to do so but for a small problem. To begin with, he had no interest in conventional dates and festivities. He had never attended any of his graduation ceremonies, declined to have a wedding with his previous wife (would never have married a woman who required one in the first place), was indifferent to Christmas and other holidays, and regarding his own birthday, Bonnie had to remind him every year or he would forget it. As a nod to convention and his affection for her, he acknowledged her birthday and allowed her to acknowledge his, which they would celebrate with a quiet dinner out. He wasn't prepared to break this tradition and celebrate his birthday with another woman. Kikuko was upset but forgave him, though the fissure, and his subsequent refusal to find the time to travel with her to Japan, was to cause their breakup. This was sad, he felt, but such is life that we must continually choose one symbolic violation over another. If the world were different and more in line with his vision, these dilemmas could be resolved simply and elegantly: let the three of them celebrate each of their birthdays together, with love, gifts and gratitude! Now *that* would make the birthday meaningful. Needless to say, both Bonnie's and Kikuko's understanding of polyamory didn't extend to this elegant simplicity. Isham took it in stride with a forlorn yet optimistic hope that he was merely a little ahead of his time. If he had this vision, surely there must be others out there who had it too.

Likewise was Kitty loath to let Isham celebrate his birthday with the enemy, but she knew his limits. She merely expressed her displeasure and refrained from an ultimatum. Still she hoped he could make it to Qingdao in time yet was resigned to his arrival the day after. What she was not prepared for was that he had reserved his own hotel room.

"Why did you do that?" she asked.

"What am I going to do if you suddenly explode at me just when I arrive and I have no place to stay? It's a budget hotel so if I make it to your friend's resort, I can swallow the first night and cancel the others. I'm just being rational and not trying to provoke you."

Provoked and dismayed she was. She cancelled the train ticket she had booked. Fanny did her best to intervene. She was torn between inviting Isham alone to her resort and loyalty to Kitty, and transparently conveyed these thoughts to both of them. Kitty now grew suspicious Isham's only motive in going to Qingdao was to massage Fanny. He tried to reassure Kitty he couldn't care less about the massage, as the mood was already spoiled. A keen strategist, Fanny went ahead and not only ordered a birthday cake but invited several of her female friends to the party — hot friends, she told Isham. He told Kitty in turn he was planning to attend after all, with or without her, and though he didn't need to massage Fanny, he would give her the greatest massage of her life should she insist.

The day before Fanny's party and the day of Isham's actual birthday, Nathan contacted him. "Happy birthday. I'm in Macau with Kitty. She flew in yesterday. You know those four paintings of hers?"

The four paintings in question were Isham's latest favorites. Kitty had grown more skilled at the brush with each fight they had. She had painted since childhood but it took a tormented relationship to catalyze her art. Still in search of her own style, she was all over the map, though she favored fast-running Chinese inks on rice paper. One of the paintings showed a woman's juicy upper lip and glinting pearl-white incisors biting into her lower lip, surrounded by red spots and pink stains and smears: a messy, arresting image. Another showed a female figure sitting with knees up and head downcast, depicted entirely in strokes of red and appearing to melt in a pool of blood as if made of wax. The third showed a black-ink drawing of a masturbating woman. So concentrated was the positioning of her hands — index finger of one on her clit and middle finger of the other lower down — it looked like she was playing a musical instrument.

The fourth painting showed two naked men lying spoonwise. They were faceless, which shifted the emotional expressiveness, again, to the genitals and the placement of the hands, the guy in front reaching back to grasp the other guy's balls and help guide his cock up his anus. It was not just the Egon Schiele-like hyperrealism that stamped the painting as special; it was its displaced qualities, its angularity. On both bodies were large tattoos of roses and chrysanthemums. Some of the tattoos were on their shoulders or ankles, but others appeared in odd places, on a knee or back of a thigh — less tattoos than a design motif suggestive of LSD hallucinations. It was this work most of all Isham had hinted to Kitty he would like to have, especially as she had painted it with him in mind, his desires in mind, so uncannily figured into it, a painting he would gladly have paid her money for, though she had yet to provide him with any of her works. The painting would thus make an appropriate birthday gift.

"Sorry if this wasn't the birthday gift you were expecting," Nathan continued, "but Kitty came to my hotel room and sold me the paintings for 25,000. She also let me massage her naked. We didn't have sex but I got her wet. I hope you don't mind. Then she went to a casino and won 100,000 MOP with the money. She's now flying back to Shanghai."

Fanny persuaded Kitty to relent and come to Qingdao with Isham. She agreed but with conditions attached. She revealed these to Isham just before boarding her flight to Qingdao the next day and as he was already heading there on the train: she would attend the birthday party only if they sat separately and pretended not to be involved, as she didn't want to stand in as his so-called girlfriend. And they would sleep in separate rooms.

If Isham had been in a calmer state of mind, less apt to allow a paroxysm of anger to short-circuit his rational faculties, he might have found some advantage to this arrangement. The dramatic ironies were readymade and intriguing, and if anyone should have appreciated them it was himself, the novelist, who could act as if he was only casually acquainted with Kitty while everyone there knew otherwise, or at least Fanny did; the two of them not knowing what would happen later that night, who would be attempting to sneak into whose room; the delectable suspense of the occasion, fraught with the possibility of another momentous upheaval to be woven into the tapestry of their tale. Instead, as Kitty's plane landed in Qingdao,

Isham's failure of the imagination landed with a thud on her cellphone:

"As I told you before, I can deal with not massaging Fanny, just as I can deal with not massaging any of your friends, who are all eager to be massaged. Nor do I care about Nathan massaging you or your selling him the paintings, even though I have yet to see any of your paintings except in cellphone photos. I can even deal with the cancellation of the book deal, though you should perhaps consider all the others you are letting down. I can deal with your usual emotional blackmail. But what I cannot deal with is this last-minute trickery of yours, guaranteed to spoil the evening, after Fanny went through the trouble of arranging a birthday party."

"What's wrong with you? I didn't get angry when I knew you would meet Fanny alone," she remonstrated.

This went unanswered, but not the photo she sent him later that night (the other guests having deftly been disinvited) of her and Fanny attacking his birthday cake with relish.

"Take your psychological problems and get the fuck out of my life," he told her.

The next day came an email from Etty:

Mr. Cook,
    Hi again. Kitty showed me the message you sent her yesterday and I'm afraid to say I can no longer work with you. I've cancelled your book talk. It's really a shame because it could have been a success, but I don't have any confidence in your professionalism and reliability.
    Regards,
    Etty

Sometimes things get nasty enough that we just want to wash our hands of a group of people, the whole annoying lot of them, and retreat to our former life. This isn't always easy to do. Fanny had been nice to Isham and tried her best, not to mention she had a rare sexual openness. The most compatible women he had known over the years had been bisexual, which invariably implied a philosophical sophistication. Well, maybe there was no basis at all to the correlation except it's what he wanted to be the case. But Fanny was someone Isham felt worth getting to know.

Another of Nathan's coterie was trying to get to know him, the flight attendant Candy. She had been less responsive than the others at first, more reserved. She was still smarting in the aftermath of Nathan's seduction, upon realizing their relationship had amounted to no more than a quickie every month or two. Single and already relegated by her society to the category of aged spinster despite her impressive physical capital, she shifted her priorities to sprucing up her cultural capital and accumulating inner resources. She returned to the piano, abandoned since childhood, and was interested in classical concerts, though unwilling to attend one with Isham as long as he was in a relationship with Kitty. She liked his book and asked him lots of questions about it. She was again considering being massaged by him, Kitty present as photographer of course. She already idolized Kitty for her talents but didn't know her well enough to feel at ease with her. Perhaps it was this stalemate, as it was for all of the women in Nathan's and Kitty's expanding circle, that released Candy to engage privately with Isham the more freely via WeChat. Bored and horny on her longer hauls, she started dipping into the cabin toilet to loosen her striped blouse — he recognized her airline's uniform — and show him her erect nipples. How could Isham cut off yet another highly attractive woman for no valid reason, who so far had been only friendly to him?

He even found himself communicating with Daisy again, of all people. Nathan was still sleeping with her on his Shanghai visits and they seemed to be getting along splendidly, not to mention the necessity for Kitty to get along with her subordinate. Surely it would be better if everyone set aside differences and got along, wouldn't it? Nothing good can come out of enmity. They reassured

Isham that Daisy was genuinely contrite about her irresponsible, indeed terrible act of revenge porn. Isham gave in and unblocked her on WeChat. She was enormously thankful for his forgiveness and showered him with fresh pics, some of them snapped in her company's bathroom stall.

But it was the latest female to join the cohort, Kitty's close friend and colleague Glory, which gave renewed urgency to reconciling the two and kick-starting the massage photobook project. Glory was a fellow manager and Party member of the same rank as Kitty in a different department in the investment firm. The well bred tend to watch out for each other and she was as attractive as the rest, if petite. The pair traveled a lot together and when not, picked up deals for each other on luxury apparel and handbags. Glory and her husband were well off indeed but constantly fought and lived in distant bedrooms in their spacious house. When she wasn't with her son she spent much of her time with Kitty — and posing nude for her camera. She kept hearing about Isham and insisted on being introduced and massaged. Not having had conjugal relations in seven years she was, if anything, too eager to meet him. Kitty was careful about which photos of Glory to free up to Isham as teasers, not wishing to overly enflame either of them.

He got to see more as soon as he hooked up with Glory on WeChat. She showed him one shot of a fancy Japanese vibrator lodged inside her and another after removing it, drawing a stream of secretions down her thigh. She got Isham to take videos of him and Kitty and share them with her (and Daisy, who had been clamoring for the same) during the very act, though it took some practice to hold his cellphone at the right angle. She was insatiable. She persuaded Isham to show her every photo of the two of them he still had on his phone. She frankly admitted to Kitty that if Isham got his hands on her she'd be unable to control herself. Kitty could accept watching Isham massage a friend in her presence but not fuck her. She reluctantly gave them permission to meet alone. But as Glory was unwilling to meet Isham without Kitty present, he remained stuck in the old stalemate.

*

"The strangest situation was with this Glory. Not long after they were acquainted, he got into one of his epic fights with Kitty and they blocked each other on WeChat."

"What is 'epic'?"

"Huge. Kitty relented but had no way to reach him; he had blocked her on Messenger, email and SMS as well. She started relaying messages to him through Glory. Glory played Kitty's surrogate mom – dispensing Kitty updates by the minute and expanding on them with commentary. He took a business trip to Taiyuan and found out Kitty was also there on her own business trip. What's the likelihood of both of them being in that provincial city on the same day? He didn't think much of it at the time and they were both too busy to meet anyway. Then he goes to Kunming on vacation. From there he was going to take the bus down to Laos and Thailand and rendezvous with Bonnie, his live-in, a few weeks later. Kitty was again saddened that he couldn't travel with her. The next thing he knows, she and Glory are in Kunming on a business trip together. Glory was begging him to come over to their hotel and massage her. He was still too angry with Kitty to see her and nothing came of it. But here's the thing. They showed him a map of directions from his hotel to theirs. He had never mentioned his hotel to them, but they knew where he was staying. He found this odd and unsettling."

"She was arranging her business trips with him in mind."

"It happened a third time. The cold war was still on and they hadn't communicated in a while, though I guess things were thawing and they had unblocked each other. He was on a business trip to Dalian. He discovers upon arriving that the two of them are not only in Dalian but in the same hotel, and not only that, they're staying in the room directly below his! It's a big city and has plenty of five-star hotels. It's too impossible a coincidence."

"Maybe he told her the hotel earlier and forgot?"

"Why would he have if he wasn't expecting them in Dalian? He was starting to freak. He had a fear of stalking, after his experience with that other woman Luna, and now it was happening with Kitty. Kitty freaked too but for a different reason. They were hoping to meet him for dinner but he already had a dinner date with a female friend who lived there. Naturally Kitty assumed the woman was one of his lovers, though he fiercely denied it. Yet if that was the case, why couldn't he blow off the Dalian girl for the sake of her and Glory? Why couldn't he get his priorities straight? Once again, they got caught up in a mutual rage. He accused her of stalking him. She threatened to contact his workplace and get him fired. They blocked each other and he also blocked – "

"Why she threatened his job?"

"I don't know. Haven't figured that out yet. She was very apologetic the next day. He unblocked her email because he wanted to keep a channel open; he worried she might very well be capable of carrying out the threat. In tears she begged him to forgive her. She would never cause trouble with his job. She was not a bad person and she loved him. She loved him deeply. If someone really wanted to get him fired, she said, they wouldn't warn him ahead of time but would just do it."

"She already had the idea to do it just by saying that."

"The thing I don't understand is how she could possibly know which hotel he was staying in if he hadn't told her."

"You can use GPS to find out where someone is."

"No. You need to turn on the location finder in your cellphone and then give someone permission to locate you. WeChat has that real-time function where you can see someone on the map but both of you have to enable it. He would have had to give her permission."

"In China there are always ways. Especially she's a Party

member. You don't know what powerful contacts she has, maybe in tech field. And you said she's expert in e-banking? She can find him. Did she have his other information? Credit card? Passwords?"

Marguerite shook her head. "No. There are apps for jealous people to track their spouse but you have to secretly install it on their phone. The only way to do that is to surreptitiously memorize their pass code when they unlock their screen and then quickly download the app when they leave the phone unattended."

"Many Chinese couples just make each other give them their passwords."

"Yeah, they monitor each other every minute of the day. I don't understand that. What a hellish way to live. You're a bit like that, you know, with all your messaging."

"I am not like that. I just express my love for you. I don't get jealous."

"It's smothering and oppressive. Anyway, I still don't see how Kitty could know which hotel Isham was staying in. I'm concerned about this myself since if it's so easy to find this out, who knows how many people could be tracking *my* cellphone this very minute."

"You don't know nothing is private anymore?"

"Of course I do. I just didn't realize anybody — not just the authorities — could track my location without my permission. In fact, I don't believe it. And you shouldn't either. Once you let the paranoid mindset infect you, you'll be living in a permanent state of fear. Lots of Chinese are already like this. They go about their lives avoiding controversial thoughts like they're in a minefield. It's only a few steps back to the Cultural Revolution, when the state had everyone's balls in its fist and people were ashamed to make love with their own husband or wife. *You* aren't tracking my locations, are you?"

"No, Marguerite. You know I'm not like that."

"How can I be so sure?"

"You're paranoid too!" Lixin laughed. "Fuck you."

"Getting fresh with me now are you. How do you know people can do this, then?"

"In China, law is hazy. But only VIP people need to worry about it. Political enemies can destroy them at right time. Police don't care what ordinary people do, unless you give them good reason."

"I guess I'd better keep treating you well," Marguerite demurred. "You know too much about me."

"I take risk living with you. What happens to me if cops find the *baijiu?*"

"I know, dear. Just so that we're clear where things stand. We do need to be careful about what we say on WeChat."

"Even you don't have drugs, you can get in trouble for kinky sex."

"You're the one who likes being tied up, not me."

"I want you to tie me up again and bring more people here."

"Why?"

"Why you are the way you are? This is how I am. I can't explain it."

"It's called exhibitionism."

"I know. *Biaoxianpi. Luolupi.*"

"Okay, how about I organize a party with some of my more openminded friends? You can be the main attraction. You could do that?"

"No problem."

"Wow."

"But not Chinese friends. Foreign friends okay."

"Why not?"

"They will think I have mental problem. Too embarrassing."

"Oh, come on. No. Either we go all out or not. I can't disinvite Chinese who want to come. That's discriminatory. I can make it clear to everyone it's performance art. I'll hang you up, suspend you from the ceiling. They will be envious of you. They will idolize you."

"You have to do something too. Not fair it's just me.

Something shocking."

"How about I fill up the tub and invite guests to join me in it while we watch you?"

"You will do that anyway. But you can't take photos. That's dangerous."

"I'll tell everyone no photos will be allowed."

"Someone will. Slyly. You can't control that. Tell guests to leave their cellphone in box by your entrance?"

"That's treating them like high school students. The only way is to carefully screen guests and make them swear, or sign a statement, that they won't take photos. We'll just have to trust them and take a chance. What's life without a little danger? That's the problem. You can't have fun anymore in the cellphone age. I keep thinking about the huge mess caused by a single topless jacuzzi photo Isham Cook took of Kitty. Due to a simple misunderstanding between her and his friend Jim, she was convinced he had sent the photo to every person he knew. This idea got stuck in her head and she couldn't let go of it. It kept growing and eating at her. It caused their disaster."

"What disaster?"

"I'm still working through all the material. The story has a lot of complicated threads. I want to finish it first. My point is that obsession is a really bad thing if you allow it to grow. It eventually takes over your life. That's why I'm trying to kick you of yours."

"Kick my what?"

"Kick you of your messaging addiction."

"You keep mentioning it."

"Because you still keep firing messages at me like a machine gun."

"You know I'm just teasing you when I send you all those messages. Why you so annoyed by them? Isn't that a problem? You're obsessed with my obsession. You have obsession."

"Good point, darling. But no. I have passions. I turn my obsessions into creative use. That's the difference. Creative obsessions are productive. Destructive obsessions are wasteful and don't go anywhere. If you're aware of your obsessions you can either eliminate them or find creative outlets for your energy. The problem is most people are not aware of their obsessions. They remain in the vise grip of obsession until someone comes along and says, 'You have a problem. You have OCD. You know what that is? Obsessive-compulsive disorder. It's ruining your relationships and it's ruining your life.' But it needs to be a person they respect who points it out because it's very hard to convince an obsessed person there is something wrong with them. Only the people around them are aware of it. Unless, of course, everyone around them also has OCD, which is often the case. If your parents have it, you're going to have it."

"I know what OCD is. Many Chinese do. I saw a woman reading book about it in café the other day. We aren't so ignorant."

"That already shows how common it is in China."

"Not all Chinese have OCD."

"But many do. The housewife who sweeps the floor several times a day when once a week is enough. The grandma who spends every day in shopping centers and supermarkets hunting for deals even though she ends up spending more money than if she just stayed home. The businessman on his cellphone the whole day yelling at his partner to no purpose. The boss who forces all his staff to keep their cellphones on twenty-four hours a day or be fined; this is true, some Chinese friends told me about that. The son or daughter who slaves away at their homework every minute of the day from grade one through twelve. No free time, no play time, no time with friends. They're not even allowed friends, not allowed to read a book for pleasure. Riddle them with guilt, make them terrified of letting their family down, terrified of giving their parents a nervous breakdown if they fail to get into the very top university in China."

"My family wasn't that bad."

"You were lucky. Anyway, you know what I'm talking about — 'study hell.' China's famous for it. But all that study, all those thousands of hours of study, never produces any real learning or knowledge. It's just rote memorization. What effect does it have on a person's mind to think the same thoughts again and again, memorize the same formulas over and over? It's a recipe for OCD, it's training in OCD — masquerading as learning. You know why Chinese students have an edge over American students? Because they have study OCD. They're compulsive. They're energized. They're frantic. How can lazy addle-headed American students compete with frantic students? To have OCD is to be in a perpetual state of emergency. See all those frantic, goose-stepping military parades on TV? That's OCD at the top, state-sanctioned OCD. And it all starts with the floor-sweeping mom who drills her kid in the same habits, because it's the way she was drilled, and the way everyone is drilled. Instead of holding brooms they're holding rifles."

Lixin was laughing.

"Take that mom again. Why is she constantly sweeping a floor that's already so clean you can eat off it? Clearly, sweeping makes her feel good, as long as there are at least a few specks of dust. Each speck she finds provides a ping of pleasure. In her mind, the pleasure comes from the satisfaction of restoring the floor to perfection, down to the last microbe. A perfectly justifiable reason in the name of sanitation. From a psychological standpoint, however, something else is going on, something more disturbing."

"I *don't* have OCD."

"I'm not finished. Let me explain. The world each of us perceives is more than just physical objects. It's chock-full of symbols, packed with symbols. Unconsciously what she is doing is externalizing her mental state into the world around her, the world she can control, her home. She's injecting symbolic value into certain objects and projecting her negative emotions onto dirt. Each speck of dust represents an unpleasant thought, absorbs an unpleasant thought. By sweeping the floor she can rid herself of all her unpleasant, disturbing, hateful thoughts. She doesn't reason it like this, unless she's studied psychology. She just knows that it works. It does the trick. For a few hours at least. Until the unpleasant thoughts start accumulating again and it's back to sweeping the floor."

"My mum is not like that."

"This is just an example. For other people, it may be compulsive handwashing, or shopping, or checking your cellphone, any compulsive activity: because it allows a symbolic discharge of negative energy. Just like your frequent messaging of me. Each message you send is a speck of dust you're sweeping away. It doesn't matter what you write, whether it's a hateful or a loving message. What's really going on, psychologically speaking, is your messages have nothing to do with me. They're just repetitive actions that help you restore your sense of mental equilibrium."

Lixin was glowering. "No, you're wrong. What's really going on is I'm trying to provoke you."

"I know. But I'm not always in the mood for slapping you and tying you up. I'm sorry, dear, I don't mean your messages aren't loving. I'm just explaining the OCD mindset. And you're not that bad. You're also right that I need to go with the flow more and get used to your style. We all have mild forms of OCD. Everyone does. What I find interesting are the more serious cases, like constant arguing and blowing up at people, beating, or stalking. What stalkers are doing is nothing other than sweeping the floor, but instead of finding fresh specks of dust, they're constantly hunting down the targeted individual like a speck of dust. The trouble is not all stalkers are content merely to monitor the whereabouts of their big speck of dust. Some are compelled to take more extreme action in order to get rid of it."

"Arguing is OCD?"

"Sure, it is."

"Maybe it's just being frank and direct. You taught me how to stand up for myself and my rights."

"Only if you keep your cool. As soon as you lose your temper, it's OCD. People quarrel to discharge negative energy. To blow off steam. That's the idiom we use and it exactly describes it. It has nothing to do with the other person. People who argue are just arguing with themselves. They're only under the illusion it's with the person facing them and it's that person's fault. That helps them externalize it. It's classic psychology: attributing to others what you're unable to deal with in yourself."

Lixin was laughing again. "Is that what you're doing when you slap me?"

"For a moment. Then I calm down enough to tie you up. Back again to this party idea. I'm becoming keener on it by the minute. I just thought of a way to disguise you. We could paint up your face like a Peking Opera face. That's the solution!"

"I'm tied up naked wearing Peking Opera headdress?"

"That's an even better idea. A headdress. Where can we get one?"

"Easy to find on Taobao. But if that photo escapes it's even more dangerous. Some Chinese will really take offense. You will serve guests the *baijiu*?"

"I can offer it. But if the wrong person shows up it's all over for us. So better not. We'll just have to watch and make sure no one goes near it. I can ask one of my friends to watch over the *baijiu*."

"I have idea. I can buy one hundred more bottles of *baijiu*. Same *baijiu*. We put them where those are now. And we hide the LSD bottles in another place."

"Where? This is a loft. There's no hidden storage space."

"We rent storage space somewhere."

"In that case what's the point of buying a whole new set? Just keep these in storage. Except that I like them here now. I like the museum effect. I put a lot of time and money into the new shelves and lighting. I also like the danger of it, the knowledge of how many life-changing sips are contained in each one of those bottles. A wall display shimmering with

significance and foreboding. Chinese guests who have no
idea what acid is, when they try it at last, that wall will glow
and pulsate like the inner chamber of a primordial temple.
How cool is that? An oracle for the modern age. They will
come back to my mecca, their faces stretched with awe and
friends in tow. I can almost fantasize being in the news,
already infamous and legendary, when we're finally caught.
You sure you're content to live with me and be my accessory
in crime?"

9

"Where did you learn to do that?"

"Peking Opera club when I was teenager."

"I thought high school students have no time for stuff like that."

"My parents made me do something traditional."

"You're gorgeous. The eyeliner has turned your eyes into giant almonds. I want to eat your eyes. I can no longer recognize you. It's perfect. And you got the peach rouge to shade so evenly into the white on your cheeks. The headdress is a bit tacky with the pom-poms and the fake pearls but who cares? Your beauty rules."

"You're handsome."

Marguerite had added a touch of mascara to her mustache and gelled back her wavy shoulder-length hair to accommodate a white fedora with her three-piece pinstripe suit. "Are you ready?" she said.

"Don't we want to wait till first guests come?"

"It will make a stronger impact if you're already in place than if you're sitting around waiting for enough guests to arrive. Then it's just a performance. You'll be uncanny and more mysterious this way, like it's how you've always been and always will be. The real drama will begin when I fill up the tub and invite people to join me and you're dangling right above us. We need to practice a bit more now anyway. Guests may be arriving sooner than expected since they won't want to miss anything."

Marguerite had once attended a suspension bondage event and remembered some of the finer points. Though hardly a pro, she concocted a simple and graceful setup, employing the minimum of gear to achieve the desired effect: two suspension rings attached to ceiling beams by chains, and four six-meter lengths of silk in the flashy hues of Peking Opera costumes – red, blue, gold and silver. Standing in the big glass bathtub, Lixin's arms were attached to the rings by leather wrist cuffs. Marguerite looped two lengths of silk through each of the rings and knotted each length together at its ends, forming four slings. Passing Lixin's legs through two of the slings under the knees and hooking the remaining two around her ankles, she then hoisted her up by her legs. By pulling on one sling or another she was able to move her body into different positions and shapes, even turn her over. Once things were underway, the guests would take over. The daring few who joined Marguerite in the tub would witness closeup perhaps the most original collision of the Chinese and Japanese theaters ever devised, as this female Dan role from the Peking Opera revolving naked above them was transformed into a butoh dancer entrapped by a shibari master. Lixin even agreed to be videoed now that her face was sufficiently masked.

For now, Marguerite suspended Lixin in place and securely knotted the slings while she finished tidying up. Lixin's legs were pulled up by the knees and splayed apart, the headdress her only article of clothing. Marguerite put a Peking Opera CD on her surround-sound stereo. Lixin sang along to the music.

"You can sing that?"

"It's famous aria. We studied many arias."

"It would be fantastic if you could sing along. You comfortable so far, dear?"

"Not too bad. Maybe keep my legs closed at start and open them later? You aren't worried we shock people?"

"Yeah, good idea. I'll adjust you in a minute. I just want to get a few more things in order. We need more floor pillows for people to sit on."

There was a knocking at the door.

"Oh, someone's here already."

Marguerite opened the door and found herself face-to-face with Louisa and three police officers.

"What's going on?" exclaimed Louisa.

The officers, two males and a female, looked equally confused. "Is this the residence of Marguerite?" they asked in Chinese.

"Yes, that's me," she said as she let them in. She took off her fedora.

"No, no. It's not what you think, Marguerite," said Louisa. "I didn't come with them. I arrived first and knocked and you didn't hear me and I knocked again and they suddenly came up. Looks like I got here a bit early."

The cops were headed over to the shelves of *baijiu* when Lixin caught their attention.

"What this?" one said.

"It's a performance. Performance art."

The cops looked around and noticed the chairs and floor cushions. "You're inviting people here?"

"Yes."

They were frowning.

"Take her down," said the lady cop, as she positioned the video camera attached to her uniform toward her.

Marguerite untied one sling at a time and lowered and released her. The cops were videoing the *baijiu* display as well.

"We're so sorry, officers," said Lixin after she removed her headdress. "I know it looks a bit strange but it really is a performance. She's an artist. I won't be naked in the real performance. I was just like this because I need to limber up without clothes and get used to the positions."

"And the *jingju* headdress? Get dressed," said the lady cop.

"Are you charging money for this?" another asked Marguerite.

"No."

"What are you doing with all of these *baijiu* bottles?"

"It's a display," said Lixin.

"We were notified by your building management that you might be selling *baijiu* illegally."

"Absolutely not."

"Are you storing more bottles anywhere?"

"No, this is it. It's just my personal interest."

"You can see every bottle is a different brand," said Lixin. "I introduced her to *baijiu* and she became interested and started collecting them. Everything she does is art."

"And who are you?"

"I'm her roommate."

"Let's see your ID and her passport. And who is she?" a cop pointed to Louisa.

"Just a friend. She didn't know anything about the performance. It was going to be a surprise."

"What about all these rugs?"

"I do sell rugs."

"From Henan?"

"No, they're imported from Iran. I sell mostly to foreigners in Shanghai and some local retailers. Here, I'll show you my import license. I definitely don't sell *baijiu*."

The cops were picking up the bottles and examining them. "They've all been opened."

"That's because we're not selling them. We're drinking and tasting them, little by little," said Lixin.

"I'm sure you've heard about the problems with fake and adulterated *baijiu*," said one cop who opened a bottle and sniffed the liquor. "You haven't added anything to these?"

Lixin took the bottle out of his hands, filled up the cap

and tossed the shot down her throat. "Of course not." She capped the bottle and placed it back on the shelf. She picked up another bottle and opened it for the cop to smell. "Can't you tell how strong and pure the fragrance is? You can't fake that."

"What's this?" the female cop asked, pointing to Marguerite's jars of colored powder.

"Those are dyes for my rugs." She showed them a vat with the remains of purple dye and the dried yarn hanging next to it.

"You make them too?" they said, confounded.

"Yes."

"We're not happy about that obscene display of yours and want you two to come down to the station with us."

Louisa, who had been trying to make sense of it all, caught Marguerite's eye and mouthed something as she pointed toward the chairs.

"Louisa, can you stay here and explain to the guests and apologize? Thanks a million. There's beer and wine. Don't let them have any of the *baijiu*, though. It's too expensive. I'll text you when I think we'll be back."

Marguerite and Lixin were deposited in the police station foyer and told to wait. The cops held on to their passport and ID while they considered on police time, as opposed to civilian time, what to do about the case.

"Will you be okay?" Marguerite whispered.

"I think I can handle it."

"If it gets rough, just hold my hand. We don't know how long we'll be here. Best not to talk."

They were joined by a stream of visitors to the station — relatives of the detained, feuding parties, people with grievances — who came and went. They all tried not to stare too openly at the unbelievable couple, the mustached foreign woman in the gangster suit holding hands with the Chinese woman and her tear-streaked mess of rouge, black eyeliner and white greasepaint. Some may have noticed that Lixin had the blackest pupils they had ever seen. Four hours later a cop summoned them into the reception area. Lixin's tears may have done the trick, for they were interpreted, none too accurately, as a sign of contrition. They got off lightly, after they wrote out statements of apology and promised not to plan such a party again.

"How strong is it?"

"Much stronger than last time," said a shell-shocked Lixin as they left the station. "I already died and came back to life. I don't know how I survived in that place. I'm still in the middle of it."

"Let's get you back home. That 'obscene' performance of ours possibly saved our skin. It distracted them. I almost peed my pants when you tossed back that shot of *baijiu*. That was really brave of you. You weren't worried he might also want a shot?"

"I knew he wouldn't drink any. The scary thing is what if they took a bottle back with them? I tried to reduce that chance."

*

She started off with each bathroom article, including the shower floor and walls before moving on to the bedstead and inner sheets, end tables, desk and desk chair (front and back), coat hangers and wall behind the hangers where clothing made contact, and of course the handles and knobs, all wiped down with the disinfectant she brought whenever they stayed in budget hotel chains, such as the Hanting branch Isham had booked in the Dawanglu neighborhood smack in Beijing's Central Business District. Not that these places were flagrantly dirty; you needed a trained eye. Isham never had a problem with them — the noisy guests who kept their door open as if it were a dormitory, their cigarette smoke permeating the entire floor, and the hard beds excepted — and couldn't fathom Kitty's insistence he always bring his own towel and washcloth. He just couldn't justify the price differential when the Hanting was good enough.

Why not spend the money on a nice restaurant and a bottle of wine? She regarded it as one of her many sacrifices for his sake, along with his requirement to start off each morning with a proper coffee at a proper coffeehouse rather than the hotel restaurant whose rice gruel was palatable enough for her. In turn, he let her decide on lunch and dinner, invariably Chinese cuisine, which he was fine with, and occasional Japanese or Korean.

They wandered down West Dawang Road toward the glitzy SKP shopping plaza. He disliked windowless mall cafés and instead of heading inside they turned east. The bike-share explosion was then in full riotous bloom, worse even than Shanghai's. Thousands of dockless rental bikes were lined up, dumped and piled up on every sidewalk, pushing pedestrians out onto the street. The aggressive companies grabbed the attention, as outdoor Chinese opera once did, through a cacophony of color — Ofo yellow, Mobike orange, and BlueGogo being the main players, and a rainbow of other competitors including Coolqi's imitation gold-plated bikes with a cellphone dock in the handlebar that charged while pedaling (bikes that were stolen almost as quickly as they appeared).

They found a Costa Coffee across from a Ritz-Carlton and a Marriott — Kitty's preferred hotels. It was their first trip since Macau, and while they only had a few days together it would constitute a significant victory if they could get through it without a fight. Kitty had been stressed out to say the least, demoted at work after claims of having harassed two women on separate occasions, the girlfriend of her ex-fiancé and a woman Isham had been involved with, Luna. This person had blindsided her with a bewildering accusation of hacking into her electronics in order to drive her insane, a woman she had never met and had at first assumed to be Isham's live-in, Bonnie, when he spilled the news about her.

As the pressures mounted, she tried harder than ever to get along with Isham, and he made efforts too. He paid for a

massage for both of them at a luxury spa attached to an
elegant café, and she agreed to befriend on WeChat one of
Nathan's recent acquaintances for a massage photo session,
one he had, amazingly, not succeeded in getting into bed
and hoped Isham might have better luck with, Holly, a
lesbian. It looked as if Isham might even succeed, for though
she had to inform him she was not up for sex, she grew
more interested in Kitty by the day, her glamor and talents,
and would happily allow him to massage her if it meant
being caressed by Kitty's camera. The owner of an apparel
business in her mid-thirties, she was handsomely alluring,
with intelligent eyes, messy bob of wavy hair, and
understated yet tasteful dress. As Holly's fantasies took hold,
she wondered if Kitty would be up for a massage herself. The
sooner it was all arranged the better. She goaded Isham by
sexting him her shower pic. Her body, by his criteria, topped
all the other women in the Kitty-Nathan circle: a lush-bellied,
brashly hipped and bosomed *fengmande* figure even by
Chinese standards, and underarms — she knew her erotic
worth — luxuriantly unshaven.

The Beijing excursion was triumphantly uneventful and
they returned to Shanghai. To prevent any further damage
to her job, Kitty established contact with Luna to see if they
could hash things out in a friendly way over coffee. It did
not go as expected; Luna assaulted her, knocked her down
to the floor. Isham rode up on the subway to meet Kitty the
next day. She was still shaken but didn't blame him for the
crazy woman's actions, though he had decidedly been at
fault for carelessly revealing her name and workplace to her.
And if she couldn't trust him to keep her privacy, she had
legitimate concerns about all of the nudes and sex pics he
had of her, not to mention the rogue jacuzzi photo. That
Luna better not have any of her photos, she warned. The
Holly massage was still on and arranged for the following
Saturday morning. Isham would be on a business trip to
Wuhan during the week and Kitty planned to pick him up
at Hongqiao station on his return Friday evening and drive

them to their hotel.

Candy, Daisy, Fanny and Glory had all been growing impatient for their own long-overdue massage sessions and were jostling for position. They took out their frustrations on Isham, the primary one responsible for the flareups they believed, by firing at him a barrage of entreaties and more nude pics. But Kitty was throwing obstacles in their paths as well. Daisy and Glory were hindered by their very proximity to her, the former her subordinate and the latter her colleague and confidant. Both were too close. Fanny was a bit less so but separated geographically and could only make it to Shanghai on occasion (most recently to seduce Kitty's ex-fiancé). Candy was around when she wasn't flying. She was, like Holly, anonymous enough and had Nathan's good reference. If it seems unlikely this hot flight attendant would be sexting a foreign guy she had never met ever more shocking images of herself even after she had found a new boyfriend, you have to understand the emotional investment they all had in Kitty, that lonely, gifted beauty who deserved a man equal to her. Isham fit the bill and had a duty to comply. They were simply at a loss as to understand his ambivalence and reluctance. They were thus doing all they could to dislodge him from his live-in peasant and nudge him back into their orbit, Kitty's orbit. Their massage invitations were mere offerings to an aspirational couple's enshrinement, but they were genuine offerings of warm, expanding flesh. His refusal to perform his part was inexplicable and insulting. What the hell was the matter with him?

The relationship had indeed become frayed. They had even started dating others — Kitty a classical music reporter she met on a trip to Spain and Isham, coincidentally, the professional cellist who had once attended his music soirées. Candy wanted to know more about the cellist and asked him as he was heading back to Shanghai on the train what she had that Kitty didn't. He messaged her to say he preferred a woman who didn't get angry so easily and was relaxing to be with.

"You mean you prefer her to Kitty?"

"Yes, obviously, that is whenever Kitty is angry."

Candy took a screenshot of their conversation and promptly sent it to Kitty. It didn't take her long to confront Isham about it.

"You prefer your new girlfriend to me? I've already canceled the hotel."

"You took my words out of context. She's *not* my girlfriend. We dated twice. I haven't slept with her and I'm not even sure we'll be meeting again. *Read* what I said. I prefer a woman who doesn't always get angry. That means I prefer you when you're not angry. It doesn't mean I'm rejecting you. Your cancelling the hotel only demonstrates your anger problem."

She immediately blocked him on WeChat and his reply came back undelivered. He then informed Holly that the massage session was off. Holly, however, wasn't about to back down and campaigned hard to get the two back on board.

Now unblocked, Isham told Kitty, "I hold you responsible for this. It's your fault. You spoiled the mood just to act out your psychodrama and you knew it. Good luck with the Spanish guy."

"No. When you said you didn't want to massage Holly, I felt disappointed and sorry."

"I warned her it would be almost impossible to arrange the massage due to your games. You need to apologize to her for misleading her. All right, I can do the massage tomorrow morning. But I'm not staying in the hotel tonight. I don't want to see you. I feel sick. I want to throw up."

"Why can't you be with me tonight? I promise I won't fight with you. I don't want to stay in the hotel alone."

"You intentionally humiliated me. You are a psychologically abusive person."

"No. You kept accusing me of jealousy. I'm not. At least, I'm not jealous of Holly. Nathan told me you're not her type.

So how could I be jealous? It's me who invited her. I canceled my weekend plan for the massage."

"I've already apologized to Holly for the fiasco."

By the time they came to terms, the hotel, their usual French Concession haunt, was booked up. Holly suggested another hotel on Jiaozhou Road in the Jing'an Temple area a kilometer north, and the session was on again. As Kitty was held up at the office, she couldn't make it to the station in time to pick him up and would have to meet him at the hotel. It was a hot and humid July night and she arrived late with her camera, tripod, and a warm bottle of white burgundy. Most Chinese inns don't supply ice but the reception allowed them to chill it in their freezer. They went to bed after a few glasses, too tired to make love but looking forward to the morning.

Isham awoke to a dreaded WeChat message, one he had nonetheless been prepared for. After discussing with a friend (who had probably warned her the couple might be dangerous), Holly had reconsidered. As tactfully as she could, she said she was postponing her visit until she had reassurances that he and Kitty had straightened out their quarreling.

This was not the first time a massage session collapsed at the last moment. Isham received the news with perfect equanimity. They went right into morning sex and prepared for a relaxing weekend, now that they had gotten all the drama out of the way. Kitty had two tickets to the historic canal town of Wuzhen, some two hours away by car. Neither had been there before. After breakfast in the hotel they headed off to make it there by lunchtime.

Canal towns had long been the norm in Zhejiang, Jiangsu and surrounding provinces. The old Shanghai walled city had been crisscrossed with canals. The main reason for the cataclysmic loss of life during the Taiping Civil War of the 1860s which had ravaged the region was the mass starvation that ensued when villages were cut off to boat traffic after their fields were burnt. Many canal towns are still intact. A few of them, notably Wuzhen and Zhouzhuang, came up with the idea not only of charging an entrance fee, but more ingeniously, expanding their perimeter well beyond their existing extent to accommodate tens of thousands of tourists. Buildings in the authentic style multiplied outward and were indistinguishable from the original structures. Of course, there were no "original" structures; they had long been destroyed by flood or fire and rebuilt many times over the centuries. No one was bothered by the question of authenticity anyway and the crowds were enormous. There were huge parking lots, one for tourist buses and another for cars. Isham memorized their lot number, as Kitty could be forgetful.

A vast entrance hall, replete with a Starbucks, reinforced the impression they were about to enter to an amusement park instead of an historical town, but once released from the hall they were pleasantly surprised. The place was labyrinthine and inexhaustible, every vantage point scenic. For lunch, a canal-side restaurant served *xiaolongbao*, soup dumplings held between chopsticks and cradled in a spoon to catch the soup when bit into, and properly chilled bottles of Samuel Smith's Nut Brown Ale and Organic Chocolate Stout. Kitty was busy with her camera, and between her dashing about for the best angles and Isham's exercise addiction, they covered a lot of ground. A Vietnamese-French fusion restaurant called Nuage, with a lovely deck view of an arched bridge at a junction of canals, enticed them for dinner as dusk flattened the crowds and lengthened the lantern reflections on the water. It was late again when they got back to the hotel.

They went to the Café Français for brunch the next morning, close to their usual hotel, with its mix of Western breakfasts that had something even for Kitty's finicky tastes. They tended to hang out past noon, before Isham would delicately disrupt the peace by announcing it was time to be on his way. Kitty hated the last day of their weekend getaways. He never spent enough time with her and he should have been considerate enough to stretch the day out a bit more. If they were going to have a fight, it was usually at this juncture. It almost required a fight; a stomping out or a storming off at least had the benefit of finality and closure. This time, however, things went beyond that and into pioneer territory.

A major sticking point over the preceding year was Kitty's intransigent insistence Isham never mention her in any way, shape or form to "that woman," otherwise known as Bonnie. How ridiculous, retorted Isham. Whoever would come up with the idea of censoring people's private talk? This could only have resulted from the insidious effects of her countless Party meetings and accompanying digestion of boilerplate Party homework which created such a mindset through osmosis. While she lived her convictions on personal freedom in her many travels and even claimed to be opposed to the CCP on a few political points, when it came to Isham she demonstrated her Party affiliation through and through. He was not about to be pushed around by someone on such absurd grounds.

"Let me try, once again, to explain something I've told you many times before," he said the last time the subject came up. "*No one* censors me. I will say whatever I want to anyone I want. Our major problem is precisely your attempts to censor me. I can't be close to a person, I can't even be friends with a person I can't express myself freely with. Bonnie has known about you all along, as she has the right to, just as you know about her. Obviously, I let her know when I'm spending the weekends with you so she knows where I am. We live together. That's all she needs to know, and apart from that I never discuss you with her. I can assure you I don't talk about you, because it would distress her, given all our nonsensical and inexplicable fighting. Got it?"

Evidently not this morning. He was sitting next to her as she helped him install a Chinese app on his iPhone when a message from Bonnie popped up and he opened his chat briefly to read it. It was enough time for Kitty to notice in the same thread the message he had sent to Bonnie on Friday that he would be staying with her over the weekend after all.

When he returned to his side of the table, she blurted out, "I told you never to mention me to anyone, most of all that woman! Promise me you will never mention anything about me to her again."

He started packing up his stuff to leave.

"No! You're not leaving."

She grabbed his iPad. He reached over to grab it back. She shielded it with her arms and they struggled as he tried to pull them apart and pry it out of her grasp. He soon gave up.

"You attacked me and I'm calling the police!" she said as she dialed emergency.

He decided to remain calm and cooperative. She grabbed his backpack by the handle and stood up to wait for the police. Her arm was rigid and started shaking. A waitress tried to get her to sit down and unbend her arm to set the bag down but she was immobilized and in shock.

When the police arrived, their first question was whether the two were acquainted. Isham explained that they had quarreled; she took his iPad from him and he tried to grab it back. The streak of blood on her blouse came from a nick on her finger when he tried to pry her hands apart, and no, he never hit her. Pointing to the security camera in the upper corner, he said they were free to examine the video evidence. The waitresses affirmed the two were fine until they were suddenly struggling; it was over fast and they didn't know what caused it (two other customers, a pair of females, had quickly left). The police freed up the iPad and backpack from Kitty's grasp and asked them to go down to the station.

As a policewoman entered Isham's passport information into a computer, a male cop took Kitty outside the station reception to listen to her story. She was sobbing but later calmed down. The cop left her sitting outside. An hour later, Isham went over to see if she was okay. She was feeling heart pain, she said. The police allowed them to go. Isham called a taxi to the nearest hospital. There a female doctor found no injuries apart from discoloration on her arms; she had thin loose skin which bruised easily. To be on the safe side they gave her heart tests, a blood analysis and a CT brain scan.

After the tests came back normal, Kitty seemed confused and tired and wanted to sit down in the lobby. She started speaking to Isham in Chinese. He was fine with Chinese; with Bonnie he spoke it exclusively. But it was unaccountable for Kitty to switch to Chinese after they had only ever spoken English with each other.

"Who are you?"

"What's the matter with you?"

"What's your name?"

"You don't know who I am?"

"I can't remember where I live. I'm afraid I lost my job and my car. I can't open my cellphone. I forgot my passcode. I want my mother," she said, crying again.

"Your car is fine. We can go back and get it now. You didn't lose your job. You've just had a shock and will be fine later. I'll contact Daisy and Glory to tell them what's going on. They know your address."

He tried calling them but neither picked up.

They got a taxi back to the café where her car was parked. He sat with her in the car. Her memory began to creep back and along with it, her anger. "I want you to leave," she said.

He got out of the car but was reluctant to abandon her. She was in no condition to drive. He knocked on the window. She let him back in — in the rear seat.

"We're going back to the hospital to get a proper report of my injuries. Then we'll present that at the police station to have you booked for assault," she announced.

"I didn't assault you. All I did was grab back my personal property. You know that. You don't have a serious injury. If you're going to be like this, I'm leaving."

She locked him inside.

In her unstable state, he reasoned, cooperating was a better bet than escalating things. He was confident he stood no chance of being charged with assault. She said her vision was blurry and she needed him to drive (she had lost her contact lenses). They returned to the hospital. Dusk had fallen, with a male doctor now on evening shift. He read Kitty's report from earlier, examined her upper body and found no signs of injury apart from the bruised arms. He printed out a report she could use for official purposes and told her to come back in three days if she was still experiencing any pain.

Back in the car, she decided not to return to the police station after all. They drove around aimlessly, until she told him to pull over. As soon as they were parked, he grabbed his backpack and opened the door to leave. She latched onto it with the same iron grip she had displayed in the café. He could have lurched out — at the risk of dragging her out and causing another scene. He decided again not to escalate things and stayed put. She demanded he write out a statement. He found a sheet of paper in his backpack and she dictated two admissions:

1) If at any time in the past he revealed anything about her to anyone resulting in damage to her reputation, he must pay her 50,000 yuan within three months. Since he had already done this (the recent Luna affair resulting in her job demotion), he therefore now had three months to pay her the money.

2) If at any time in the future he reveals anything about her to anyone resulting in more damage to her reputation, he must pay her 100,000 yuan within three months.

Of course, she had no right to pull fees totalling over $20,000 out of thin air and it was the business of a law court to decide damages. But as it was unlikely any of this could stand up in court, he did as commanded, though it took five drafts on more scraps of paper before she was satisfied. It was ten-thirty when she let him out of the car, and almost midnight when he got back home. Bonnie knew something was up from earlier messages and he filled her in on the day's events. Daisy and Glory still hadn't responded.

A reply from Daisy was waiting for him in the morning. She had been at a company event the whole day and was too busy to notice his calls and messages. Kitty had not shown up for work and wasn't picking up her phone. Nathan was now in the loop and Isham filled him and Daisy in on everything. He reaffirmed he had not hit Kitty in the café. The only force he applied was on her arms and hands, but stunned by her strength he stopped after no more than ten seconds upon realizing that not to have stopped would surely have devolved into greater violence on someone's part.

"Go see if Kitty's car was still parked in the same spot," Daisy demanded.

Isham obliged and made a detour there on his way to work. The car wasn't there. He also checked both hotels, the one they had stayed in and the other they normally stayed in.

Daisy had a psychologist friend who explained that amnesia could result from either blunt head trauma or emotional trauma. With the latter, "transient global amnesia," the sufferer filters out the traumatic event and retains only recent positive memories and associations. On this hunch, she started calling every place they had spent time in over the weekend including hotels in the Wuzhen canal town. Later in the day, she located a woman by Kitty's name in a Wuzhen establishment called Nuage and showed him a website photo of the place. It was the same restaurant where they had eaten dinner. He hadn't noticed at the time it was also a boutique hotel. The guest had checked in at two o'clock in the morning. She wasn't picking up the phone. Daisy finally got her on the line and it was indeed Kitty. She had no memory of the previous day's events or any recollection of having left Wuzhen in the first place. She was befuddled and wondering why Isham wasn't with her. Daisy and her husband drove up to Wuzhen to bring Kitty home, the husband driving Kitty's car. Her car was damaged on the passenger side from striking a guardrail.

Kitty was back at work the next day. Daisy described her as normal but "a bit slow." She was worried because Kitty would be leaving the following day for an important business meeting in Beijing to last the rest of the week and she had a presentation to give.

Kitty resumed communications with Isham several days later from her Beijing hotel. He was very relieved to hear that her presentation went satisfactorily.

"Did I say or do something terrible to you when we fought last weekend? If so, please forgive me," she said.

"I'm not angry with you at all. You and I had a bad time last Sunday. I feel awful about what happened. It's mostly my fault. It's a lesson to control my anger."

"I also feel sorry for giving you a bad weekend. I need to control my anger too. You're always the one who's more tolerant."

He told her not to worry and to focus on her job. She showed him some wine and cognac she'd picked up for when they next got together and told him she had gone braless today in Beijing's heat and revealed to him how she looked.

10

"Holy fuck! for starters. Secondly, I strongly advise you not to have any contact with her ever again," said Jim in reaction to Isham's wild Sunday.

Isham had been scouring Kitty's social media for any signs of her the day after, her Messenger as well, when Daisy informed him that they had found her in the Wuzhen hotel. But upon sending his account of the day's events to Jim, he realized he had forgotten to exit Kitty's Messenger and inadvertently sent it to her. He quickly deleted it. When Kitty contacted him on WeChat later in the week, he breathed a sigh of relief that the message seemed to have been successfully deleted. He hadn't said anything particularly bad about her. He didn't need to; Jim was aware of their constant fighting and had a pretty thorough understanding of them both. He merely described the weekend's events. Yet knowing the way she was, she might take any reference to the affair as a breach of privacy. He wanted no more trouble. He was glad to see she was coming around and her memory was coming back. He could no longer return to the relationship, however. Not after that

Sunday. If his chats with her over the past couple days were friendly, it was to help her get back to herself, not to pick up where they left off. He would make it clear at the proper time that it was over.

But messages sent on Messenger are not, in fact, deleted at the receiver's end.

"I just saw your message to Jim," she told him on WeChat. She attached screenshots to confirm it. "I want to see you right now. How did I get all these bruises on my body? If you dare talk to that ugly woman about me, you know what will happen. I'm on the way now and will be at your door soon." She showed him a map locator of his residential compound, which she had never visited before. He didn't recall ever giving her his address.

It was Saturday evening. She had returned to Shanghai earlier in the day. Isham and Bonnie had just eaten dinner and he was relaxing with some music and a book. It took him a moment to process the message. Kitty was driving down to see him. It was not enough to dissipate the dopamine stone induced by Leonard Cohen's velvety rhythms and a third glass of wine, and it was all like a movie. But he would have to confront her. He reminded her that Bonnie was with him.

"Step out into the hallway," Kitty ordered Isham when she arrived.

"Why don't you come in and we three can talk?" said Bonnie.

"And who are you? This is our affair."

Bonnie looked Kitty in the eye. "You can't just take him away from our home."

"Your home? I can't stand here and do what I want? Go ahead and call the police!"

"Okay, I will."

"Come with me," said Kitty to Isham.

"I have to go back inside and get my glasses."

"You don't need your glasses."

"Yes, I do."

Isham followed Kitty down to a nearby street where her car was parked. He wanted to talk things out. She wanted to drive him back to her side of the city and told him to get in her car. There was no way he was getting in that car again and he refused. They sat down on a ledge by the street. She asked him more questions about the previous weekend. As he filled in the gaps in the day's events, her anger rose. She then stood up and slapped him on the face. She pulled out her cellphone and pointed it at him. "I've been recording everything you've said since I was at your apartment door. I am telling you, Isham Cook, I am going to do everything in my power to have you deported from China. This is not a threat, it's fact. I *will* do this."

"What specifically did I say to make you want to do this? You're crazy!"

He started walking away. She grabbed him by his T-shirt. He pulled at the fabric but her fist was clamped on it like a bulldog's. They were in the middle of the street. He could have removed his shirt and tried to make a break for it, leaving her standing there with it in her hands, or simply marching off until she let go. But in her state, her adrenaline rage, he'd more likely have to drag her along the asphalt and they'd end up struggling as they had in the café. From a stranger's perspective witnessing a woman grappling with a big foreign guy, Isham would naturally be assumed to be the aggressor. If the cops got involved, any witnesses might second Kitty's claims she was being attacked. Such an outcome could be calamitous for him. There was only one thing to do. A residential compound gate was close by. He walked over to the guard, pulling her along by the fist still clamped on his shirt, and said he was being harassed by her and to call the police.

It took them an interminable twenty minutes to arrive. Isham said he was being held by Kitty against his will. They detached her from his shirt. Isham got in their car. One of them went with Kitty in her car.

In the station reception, Kitty lurched at Isham as he was

calling Bonnie and tried to grab his phone out of his hands. They made her sit down in the foyer. They listened to her side of the story. They listened to Isham's. They had him wait in the foyer as well. Soon Bonnie arrived.

"What's your business?" a cop asked her.

"I'm his girlfriend. We live together. I already know what's going on."

"Officer, this is my affair. I don't want this woman to be here," Kitty retorted.

"She came to our apartment. She was confrontational and she cursed me. Then she made him go with her," said Bonnie.

"She took him from your apartment?"

"Yes. I was going to call the police but was afraid it might make things worse. He later texted me and said it wasn't necessary."

"All right. You wait outside. I'll let you know if we need you for anything."

They sat there for hours. At five in the morning an officer named Sun asked Kitty to repeat her demands. She wanted Isham to sign a statement and have it stamped by the police. Her demands were similar to those of the week before, except she allowed that any damages he owed her could be assessed in court. She added a new demand: if in the future she was determined to suffer any physical or psychological symptoms from their previous week's altercation which caused her to be absent from work, he must compensate her for lost salary. Isham proceeded to write out the statement. She also made him return the wallet she had once given him as a gift; he had to empty its contents into his pocket. They fingerprinted the paper with red ink, the police stamped it with a seal, and Isham took a picture of it with his cellphone. Kitty grabbed the paper and dashed out of the station. Her car wheels screeched out of the parking lot. Bonnie entered. The police reassured them they could report any further aggression from Kitty.

Isham and Bonnie caught a few hours of sleep and spent

the rest of the day in a café. Given Kitty's threats to Isham regarding communications about her, he was reluctant from this point on to contact anyone known to her, including Nathan, Daisy or Glory. Glory had finally responded during the previous week only to blame him for the dispute with Kitty; he deleted her. But he thought at least Daisy should know the latest. He suggested Bonnie message her in place of himself; Bonnie had every right to enter the fray, as she was now involved. She sent Daisy a friend request, explaining who she was and her wish to give her a clear account of what had happened. Daisy declined the request.

On Monday Isham was informed by Nathan that Kitty hadn't shown up for work and was missing again. He needed details — all the places they had visited in recent weeks in Shanghai, and Beijing as well on their trip there, places she might have fondly associated with him and hence had returned to. Nathan confirmed she wasn't in Wuzhen. There wasn't much, Isham said, apart from the Hanting hotel in Beijing and the Costa Coffee they had breakfasted in. He recollected a few more locations they had visited while there, the 798 art district and oh, there was also the spa café where they had their massage. Isham wondered why her car's movements couldn't be tracked by street security cameras. Nathan said the police wouldn't act on a missing person until seventy-two hours had passed. He also noted Daisy was trying to access Kitty's credit card transactions for clues.

Several days later, Nathan relayed a message from Kitty's father. He apologized to Isham for the trouble Kitty was causing him. They were an educated family and would never countenance anyone in their household extorting money. They were also, as he could surely understand, very upset and would appreciate any help in locating her.

The same day, the cellist Isham had begun dating contacted him. An unidentified person had posted a mysterious and disturbing screenshot on her public Weibo page of someone's WeChat profile. It was Bonnie's and showed Daisy's response to her friend request: "I don't know you. What are you doing messing about in others' affairs with your sick business?"

Stanley was sending Isham a flurry of exasperated messages of his own. Kitty wasn't responding to his attempts to contact her. Her photo-essay travelogue was all but ready for publication and the whole affair had practically been giving him a nervous breakdown. Several weeks earlier, around the time of Kitty's unpleasant café encounter with Luna, she had told Stanley to withdraw her book's dedication to Isham. The galleys had already been set and this caused enormous hassle for the publisher. Even more worrying, Kitty was expected at several book-signing events over the next few weeks and it would be a disaster for everyone if she was missing, let alone the loss of his own outlays and professional reputation. Industry contacts of his were mightily interested in both books, hers as well as *Massage and the Writer*. He estimated he could easily sell 4,000 copies of Isham's translation alone. What in god's name was going on? But Isham was reluctant to provide Stanley with more than the sparest details, fearing anything he said could potentially be turned against him by Kitty.

Ten days after Kitty went missing, Nathan announced she had been found at the Ritz-Carlton across from the Costa Coffee they had visited in Beijing. Once again, she had no memory of the recent events around Isham and the police, no memory of having left Beijing since their trip there. This was heartwarming news. Despite being presently mired in serious psychological difficulties, that she was alive and intact, rather than found in a ditch or river somewhere, came as the greatest relief. Isham was horrified at the thought he could ever be remotely involved in a person's demise. For all her viciousness she was a good person at heart and had only become twisted by jealousy. Even if she were to spend the rest of her life attacking him, he could make provisions for that. He couldn't make provisions for her premature death, the despair of having been tangentially responsible for it, not to mention the cloud of suspicion hanging over him and the fresh investigations it would spark.

A few days later he was on his way to work when he received three calls in a row from the same number. He never answered callers he didn't recognize, and it was common for telemarketers to call twice in a row. Three times in a row was peculiar but not that alarming.

Then his boss phoned him. "Isham, I was just contacted by the *police*."

"I think I know what it's about. I'll head over to the station now and will get back to you later to explain."

He called the number back. It was the local police station, and they wanted him to come down and answer some questions. He informed Bonnie and gave her his boss's number in case he was kept there longer than expected.

"Oh, you've arrived," said Officer Sun, whom Isham recognized. He was joined by Officer Feng, a pudgy subordinate, where Sun was tall and commanding. They were buzzed through a back-office door and he followed them into a room with padded and soundproofed walls. Something was up. They took his passport, cellphone and iPad and placed him in a chair with a video camera positioned in front of him.

Feng sat across from him and started the questioning. "Have you ever sent any nude photos of Kitty to anyone without her permission?" (Kitty and the others referred to of course by their Chinese names).

"I sent a topless photo of her to an American friend of mine, but that was over a year ago. I sent the same photo to a Hong Kong friend some months later. Both were friends of Kitty's and she knows I sent them the photo. I also shared a number of other photos among her friends, and always with her permission. Apart from that I can't think of anything else. Why is this an issue now?"

"Have you ever made any nude or sexual photos of her publicly available on the Internet or any websites?"

"No, absolutely not."

Feng and several other cops scanned through the photos on Isham's phone and iPad. It was embarrassing. He had hundreds of images of Nathan's and Kitty's female friends, and many of Kitty. There were nudes he had taken of himself which he had shared with the women in turn. Feng pointed to specific photos and asked who took them and how they had fallen into his hands. Isham explained there were four primary sharers in their circle — Nathan, Daisy, Fanny, and Glory — all mutual friends. The women had deluged him with their nudes over the past year or two. Kitty was more circumspect but sent many shots of herself to him privately and, again, allowed him to share some of them with the others. She herself was a prolific nude photographer and Daisy and Glory had often posed for her; Fanny lived in a different city. They were all quite openminded about it. The photos never left the group. "Everyone sexts each other nowadays," he said. "Is there a problem?"

The cops appeared bored by his amateur porn cache. Isham was banking on the assumption it was not the possession of pornography itself, illegal in China though it was, that had landed him at the station, otherwise their whole circle would be implicated. Feng then produced a printout of WeChat conversations, including images. One of them was a photo Isham had taken of Kitty sucking his cock way back before their U.S. trip. He recognized the striking photo because he had captured her in fellatio staring at him with her eyes wide open. It was also one of the aborted massage photo sessions with Abby. Abby had begged them to photograph their lovemaking and show her, and Kitty agreed.

"Yes, I know that photo," said Isham. "I may also have shared it with the same people I mentioned, with Kitty's permission."

"Not with this person," said Feng. Isham was just able to make out the tiny profile image of Glory in the chat dialogue. "In this conversation you said, 'Don't tell Kitty I'm showing you this.' Could you explain why you're contradicting yourself?"

"To be perfectly honest, I forgot about that occasion. As I said, we shared hundreds of photos over the past couple years. Almost every time I was sharing Kitty's photos, I asked her permission. It's possible I may not have gotten her permission on one or two occasions, like this one."

Feng banged the table. "May *not* have? Do you think I'm an idiot? You admitted right here that you were hiding the fact from Kitty."

The police are practiced at raising their voice, indeed quite enjoy doing so. Isham was careful to avoid giving Feng further reason. "Forgive me for not explaining myself clearly, Officer. As you can see, my Chinese is a bit rough and things don't always come out logically. It's now coming back to me. That woman is Glory, Kitty's colleague and friend at work. Glory has shown me nudes Kitty took of her. Glory has shown me very explicit nudes she took of herself. Kitty has shown me nudes she took of Glory. Not long ago, Kitty even allowed me to take a video of us having sex and share it with Glory. The three of us have shared a lot of nude photos, and there was nothing secret or furtive about it. I honestly do not remember that conversation in the printout. I imagine what happened is this. Kitty and I were often quarrelling. Glory was constantly pestering me to show her more of our nude photos. This was also her way of mediating and bringing us back together. But it would have been awkward for me to ask Kitty's permission if we were fighting or not speaking to each other at the time. That would have been the only reason for me to ask Glory to keep it secret."

"You're saying this was the only time you've distributed her photos without her permission?"

"As far as I can remember, yes."

"Where's your evidence that she ever gave you permission?"

"I'd have to go over all my previous WeChat conversations with her, and that's going to take some time. I can't do that as long as you're holding onto my cellphone."

"You're not getting your electronics back until they've been thoroughly checked and analyzed."

"How long is that going to take?"

"We can't say. She believes you've been sharing her photos with everyone you know, not just her friends."

"That's totally untrue. Show me the evidence of that."

"We have an example right here of your invasion of her privacy. It's reasonable to suppose there will be more."

"I'm not trying to excuse myself. She is indeed fearfully protective of her privacy and reputation. But it's hardly damaged by Glory seeing that photo. And it's not like I was setting out to damage her reputation. I would never intentionally have caused her any trouble. But look at the trouble she's now causing me. I can tell you those two are not being honest about this accusation. Now I'm beginning to figure out what's going on. As you know, Kitty and I have fallen into a vicious dispute. She's trying to get revenge any way she can. She's trying to get me in trouble with this charge, because it's the only thing she can think of. Glory is cooperating with her and showed her that WeChat conversation."

They decided to summon Kitty to the station to corroborate her account. Feng was replaced by another cop, who went through the same questions, and yet another. Later a young officer from the immigration police arrived, dressed in a black T-shirt and jeans. He placidly enumerated the possible outcomes for Isham, as if he were going through his own work routine: jail and deportation, jail and a fine, a fine only, or no punishment. When he learned Isham had once taught at his alma mater, he became more amiable. They discussed their respective experiences at the university. Handing Isham his card, he said somewhat bizarrely upon parting, "If you ever need help with anything regarding immigration, you know, visas and so forth, feel free to contact me."

The afternoon was slipping by. Feng returned to report

that Kitty had arrived with a colleague and was filling them in again. "It's not looking good for you," he said. "She's flatly denying everything you've told us. I invited her to thrash things out with you in person but she refuses. It looks like the outcome of your case will hang on our boss's decision."

When they were satisfied everything useful had been gleaned out of Isham, they moved him to a prefab conference room situated in the parking lot, where he sat with a guard. Another hour or two elapsed and dusk was setting in. He had a view into the station building and observed Kitty and a woman he recognized enter the foyer from inside and sit down; it was his first live glimpse of Glory.

A cop entered with some food for him — a chicken sandwich and fries from KFC. Soon a group of cops arrived. One looked to be in his fifties and sat at the head of the oblong table. The boss's manner was avuncular, even pleasant. He asked Isham nothing about the case, only his motives in being in China and about his years of teaching and consulting. He asked him what he felt about China. Isham said he was fond of the country, the culture and the people. He would not have been living here for almost two decades had that not been the case. He asked him about his homeland. Rather than cast their countries in a contest, Isham merely characterized the U.S. as beset by a variety of problems exacerbated by the Trump White House, and he hoped relationships between the two nations could remain strong. The boss concluded with an odd question. "Do you think we're friendly?"

"Sure, of course."

They got up to leave. One cop remained and handed Isham several forms to sign. He quipped on his way out that they hoped soon to be wrapping up this "bullshit thing," employing the English phrase, the implication being Kitty's charge was too trivial for their time.

More hours passed. He reflected on the only other

involuntary visit he had made to the confines of law enforcement. He was twenty. His stepfather was in the midst of a bitter divorce with his mother. She got the house. He made an unannounced visit one day to take back some items he claimed were his. She was out at the time and had instructed Isham, on the advice of her lawyer, to under no circumstances let him in. Isham ejected him and hastened his exit down the front porch steps with a soft, symbolic shove. Though he neither fell nor was hurt, he told the police he had been "assaulted," and Isham spent a night behind bars. There was that weaponized word again, so readily deployed. He was incapable of deliberately causing another person harm, but others casually do the same to him.

The more he thought about it, the more outraged he grew. No, he was not guilty of invading Kitty's privacy by neglecting to get, on that one occasion, her permission to show the fellatio pic to Glory. Here was a circle of friends freely sharing each other's revealing photos. The first time, of course, you get someone's permission. Thereafter, you don't need their permission every time because it's understood. What are friends for without that bit of leeway and trust? Yet here she was taking the drastic step of lodging a criminal charge which she knew to be patently dishonest. Was she consciously doing this out of sadistic spite, or might there not be something else going on, moving her inexorably to action in spite of herself?

He considered Kitty's motives as objectively as he could. She was stuck on the notion, taken root from a badly phrased comment from Jim, that Isham had distributed her nude photos to everyone he knew. The power of an idée fixe to take over a person's brain like a zombie parasite, the power of obsession to reduce people to a shell of themselves, reminded him of another past ordeal, a naïve college senior and virgin he had once gotten into bed. The girl was too wracked with ambivalence for his tastes, and they only had a single sexual encounter. The next day she asked him if he had given her AIDS. Impossible, he told her. He was wearing a condom, didn't ejaculate and was free of STDs; he never even penetrated her but had merely pushed a little at her entrance. But once seeded the idea grew tenaciously. He showed her an HIV-negative test report from earlier in the year. It was probably out of date, he admitted, but assured her the possibility of her being infected was nil, nada, zilch, and no, he was not going to have another test done to appease her anxiety. If she was really adamant, she could go get her own HIV test. Isham knew how the power of denial could render a man confident when he should be concerned, but in this case, it was out of the question she was in any danger. Still she kept at him, thoroughly convinced she had AIDs. She kept at him even after he returned to the U.S. several months later. She had had plans to study abroad in Australia but was terrified of being alone, mortally ill and away from her parents. She wanted immediate confirmation she was indeed afflicted so that she could cancel her graduate study and arrange her return to her hometown to die. He relented and had another test done, scanned and emailed her the report. Next to the word "seronegative," however, a tiny wrinkle on the page was picked up by the scanner. She was certain the mark was a sign of his tampering with the paper to erase the truth. She insisted he go back and retake the test. Sorry, he told her, there was nothing more he could do, except to recommend she see a psychiatrist before she grew any more despondent. He blocked her email.

Kitty had similarly worked herself up into a hysterical state. The mere possibility her photos were circulating widely on the internet was distressing enough. If true, it was only a matter of time before someone at her company saw them, or even worse, the local media. Given the number of revenge-porn affairs in the news in recent years and her being a Party member — no other group in China sated the ravenous public's desire for scandal — this was no small matter, and she was still under discipline for previous lapses.

But there was another, more unsettling possibility. The extent of the rough treatment she had doled out to Isham over the past couple weeks, however well deserved, was now dawning on her, or at least Glory had filled her in. He must be planning an attack to get back at her. He had not just the jacuzzi and fellatio photos in his possession but many more compromising images, of Daisy and Glory as well. They too were Party members, with families, who could little afford the faintest whiff of scandal. If word got out of an in-house pornography operation exposed by a foreigner, the consequences would be unthinkable. The higher-ups might suspect Isham of being a financial spy. They could disappear into the Party's "black jails." Daisy was at least partially protected by her lowlier status in the company hierarchy, but Glory was likely even more anxious than Kitty and demanded something be done and fast. Here was their chance to have the threat deported from China and done away with, their hands washed of the matter. Thus they escalated each other's paranoia and freaked each other out.

On the other hand, surely, they couldn't be so naïve as to suppose Isham would be less lethal at a greater remove? If he was intent on causing them pain, he could accomplish it just as easily thousands of kilometers away as a kilometer away. All he needed to go nuclear was a handful of explicit jpegs and a few keystrokes on his laptop. He had more than a handful; he had tons. He had WeChat conversations going back a year or two, maybe more, with a wealth of evidence of their consensual sharing of images. The decisive factor, the fulcrum of the matter, could not possibly be lost on them: if they thought he now had reason to mess with them, just wait till he was deported. Once they succeeded in destroying his life in China, everything he had built up there over the past decades, he would have genuine motivation to seek revenge — and he would have nothing to lose. By machinating his deportation, they were putting themselves in far greater peril than if they simply let things go. So not only did their aggression make no sense, strategically speaking it was astoundingly foolish.

Unless it wasn't about strategy at all, but theater. Maybe Kitty's goal was precisely to get him deported, and if it meant consequences to her reputation and career, so be it. She was of two minds on her hateful profession anyway. On their very first acquaintance she had mentioned her plans to quit and emigrate to Canada to start a new life. Leaving China with a bang might be the very stimulus she needed. In other words, Isham's intolerable behavior had goaded her to give full vent to noble rage at his spurning of her love. She had enough soundness of mind not to resort to the ultimate crime of passion, murder. But she sought a big dramatic gesture causing them both to go up in flames. Glory, on the other hand, could have had little appetite for reckless acts. The American was deserving of a slap on the wrist, to be sure, a few days in the slammer, but not necessarily deportation. Of course, the police don't work that way. You don't lodge an accusation and expect them to agree on the outcome. She had accompanied Kitty to the station, restrained and leashed, not to vouch for her but to force her to negotiate. Perhaps they had come to drop the charges altogether and seek a safer recourse, such as a letter of apology.

Isham saw Officer Sun escort Kitty and Glory out and around the side of the building, and they were gone. A cop appeared in the conference room. "You still have to wait." He then added, somewhat reassuringly, "Don't do it again."

It was close to midnight, twelve hours after arriving at the station, when Sun, Feng, and another cop drove Isham home. They came up to his apartment and explained the situation to Bonnie, who had been pacing the whole day in frantic contact with the station, having been told not to bother coming down as they had no idea when he'd be released. Now that he was released, he could still be charged if they found evidence to bear out Kitty's invasion of privacy accusation. They took more of his devices for analysis — his laptop and an external hard drive. They gave no timeline for the return of his electronics or his passport.

The loss of the former was something he could work around. Bonnie had an extra laptop and a friend lent him an old iPhone. The passport seizure was, for a foreigner in China, a graver matter. He would not be allowed on trains and planes or in hotels, ruling out travel, and he was required to travel for work. This wouldn't be a problem for a few weeks, but anything longer than that could put his job at risk.

Isham and Bonnie had been together for over a decade and she knew him well. Such a crisis had been long in the making. It was about time he had something blow up in his face — as long as he still had a face. She was able to take it in stride. But neither she nor Isham could fathom Kitty's bizarre hatred of her, which went beyond jealous enmity. Prior to her rude encounter at their apartment entrance, the two had never met. The only knowledge Kitty had of Bonnie (having forbidden Isham from discussing her) was through hearsay. Several music soirée friends of his had gained entrance to Kitty's circle through her blog or Nathan's introduction and made disparaging remarks about her, as people tend to do when currying favor with a rival.

Linguistic prejudice was partly to blame. Bonnie was from Beijing and had spent her toddler years in the traditional alleyways known as *hutong*, stamping her speech with the cadence of old working-class Peking. But her Mandarin was otherwise perfectly sound and regularly called upon to clear up confusion whenever Isham struggled with a shopkeeper's or waitperson's woolly rural patter. A Taiwanese friend once visited Isham in Beijing when he was first teaching in China and had remarked how lively Beijing Mandarin was compared to the colorless Taipei variety, shorn of its roots. All Chinese carry the trace of their local accent; to cover it up, they seek to neutralize it through hypercorrection. Kitty, from Harbin in the northeast and conscious of stereotypes of her own local patois, exemplified this flattened, "educated" Mandarin, in contrast to the unselfconscious music of Bonnie's, which, with its guttural ligatures on the ends of words, grated on genteel Chinese. None of this posturing fooled the Shanghainese, who naturally considered their own speech superior to everyone else's. But to Kitty and her circle the rumors indelibly tainted Bonnie as vulgar.

Already the recent events were changing Isham and realigning his priorities. Bonnie was looking more beautiful than ever; not necessarily in terms of looks, though she did have the most ravishing eyes, but in temperament and character. The purity of her gaze was still there after all these years; not the infantilized "purity" of the innocent and sexually spotless, as the word signifies in China, but the purity of constancy, coupled with her straight-talking, down-to-earth manner, free of game-playing and deceit.

11

As if Cook didn't already have enough to worry about, a mere day or two later Luna sent to his many contacts accumulated over the years (when people were laxer about cc'ing friends) a mass email, in which she announced she had had no choice but to lodge a cyberbullying complaint against him and his co-conspirator, a Chinese woman named Kitty, with the police. It was this Kitty who was the chief person responsible for hacking Luna and his other girlfriends present and past, to threaten them and make it known she was now in charge of Isham's life. Luna wasn't sure how much of the blame to assign to Isham. She even suspected Kitty of controlling or confining him. Yet he had surely benefited from all the attention it drew to his blog and his books. Indeed, he had once written a story about a similar occurrence, the secret videotaping of people's bedroom activities from a rented room in a building with a facing window. She warned the recipients that they had all been hacked by the pair and were being surreptitiously recorded. The police were investigating but she was letting everyone know now so they could take immediate steps to protect themselves.

For his part, Isham was confident enough Luna was ever more in the grip of paranoid schizophrenia and possessed no evidence of remote interest to the police. But she was capable of causing trouble. He had to explain the embarrassing situation to his recipients without revealing anything which could rebound to Kitty. Thankfully, the two social circles didn't overlap. More worrisome was the likelihood Luna would again contact Kitty's workplace, and that could hardly come at a worse time.

Isham now believed he understood what was triggering the most violent reactions from Kitty. It wasn't mere jealousy, despite her relentless vilification of Bonnie. Nor was it the mere breach of her sexual privacy. She had posted plenty of her own nudes on social media (albeit absent her face), and she had willingly, or permitted to be, shared full-blown explicit images and at least one sex video among some of her friends with her face in full view. Let's further clarify this since it's a crucial point. There are those who are fully cognizant of the revolution in sexual expression afforded by twenty-first century technology and accordingly would never allow a single compromising image of themselves to be captured digitally, ever. And there are those who are less aware of this, or less concerned, and operate according to trust. Kitty fell in the latter group — the digital equivalent of not wearing a condom. She then realized, after the fact, that she would have been better off in the former group. Her violent reactions could be attributed to anger toward herself, displaced onto Isham, at allowing things to get out of control. But it was more than that. She was building her own dome of paranoia, with the difference that hers, unlike Luna's, was at least partly anchored in reality.

The breach of trust had begun with the topless jacuzzi photo. It was not so much the fact Isham had shown it to Jim without her permission, but that he had shown it to *all* of his friends, as Jim himself avowed, his best friend. And if he had shared that pic with all of his friends, he must have shared others. And he had: the fellatio pic shown to Glory, again without Kitty's permission. Since everyone he knew had this potentially treacherous information about her and she didn't know what they might be capable of, she redoubled her efforts to put a stop to it, including but not limited to having him prosecuted and deported. Short of these measures, it was only a matter of time before her images went viral and all of China knew about her.

Something also had to be done about that ugly, boorish woman who lived with him. *She* started it all, with the malicious complaint she had made to WeChat over the seminude image Kitty had posted of herself on Isham's Chinese blog, a blog she had set up just for him. What had that woman done to help out his writing career? Isham had committed another damaging breach of trust in revealing her workplace location to the woman, who had then almost succeeded in getting her fired after accusing her, falsely, of harassment. Well, she finally had to concede Luna and Bonnie were not the same person, now that she had met them both face-to-face. But they might as well be, the one having physically attacked her and the other prevented from doing so only by the grated outer door in Isham's apartment entrance. They were clearly in league. The phone call to her HR department, by the way, was the same charge leveled by her ex-fiancé's girlfriend only months earlier. She couldn't recall if she had told Isham about that, but if she had it would explain Luna's actions, once she had gotten the story from Bonnie. That woman couldn't let well enough alone. What nerve she had in requesting Daisy's WeChat contact only to stir up more trouble with her lying account of the horrible weekend. But video evidence doesn't lie, thanks to Nathan, who had rushed to Shanghai after Kitty's second disappearance to help Daisy hunt her down. Nathan happened to pay a visit to the management office of Isham's building and was shown surveillance footage of the encounter outside his door, where Bonnie could be seen and heard screaming at Kitty.

"That's not possible and Nathan is spreading a lie," Isham told Fanny, who had relayed him this information. "First of all, only the police have access to such footage, and they would never show it to a stranger walking in off the street. Second, there is no security camera outside my apartment entrance. There are no security cameras on residents' floors at all. They only exist in the building lobby and in the elevators."

Fanny was the only one of Kitty's circle he was still in contact with. Kitty had kept her in the dark, and up until Isham's detention by the police she was still begging him to arrange a massage with her and Kitty, or with her alone if he was willing, as she was planning a trip to Shanghai soon.

Holly, meanwhile, had apologized profusely for blowing off her own massage session with them. She was remorseful and uneasy, because neither had responded to her messages since their aborted encounter. Isham was afraid to refer to the massage at all. He couldn't even hint at trouble, say that he and Kitty were having another fight, or she was indisposed, or anything about her however innocuous. He finally informed her something had come up, and he couldn't go into any more detail except it wasn't her fault. But Holly had by now gotten wind of the matter, and Isham's message was returned undelivered. She fled fast, changing her WeChat account altogether. Her friend had been right all along: this was not a couple to get mixed up with.

Isham was chafing under Kitty's threats, her regime of fear. He decided enough was enough. He was as much witness to the events as she herself and had every right to set the record straight with his side of the story. Therewith he composed a long email to Nathan and Stanley and recounted all that had happened.

In it he admitted he had overreacted in trying to wrestle the iPad from her grasp, but he had acted impulsively, in the heat of the moment, to recover his property. Of course, had he known she would respond as she did, he would never have attempted it. He would have defused the situation, and he did try to defuse it after their brief struggle, but something snapped in her and she was thrust into a state unlike anything he had ever seen before, a state of shock. He was sorry to have triggered it, but her reaction was wholly unexpected.

She took the drastic step of calling the police. You don't accuse someone lightly of assault; to do so is itself a form of assault. He allowed she may truly have perceived their struggle as an assault. Live witnesses, unapprised of what started it, might also have perceived his actions as an assault. Male aggression was happening everywhere all the time and women were to be commended for standing up to it. But that doesn't make every instance an assault. Key to the definition of the word is that the use of force is offensive in nature; there is an intent, or a threat, to cause harm. His application of force was defensive — to recover his property. If the situation had been reversed and he had grabbed *her* iPad, she would have been fully within her rights to apply the necessary force, short of excessive or grievous bodily harm, to get it back, even if this required smashing his knuckles or scratching his face, whatever was required to separate her iPad from his grip, and such would not have constituted assault. Note again that he had not gone this far but had quickly given up, in the interest of de-escalating things.

He cooperated with her the entire day, accompanying her twice to the hospital to make sure she was okay. At the day's end, she confined him in her car and forced him to pen a statement admitting that he had slandered her and required him to pay her damages. Faced with her unrelenting hostility, he might simply have walked away, if she had allowed him to without restraining him. He was much larger than her and you'd assume he could easily have sluffed her off. But he could not have done so without a struggle, and this would have plunged them right back into a repeat of the café scene.

Slander, by the way, was a word she had long lobbed at him, a word she understood loosely to mean speaking ill of her to others, indeed speaking of her to others at all. She had on more than one occasion threatened to take him to court over it. He had to point out to her that her use of the term was very far from the legal definition of slander, namely a lie about someone intended to damage their reputation. An opinion about someone, however hurtful, is not slander; a truth about someone, however damaging to their reputation, is not slander. He had never told a lie about her, and he couldn't imagine intentionally damaging anyone's reputation. But she took the idea of slander to an extreme, to encompass the mere mention of her name in conservation with anyone, regardless of what was said about her.

That's apparently what sparked Kitty's rage in the first place: her viewing the content of his private correspondence, his message from Bonnie, followed by a second instance a week later, her viewing his private correspondence to Jim. Since the latter instance was hardly reason to go back to the police, she needed something else to get him in trouble, and this was provided, courtesy of Glory, by the explicit photo he had shown to her without Kitty's permission (a disingenuous accusation given all their pics Glory had seen with Kitty's permission).

Because of her actions, Kitty had now put everyone in danger. The police were examining countless sexual images in his cellphone, iPad and laptop that had been freely sent to him by Kitty and her female friends and by Nathan as well of his female friends, many without their permission. Of greater concern was that if Isham were jailed, he would be visited by the U.S. Embassy (per diplomatic procedure). If any foul play were suspected, it could potentially get into the news. Isham stressed that's the last thing he wanted, but it was already out of his hands and out of his control — again, as a result of Kitty's actions.

Isham and Bonnie paid a visit to the police station a

week later to get any updates about his case. They were arriving from different parts of the city and he got there first. By coincidence, Kitty was at that very moment standing in the front lot talking with Officer Sun. She quickly departed upon seeing him. Bonnie arrived a few minutes later. Sun proceeded to show them a printout of Isham's letter which Kitty had just brought to him (forwarded to her by Nathan via Daisy, he later learned). She was furious, Sun said, and he was disappointed as well. She had been planning to visit the station anyway to check up on the case and see if Isham's conviction couldn't be sped up, but then she received the letter. In it was all the evidence of Isham's nefariousness and vengefulness spelled out in the plainest terms. She had made it crystal clear to him — and had his signed statement — not to talk about her to others. Not only did he break this promise, his letter was full of slander and vitriol and utterly lacking in remorse. She was particularly upset at the wrecking of her relationship with Stanley, her publisher, by revealing her recent afflictions; Stanley had accordingly cancelled her upcoming book talks. Isham had invaded Officer Sun's privacy as well by mentioning him by name in the letter. On top of it all, Isham was threatening to spill everything to the media.

All wrong, Isham protested. The letter contained only factual information of public knowledge to everyone involved. Stanley had been frantically trying to find out what was going on and had a right to know what was going on. If he determined Kitty wasn't reliable enough to fulfill her book contract agreements, it was due to her problems alone. There was nothing at all vituperative in the letter. He had made not the slightest threat to anyone. The affair getting into the news was a distinct possibility but only because Kitty lodged a charge with the police in the first place. As for his mention of Officer Sun, he apologized for that but had only mentioned him incidentally.

Sun brushed all that off. The police were busy. They didn't have time for annoying, petty cases. Kitty had been considering dropping the case and as soon as she did, they'd return his passport and electronics. But now after his irresponsible letter, she was adamant about pursuing the case to the end. Since she wasn't negotiating, they had to follow protocol and investigate. It could take them six weeks to reach a decision. His electronics had been bumped up to district level for a thorough analysis. If incriminating evidence were found, he could be formally charged. In the interim, his only option was to try to persuade Kitty to soften her stance. If he couldn't contact her because she had forbidden it, he should contact her friends to act on his behalf.

Fanny stepped in to do just that, after Nathan shared the letter with her. She had the independence of mind to regard the conflicting claims and counterclaims with some perspective and dispassion. The facts of the case just didn't add up and could only have arisen from a series of massive misunderstandings that served no one. She also realized they were all implicated to some extent. She felt obligated to intervene but stressed to Isham she was taking a risk in mediating; Kitty had threatened to terminate their decades-long friendship if she so much as mentioned him. The letter he had written was calculated to press all the wrong buttons and he needed to start over with a sincere and heartfelt apology. He could send it to her, and she'd look it over and forward it to Kitty if it passed muster.

Isham cautioned Fanny on this score, thankful though he was for her help: Kitty would regard any apology of his as an empty gesture. The more sincere he was, the more insincere he'd seem. Second, in the absence of any communications from her, he had no idea what to apologize for. Trying to grab his iPad back? The photo sexted to Glory without her permission? The letter to Nathan and Stanley? All of the above? Third, any apology could put him in further danger by his admission of guilt. He didn't believe he was guilty of anything, apart from the failure of their relationship. He suspected she wasn't even interested in his apology; she only wanted more evidence to incriminate him with. If that was the case, an apology could undo him.

Fanny reminded him he had no choice; his deportation from China was at stake. He had to try to see things from Kitty's perspective. She had legitimate concerns for her reputation, particularly since he now seemed more hostile toward her than ever; the vengeful and threatening tone of his letter proved it. Kitty had reason to believe he was at that very moment continuing to "spread her privacy" with more offending images. In fact, she believed he had used her ever since their "fake" relationship began for the sole purpose of entertaining his friends with her nude images. All evidence pointed to this.

Wrong, Isham protested. All of it wrong. Nevertheless, he was persuaded to give the apology a try in case it helped. After several drafts, she sent a version she deemed acceptable to Kitty.

No response was forthcoming.

Meanwhile, a restructuring at Isham's company placed him with a new boss. His previous boss, Richard, had been a dapper middle-aged Englishman. His new boss was a Chinese woman with the adopted English name of Rose. Richard was an ideal boss. He had the calm temperament of the born manager, commanding respect with a minimum of fanfare (sharp shirts, tan quarter-brogue oxfords, a friendly gait). Rose had worked at the company for years and Isham knew her well. She was also hands-off in her managing style. An organizational genius, she triaged her daily tasks and had little patience for people who wasted her time, yet could attend with laser-like empathy on those with an urgent problem.

It was a busy Monday, with new training for everyone. Rose was missing from her scheduled team meeting. When she later caught up with Isham, she said a woman named Kitty had visited to complain about him. She sat down with the woman in the elevator area. Her story tumbled out in a jumble and it took Rose a few minutes to work out what was going on. The upshot was that if Isham followed through on his threats to expose Kitty to the media, she would do the same, and she would identify his company by name as well. In fact, she would go to the media if he so much as tried to contact her or any of her friends again. Isham emphatically reassured Rose he had no reason to do so.

Fanny was back in touch when she learned, again through Nathan, of Kitty's visit to Isham's workplace. To prevent Kitty from taking even more drastic steps, she urged Isham to make another straightforward appeal. Nathan was also putting pressure on Kitty to negotiate. They acknowledged that the worst-case scenario for Isham — losing his job and being kicked out of the country — was disproportionate to the crime. They recognized as well he had not been formally charged with a crime and might never be. But what had taken place was, from Kitty's perspective, even worse: she had lost face over their relationship. In China, loss of face demanded proportionate restitution. Kitty would continue her scorched-earth campaign until Isham was destroyed. They were working out a way for him to save her face without going to that extreme.

A week later Kitty unblocked his email and sent him a message. "Nathan put pressure on me to meet with you. If you want, next Thursday afternoon in the Café Français."

Isham had deep misgivings about meeting her in person. It would be a minefield. That she would present a harsh front was certain. Of greater concern was whether their meeting had any point. He worried she had no intention of negotiating or reaching a compromise at all. He feared her only purpose was to get him to prostrate himself at her feet in order to extract an abject confession or otherwise entrap him into further incriminating himself. Or she'd dump on him a comical list of demands he'd have no choice but to reject out of hand. Any hesitation on his part to agree unconditionally to her demands would not just cause things to grind to a halt; it could incite another violent response from her. She might again attempt to detain him.

Isham replied that he had reasonable concerns for his safety if they met. He asked her to agree not to record their conversation, force him to commit anything to paper, or prevent him from leaving. It must be a civil face-to-face rapprochement. He had one more request: whether she could give him some idea what her demands were and help him prepare a response so as to ensure the meeting would be productive. Any one of these requests alone risked sabotaging things at the outset. Better that than repeating the café horror again. At least he could gauge her reaction and determine her interest in resolving things.

She sent him a stark reply: "It's *you* who wants to meet. If you have these concerns, we don't have to meet."

Kitty's hard bargaining again brought impasse. Nathan now stepped in and managed to mollify her enough to agree to what were after all reasonable ground rules. He forwarded her response to him to Isham: "He wants to meet but with conditions. I promised and unlike him, I will keep my promise. Unless we reach an agreement, I won't drop anything." In spite of her stonewalling, Nathan assured him the meeting was still on.

At work the following Monday, Rose called Isham to a private conference. Richard was there as well. There was a problem. Kitty had paid the company a second visit on Friday. This time she submitted a lengthy complaint. While they couldn't show him what she had written due to privacy restrictions, they paraphrased its key points. She readily owned her intention of getting him fired. She believed his morally and possibly criminally negligent behavior disqualified him from employment in such a reputable company; to this she enumerated everything objectionable he had done to her over the preceding month and well before that. Rose reassured Isham, and Richard concurred, that all of Kitty's accusations which concerned their private affairs were of no relevance to his job and he need not worry, with the exception of her publicizing the company's name in the media in connection with his person (and the media were interested enough to make it newsworthy). In fact, someone in the HR department, through which Kitty had reached his boss, spread a rumor about his affairs among a number of staff. That was not his fault, and the person in question was being dealt with. However, it meant unwanted attention and might force the company to take action to protect itself, whatever that might entail.

But there was more. Kitty claimed Isham had once given her confidential information about the company which could potentially be of interest to business rivals. They wouldn't reveal any specifics, but Isham suspected he knew what was being referred to. He explained that the alleged leak had taken place several years earlier when they had first met and was inadvertent, insignificant and of no possible value to anyone. Nevertheless, as the leak involved the company, they had to follow up. Isham was thus now under investigation by both the police and his workplace.

He was better off with Rose than Richard as his boss. Richard would not have known what to say to Kitty; they would have intimidated each other. Rose was the same age and could engage her as a fellow female on familiar territory. As she told Kitty when she sat down with her on her second visit, "Of course, we're not discounting your accusations and are taking them seriously. But I've known Isham for over ten years. He has a spotless record. He works hard and is a straightforward and honest employee. There has never been a complaint about him from anyone. I have absolute trust in him. None of what you're saying seems to be about the same person and I'd be shocked if any of it were true. The stress is taking a toll on him. You can see how he's lost weight."

Kitty's hard front faltered and she looked away. "I've been torn up lately as well. Sometimes I think I'm going crazy. Some of my friends say I should forgive him and move on but others say I shouldn't. And I really can't forget how he hurt and humiliated and used me."

That evening Nathan confirmed Kitty's second visit to his company. She was back in form, her tone bordering on boastful and triumphant, and he cited her: "I showed his boss all the evidence. If he's convicted by the police of invading my privacy, he will be fired. And he'll probably be deported. I don't need to do anything else now."

"You don't deserve this," Nathan told Isham, "but she doesn't listen to me and insists you hurt her deliberately. Also, her two friends you know of are encouraging her to be aggressive with you and don't want her to meet with you. They're afraid she might soften and feel guilty upon seeing you in person."

"You mean Daisy and Glory?"

"I can't reveal their names."

On top of this, Nathan added, Kitty had retained a lawyer and was preparing a lawsuit against him for invasion of privacy.

In other words, Isham realized, at the very moment Kitty was pretending to negotiate a meeting and a possible reconciliation, she had been marching ahead with her destructive plans all along. He therewith informed her he was scratching their planned Thursday meeting and would have no further contact with her. Rose agreed that under no circumstances should he meet with her. She also reassured him that Kitty had made her case and had no more reason to pay another visit to the company. If she did, they would consider having her removed from the premises.

A few days later, Isham was interviewed by senior management as part of their investigation. It was a short, fact-finding interview, just a list of questions. He was able to read between the lines a better idea of the evidence Kitty had assembled against him. Most of her so-called evidence consisted of laughable fabrications pulled out of thin air. He then scoured his email history with her and dredged up several conversations which severely weakened her allegations; these he presented to the committee.

But Rose reminded Isham there was now a graver problem besides the investigation against him. She had confirmed with HR about a provision in his contract which would make it instantly void upon the voiding of his visa. His visa expiry date happened to be coming up soon, in three weeks. He could not submit his visa renewal to the Public Security Bureau without his passport, and the police had his passport. No matter how much the company valued him, he would have to be fired the day his visa expired. And every day he was in the country on an expired visa would incur significant penalties and could lead to a criminal conviction as well for being in the country illegally. Absurd as it sounded that the police themselves could be responsible for his criminal conduct, this possibility was staring him in the face. It had been more than six weeks since his detention and the originally stated timeline for concluding the investigation, and still no word from them. What if they dragged it on indefinitely while he was accruing hefty visa-expiry fees? Even if the investigation concluded in his favor, he might be thrown in jail for overstaying his visa — and then deported. Kitty might succeed in her endeavor to get Isham booted out of China after all, but not for the reason she imagined.

The aggrieved couple made repeated appeals to the police to return his passport, after which he'd gladly give it back to them once his visa was renewed. They declined to respond. As the days to the expiry date counted down, Isham prepared for a possible imminent departure from China.

Then came a disturbing phone call from the Bookworm, an expat bookstore and performance venue in Beijing, the counterpart of Shanghai's Aspidistra Books. Where the latter was government-owned, the Bookworm was privately run and had not objected to Cook's books being sold there. Sales had been doing quite well, in fact; over the past few years he had arranged several boxes of shipments directly to the bookstore from his U.S. printer, conveniently bypassing vetting by Chinese Customs. Now he learned the bookstore had been visited by officers from the Ministry of Culture and his books spirited away. The manager had no other information except to say that someone had complained his books were "offensive both politically and sexually" to China. She had no idea who that someone might be.

There was an irony here which Kitty could not have failed to appreciate in this her latest attempt to get Cook removed from the country. He didn't have proof she was behind it, but as it stood as good a chance in succeeding as her other attempts, it was only surprising she hadn't tried it sooner. He'd be the first to admit his books were offensive and proudly so, not overtly to the Chinese state but to community standards, the average person's sensibility. He believed the sex he wrote into his fiction motivated his characters and propelled the action and was therefore dramatically justified. He also knew this was a fine point lost on many readers, for whom the merest graphic sexual description was obscene, but those readers couldn't be helped. "Offensive" was, of course, a relative word. By it he meant those nuggets of gold mined by any writer worthy of the name, ideas alone, in all their outrageous oddness. Could any fresh idea not be offensive, indeed violent, in the uninvited shift it forced in perspective? Whatever the case, the censors could have found ample grounds for confiscating the books and deporting him. This would moreover be an inevitable outcome, were his story to become newsworthy.

As citizen-subject of the state, perhaps Kitty even saw a duty to report his publications to the authorities. Her act would have had an ulterior purpose, that of sending him a message: don't even think of writing a book about our affair. It can confidently be stated that Cook would proceed to do exactly that; one would lose respect for him as an author if he didn't. But could Kitty be so naïve as to imagine she could intimidate him into not writing about her? An author is just as aesthetically obligated to write about his life and those caught up in it as the state is morally obligated to censor him.

An investigative reporter writes about a real-world event

with strict fidelity to the facts. A novelist writing about real-world events has the same starting point, strict fidelity to the facts, but with a key difference — a bit of leeway to alter and fictionalize, condense and expand for rhetorical effect. Kitty would be right in assuming she'd loom over his novel as a larger-than-life character. She'd be wrong, however, in assuming he'd write the novel with revenge in mind. Nothing could be more uninteresting to Cook than revenge writing, which stooped to the same level as revenge porn (this is not to write off revenge through other channels where it was due). To contemplate such would disqualify an author as a novelist, at least one with any literary pretensions. Kitty had betrayed her own misunderstanding of the art when she once tried giving him advice on a novel he was working on at the time, namely to draw out the central characters' love story for the sake of reaching a wider audience. No, he said, the story must reach an audience through its organic integrity, not the application of generic formulas.

Kitty was indeed prime material, not as a flawed but rather as a fantastic and colorful persona. In this he'd have to thank her for being such a force to reckon with and convert into fiction. She played her part perfectly, even at the risk of dragging herself down with him. Not that this was the love story she would have imagined, but then neither was *Macbeth*, Shakespeare's finest love story, though one not conventionally regarded as such, being too disturbing and nihilistic. But a novel without a touch of the latter is like a bottle of non-alcoholic wine — unpalatable and loathsome not for what it is but for what it is not.

12

"Oh, hi honey. Come in," said Marguerite, greeting Louisa at the door. They embraced with kisses on the cheek. "Thanks so much again for rescuing us the other night."

"I'm really sorry I left before you guys got back."

"Hi Louisa," said Lixin, embracing her as well.

"Totally understandable," said Marguerite. "You had no idea when we'd be back and we didn't either. So I guess a lot of people showed up."

"Yeah. You really invited a crowd. I let them in and explained the situation as delicately as I could. A few hung around for a drink — you know, coming all that way for nothing. It was so confusing when the police came. I thought for sure they must have gotten wind of that enticing party notice of yours, 'Peking opera beauty suspended in space.'"

"We were getting Lixin all set up and ready to go when you arrived early with the cops."

"I *know*. Such a bizarre coincidence. They were investigating the *baijiu* and not the party, right? I'm still unclear what happened. You were visited earlier by your management about it?"

"When they came to check up on my papers and noticed all the *baijiu.*"

"They didn't say anything at the time? Or looked at the bottles suspiciously?"

"Not that I recall. You didn't give the guests any of it to drink, I hope?"

"No. Not into it myself and most people I know aren't either. It's true you can't sell something without a business license for it."

"That's right. Alcohol particularly attracts attention because so much fake and adulterated *baijiu* is circulating around, including toxic, poisonous stuff. There's such an incentive, when top-notch Maotai and Wuliangye can go for over a 1,000 kuai a bottle. Even ten times as much."

"I've heard stories of people dying from tainted alcohol. But not recently."

"They've been cracking down."

"What is all that for anyway though? It wasn't here before. It's quite striking, with the glass shelves mirrored on both sides and the brick backing and track lighting. I never realized there was such a variety of *baijiu* brands."

"If I tell you, can you keep it secret?" said Marguerite, with a glance at Lixin.

"Sure, of course."

"There's enough acid in those bottles to get a small city high."

"You're kidding. Why?"

Marguerite recounted the story of the unconventional medium she had used to smuggle in her gram of LSD and the challenges of divvying it up into 10,000 hits.

"My god!" laughed Louisa. "I thought you had enough DMT to keep you busy for a while, and you need all this too? I bet you were scared shitless when the cop was examining it. What if he had drunk that shot Lixin offered him?"

"We would have been fucked."

"Fucked? You'd be more than fucked."

"Yeah, I know. Capital punishment."

"Oh, you'd be executed for sure. And you'd be executed right along with her, Lixin. What a news story that would be. The biggest scandal involving a foreigner since the Bo Xilai affair: exotic Afghan American woman running a drug ring and a sex cult who strings up naked Chinese beauties for amusement. And insulting Chinese culture on top of it by dressing them in Peking Opera costumes! Anywhere else in the world it probably wouldn't be so sensational, but not China. There's too much historical baggage here. And the cops can come back here at any time. They already have reason to suspect you." Louisa cast a worried look at the wall. "Is it worth it, Marguerite? Wait. Lixin, how much did you sip from that bottle in front of the cop?"

"Not so much, but still a lot."

"That was one brave move."

Lixin went over to the wall and grabbed the bottle she had drunk from during the raid. She opened it and filled the cap. "The cap is not so big."

"I'd say it was about three hits. Enough to slam you but not unhinge you," said Marguerite.

Lixin proceeded once again to toss the shot down her throat.

"What are you doing!" they exclaimed.

She poured another shot into the cap and offered it to Louisa.

"No, thanks, Lixin. I know we should be celebrating your surviving the police, but I just can't."

"It's safe. You won't get high."

"What do you mean?"

"I ordered new *baijiu*, all the same bottles. I hid the LSD bottles in another place. Not this apartment. They are safe. We are safe, Marguerite."

"You replaced all the bottles with new ones like you said? When did you do that?"

"When you weren't here."

"Well, aren't you the industrious girl. The exact same brands?"

"You should really be careful about where you hid those bottles," said Louisa. "Are you sure no one could accidentally get their hands on them? Any children?"

"Not possible. I know how dangerous it is."

"So what happened when you took that acid? How did you survive in the police station?"

"It wasn't her first time. She was already a pro," said Marguerite. "She had her first trip before that."

"How did you like it?"

"I can't say I like or dislike. It's not play. It's work. Hard work. It produces something. It changes you."

"I only dropped acid once and don't think I could do it again," said Louisa.

"It's not for everyone."

"*I* will do it again."

"She says the drug is a spirit telling her to finish what she started. I told her when she's ready she can try hitting the deems while peaking on acid," said Marguerite.

"You mean smoke DMT while tripping?"

"She's a pro but not yet a psychonaut."

"I tried smoking pot on acid and it blew up in my face. I was at a party. It was my first time to drop and nothing was happening. When I smoked a joint, the acid jumped out like a jack-in-the-box. I was hit hard and stayed that way till dawn. And ever since whenever I smoke pot the acid comes back. The more I smoke, the more it comes back. Even thinking about it makes it come back. Maybe if it was the right setting with a lot of good people tripping together, I could experiment again. But you've got all this drug paranoia in China and it makes for an ominous atmosphere."

"The acid keeps coming back because you never finished processing it. Try it with us. I guarantee you you'll have a better experience. I'm curious, but do you ever deal with drug cases among foreigners at your law firm?"

"Yes, a few. Believe me, it's the last thing you want to get caught with. The Chinese Government is obsessed with stamping out drugs. A holdover from the Opium Wars, I think."

"Yeah, it's that and a few other things, I think. Not just China but many Asian countries are fanatical about drugs — Japan, Korea, Singapore, Thailand, Malaysia, Indonesia, all of them. They tend to be fanatical about working the asses off their populations as well, and there's a connection there. What's different with the rest of the world is that Western culture, Enlightenment culture, has seeped down over the centuries and taught people the good life, the quality life, even in countries with draconian drug laws. The East allows some drugs — alcohol, tobacco, the betel nut — which have a long tradition of use. But that's it. The most hated drug to these regimes is precisely the most popular drug everywhere else: marijuana. It's a symbol, and a bad one. It stands for everything they don't understand about the West. It's anathema to authoritarian ideology. Pot rubs your face in reality and forces intense self-awareness and self-reflection. Pot makes things interesting. It turns the serious into the ridiculous and makes people laugh. One of the things they laugh at is their own brainwashing. Of all the cons people in the East have been suckered into believing, the biggest is that life is all about work and nothing but work. Now, life *is* work if you do creative work. Once you have that insight, it's all over for normal work — the Asian twelve-hour day. That's why weed is so threatening and why it's punished as severely as hard drugs."

As if to underscore her point, Marguerite got out the bong.

"You should think about your using that too, Marguerite, if the police were to come back. They deport people for simple marijuana possession. I'm sure you've heard how they started going into bars and brewpubs rounding everyone up and testing them. They used to take people's urine samples but now it's hair samples and DNA analysis. This can show traces of cannabis in your system going back three months. I heard about a case recently, an American who had just arrived in China, and after a DNA hair test he was jailed and deported for having legally used medical marijuana back home."

"Eventually they're going to have to come to terms with the global trend toward cannabis liberation."

"They don't care. You've illegally used it as soon as you step on Chinese soil."

"Yes, I'm aware things have changed. A friend of mine who lived in Shanghai in the nineties told me the waitstaff in the Uighur restaurants used to openly peddle homegrown hashish to their foreign customers. We're lucky the cops didn't search my place when they were here as they would have found this. You're right. The bong and the weed are risky. But I just can't allow fear of the state to alter my daily routine. Once you go down that road, you'll be afraid to masturbate in your own bedroom."

"And your jar of DMT?"

"It's disguised in my spice rack."

"Didn't you say you made it? You extracted it from something. What chemicals did you use? Anything like that can implicate you, and it would all turn up in a thorough search. I mean, Marguerite, if they carried out another bust, anyone that happens to be here, including myself, could be whisked off to jail. You have to think of the consequences."

"I'll consider what you're saying. But I can't throw out the deems. That would be sacrilege. We can smoke up the rest of it. There's one thing I will never give up, and it will never be found since it's hiding in plain sight."

"What's that?"

Marguerite went over to her jars of powdered dyes. "The curry-colored powder is Syrian rue, a traditional Persian herb and rug dye. It looks a bit like turmeric, doesn't it? And this rust-colored powder is mimosa bark, also a traditional dye. If you boil down these two together, there's your ayahuasca — drinkable deems. No need to extract it."

"Really."

"There's a chemical reaction when they're combined."

"Wow."

"Which reminds me. I have a question about the laws in China. How easy would it be to get kicked out of the country for selling a banned book or a book about sex or politics?"

"Only if it's clearly a political attack on China or the Government. And you are the author. Merely possessing a banned book won't get you into trouble. They'll just confiscate it. People are bringing in banned books all the time. They can't be too strict about that."

"And sexual content?"

"They're not interested in that either. Unless you're discovered to be in the porn business and are manufacturing or distributing stuff."

"You know that writer you mentioned who was rumored to have beaten up his female translator in a café? I found out all about him."

"You did? How?"

"With Lixin's help, I put it all together. Or most of it."

"I want to hear about it."

"In a nutshell, she lost face over their relationship and just lost it altogether and called the police when they struggled over an iPad. His iPad. She wasn't injured. She got short-term amnesia but that seems to have been caused by rage or some other emotional shock. And she wasn't even the translator."

"She wasn't?"

"It was a different woman, named Kitty. She had connections in the book world and was helping him promote his books. The translator was a woman named Luna. He was involved with both of them, and living with a third woman named Bonnie. But what happened in the café was only the beginning. Kitty proceeded to do everything in her power to ruin his life. Nobody knows where he is now."

"How did you learn all this?"

"Lixin happened to have the Chinese translation of his

book, *Massage and the Writer*, and we found the original English. His name is Isham Cook. We tracked down the woman he was living with and a close male friend of his in the U.S., named Jim. I visited him on a recent trip there and he gave me the whole story, plus reams of stuff Cook himself wrote about everything that happened before he vanished. Easily a book's worth of material. I've already gone through most of it but there's so many threads I'm unsure how to put it all together. And what a wild story it is."

Lixin handed Louisa copies of the English and the Chinese.

"I haven't heard of this guy," said Louisa. "He also got in trouble for this book?"

"You've heard of the Bookworm in Beijing? His books were being sold there until the police came one day and took them."

"What about Aspidistra Books?"

"We found this English copy there. They weren't even aware they were selling it. He planted it there himself. I'm wondering if he might have gotten the boot from China as a result of his books."

"This doesn't look like a political book. It's about massage and sex. It's not even about China. Wait. I see there are a couple essays in it about Chinese massage."

"It's not bad. I read it. I checked out his other books online. He mostly writes novels and essays. There's a lot of sex but it's treated in a literary or philosophical way. His books aren't political."

"Then it's unlikely he would have been deported for his books. At least not for the content. But they could have nabbed him for *selling* his books."

"Why is that?"

"Chinese labor law. You can't earn money from a source other than your job. You almost got in trouble yourself for the same reason — with all your *baijiu*. Presuming he had a job and was on a working visa."

"Even if the bookstore was selling his books and not

himself?"

"As long as he wasn't earning any Chinese currency it would probably would have been okay. Were his books on commission?"

"No idea."

"But what happened when this Kitty called the police on him? Was he arrested?"

"No. They were taken to the station and released. A few weeks later he was called in for questioning, after she accused him of something else altogether — sharing a nude photo of hers online. The only evidence was that he had shared the photo with her best friend, who was already in on their sharing of each other's sex pics."

"He was interrogated just for that?"

"Yeah, and they took his electronics and passport and kept them for months. He almost lost his job when his visa was about to run out, since without his passport he couldn't renew it. Jim told me he did manage to survive that cliffhanger. The cops returned his passport the very day his visa was expiring; he had to bring it right back to them with the new visa in it. But Jim didn't know what happened to him after that, only that the police were still investigating and he was under threat of deportation."

"He was never charged with anything?"

"We don't know. Kitty threw everything but the kitchen sink at him. She had often accused him of slander and invasion of privacy even before this all started. She was stuck on the notion he was secretly out to destroy her. So she went to the police to try to destroy him."

"Well, was it slander or invasion of privacy?"

"Isn't slander about destroying someone's reputation? She was obsessed with her reputation, understandably as she was a Party member, with a high-level job in an investment firm."

"It can be slander or invasion of privacy but not both, at least not for the same photo. If he had faked or photoshopped a pornographic image which purported to be of her and it was leaked to her workplace, that's slander. Defamation. If it was an actual nude photo of her, that's invasion of privacy. If he was responsible either way and he had done so deliberately, and she could prove it, she could nail him. At least take him to court. Though that would be harder if her bosses and coworkers all sympathized and stood up for her. If not and she lost her job because of it, she'd have a strong chance of winning a lawsuit."

"She was indeed preparing a civil suit against him, it seems."

"She would have been holding off on a civil suit until the outcome of the police investigation. There would have been no point in a lawsuit if they ended up deporting him. And a lawsuit for what? The same frivolous invasion of privacy charge based on a nude photo no one saw except her best friend? No lawyer would waste time on that. Again, she'd have to prove damages. That's why you go to court: to be compensated for the loss of your livelihood. You won't get very far in a lawsuit merely because you have some evidence someone slandered you or invaded your privacy. You have to prove you suffered. That doesn't mean you can't try suing someone, of course. Lawyers are happy to bill you for their time. Did Kitty suffer any reputational damage from the naked pic?"

"It seems it never got out in her workplace. She *was* demoted not long before the café thing, though, after Luna, the translator, contacted her workplace and accused Kitty of harassing her."

"Really. Was she?"

"Apparently not."

"How did *she* get involved with them?"

"Isham once let it slip to Luna where Kitty worked, but only incidentally and well before the eruption of events. Not long before the café incident Luna developed this paranoid delusion that Kitty had hacked her identity and was spying on her through her computer and cellphone cameras. Kitty never blamed Isham for her demotion and never brought this up with the police, but it contributed to her stress at the time and her worries about her job and reputation."

"Now this is getting interesting. Kitty would certainly have had grounds to sue. Though Luna might wiggle out of it if she confessed on grounds of mental illness. In that case, she wouldn't knowingly have slandered her and thus had no malice aforethought. On the other hand, if Kitty really had hacked her computer and was doing what Luna claimed she was, Luna could sue *her* for invasion of privacy. But she'd have to come up with evidence. You sure Cook wasn't in on it? If he was discovered to have colluded with Luna in harassing Kitty, she could nail him on that. That would be a good example of slander."

"Actually, Luna accused Isham of colluding with *Kitty*."

"How is that?"

"It was part of Luna's delusion. In any case, Kitty caused him huge trouble at his job."

"What trouble?"

"She visited his workplace several times to try to get him fired."

"For what?"

"She had some evidence he had shared confidential information about the company with her."

"Why would he do that?"

"Not sure. He was put under investigation by his company. Jim said Isham told him the evidence was on the flimsy side and he didn't think the infraction or whatever it was, was serious enough to get him fired. He came a lot closer to being fired over the visa that almost expired."

"If the police decided to charge him, his company almost certainly would have fired him because of the ensuing criminal record, however minor. As long as he wasn't charged and they found no serious misconduct at work, and as long as they were a professional outfit and valued him, his job was probably safe. What company was it?"

"I don't know anything about his job or the work he did. Something to do with English consulting."

"There are thousands of English 'consulting' companies in China. Most of them are just tutoring and other fly-by-night operations. If he still had his job, and she still had her job, there wouldn't be much she could do to him except wait for the police to nail him, and I don't see them doing that based on what you described. You're sure she didn't suffer any medical injuries when they fought in the café?"

"No. He took her to the hospital and found no problems, apart from some bruises on her arms from their struggling over the iPad. It seems to have triggered her amnesia but it was psychological, not due to any head injury."

"Anyway, if he had assaulted her and there were witnesses, he could have been jailed on the spot. The fact she went back to the police with an unrelated charge means physical injuries and assault weren't involved."

"What about the amnesia? Could she use that to sue him? For emotional shock or distress?"

"Emotional distress is usually linked to psychological abuse. In a relationship among equals? And no accompanying physical abuse? Not easy to prove. She'd have to show he had been abusing her over time, did so intentionally and beyond what any normal person would put up with, and the abuse was so extreme that she couldn't work or was otherwise incapacitated, medicated, and so forth. Was that the nature of their relationship?"

"No. They just fought constantly."

"They set a high bar for psychological abuse, otherwise anyone could go to court out of resentment or grievance over a failed relationship. You don't sue someone just because you broke up. This high standard also protects those who have been the victims of real psychological abuse."

"Is there such a thing as passive-aggressive abuse, you know, when someone doesn't obviously abuse you but is just cold or uncooperative?"

"No. There is negligence and neglect, in a relationship with someone who's dependent on you — a child or an elderly or disabled person. For ordinary couples, the abused partner has to have the courage to take action and report it. But it has to be bad enough to report it. Again, you don't report abuse merely as a means to get back at someone. I don't mean to say people can't become psychologically devastated in a relationship without actual abuse. You invest everything in a person and work at it for years and then one day the rug is yanked out from under you and you're just floored and can't recover from it," said Louisa, swiping a tear from her eye.

Lixin went over to the bathtub and turned on the tap.

"You can't take someone to court over that but you can do other things to get revenge."

"From everything I've read about the relationship, he never treated her badly, I mean abusively. That wasn't his style. He was always honest with her and made clear his poly inclinations to her from the start," said Marguerite.

"Poly?"

"Polyamory. You know, people in communal relationships."

"Oh, yeah."

"She tried to understand him. She let him open her up in many ways. Her main complaint was he spent so little time with her, only a weekend or two every month, less if they were fighting, and they were always fighting. He might have gone a long way to mollify her had he simply worked things out with Bonnie to spend more time with her. And showed her more sympathy and affection instead of hostility. Mutual hostility is a vicious circle and they constantly set each other off. She tried hard to break the cycle and was often very apologetic. It was harder for him to do that. Jim said Isham was normally charming and friendly, but he could also be distant with people and would just shut down as soon as things heated up. There must be something at the bottom of it – Jim mentioned his bad relationship with his mother – causing him to grow cold toward women who challenged or provoked him. And Kitty was a tough cookie who stood up for herself with anyone who challenged her.

You can see why the sparks flew. Hot-tempered people can usually be turned around with a bit of softness and charm, and that's exactly what he couldn't do. He couldn't unbend but retracted into his shell of male pride. Maybe if she had been the only one in his life instead of splitting himself among several women. That's what it really boils down to, I think. She was angry at him for having other women and he was angry at her for being angry at him. He thought it was enough that he was honest with her about his polyamory and was frustrated she couldn't accept that in him. And she couldn't accept it."

"It sounds like a lot of relationships I know of — without the polyamory," Louisa laughed.

"Polyamory was part of his sexual identity. To not accept it was like someone not accepting you're gay or bi."

"Of course, you're not going to accept if it directly threatens your own relationship with the person. I don't know. Seems like they had so many problems they should have split up a lot earlier."

"Jim could see that and frequently chided 'King Lear,' as he liked to call Isham, for wallowing in his little Shakespearian tragedy over Kitty."

"What did the woman he was living with think about it all?"

"Bonnie? She wouldn't talk about it. Apart from a few scenes when she tangled with Kitty and the police, I don't have any email or WeChat conversations between them, obviously, as they were living together."

"What was she like?"

"Dignified. Attractive. But reticent. Very different from Kitty's portrayal of her as ugly, uncultured and boorish. They never in fact met, except for a brief scene at his apartment door."

"And she had no idea where he is?"

"Not unless she was hiding something."

"She was still living in the same apartment?"

"Yeah. A nice place. One whole wall was lined with

books, another with CDs. He had an expensive stereo
system and a couple large Oriental rugs, which I could see
were made in Henan. He had an unusual collection of art
on the walls and I asked her about them. I have a very good
visual memory and can tell a lot about him from his eclectic
tastes. There was a nude drawn on brown-bag paper in an
odd-shaped frame made out of colorful patches of discarded
clothes, some Chicago artist from the 1980s. There was an
imitation fourteenth-century Madonna and Child painted
on wood he had picked up in Venice. There was an
exquisitely rendered street view of Philadelphia from a
couple hundred years ago — a family heirloom. There was a
curious painting of two figures merging into one with a
penis like a man's face with a large nose. And there was a
painting of a vagina made to look like a sea plant
underwater, with its lubrication seeping out and a fish
swimming toward to it. The last two paintings, she said were
done by a female Chinese painter he bought them from
because he was attracted to her. Come to think of it, an idea
just occurred to me that might get his attention and flush
him out of hiding or captivity or wherever he is."

"What's that?"

"I could write it all up into a book and publish it."

"A biography? An exposé? You'd better be careful. You
might get Kitty's attention too, and she doesn't sound like
the kind of person you'd want to mess with in a lawsuit."

"How would I be able to write about it without being
sued?"

"The problem is it's not your story. All your sources have
been privately obtained without either Cook's or Kitty's
permission."

"Could it be disguised as a novel?"

"Perhaps, but you'd have to change a lot. If anyone
reading it recognized anyone involved and informed them,
they could take you and your publisher to court and sue you
for invasion of privacy. Though the likelihood of that
diminishes the more you disguise things and present it all as

fiction. However, if Kitty read it and felt the picture of her was false and painted her in a bad light, she could try suing for libel. But she'd have to show exactly what was false. I doubt she could win a lawsuit unless it was public knowledge that the book was about her and, again, her reputation suffered because of it."

"Since he's a writer, I'd expect *him* to write a book about it."

"Maybe he is, and it's not yet written. Or he's waiting for the right time."

"If he does write a book could she sue him?"

"Only for libel, if he were to falsify anything about her in the book. If he sticks to the facts, she won't win a lawsuit."

"Not for invasion of privacy?"

"No. As long as it's confined to their relationship, everything she did also happened to him. It's his story too. He has a right to tell his story. There's an old piece of wisdom that you should never get involved in a relationship with a writer, since you're going to get written up."

Lixin took off her clothes and started doing the same to Louisa's T-shirt, bra, and the zipper of her cutoffs.

"Lixin — "

"Come. Take a bath with us."

"Good idea," said Marguerite.

"You guys! You didn't prepare me for this. I'm body shy."

Lixin led a naked Louisa over to the tub and the three of them got in. Lixin sat Louisa between her legs and cupped and kneaded her breasts.

"Oh, come now, Louisa. You're hot and you know it. That sumptuous red hair and those hazel eyes and freckles of yours," said Marguerite as she filled up the bong.

"A blizzard of freckles and my boobs are small."

"I like them," said Lixin, who nibbled Louisa's earlobe and stuck her tongue in her ear.

"Are you really going to write it all up in a book? How much writing experience do you have?" Louisa continued.

"I do have writing experience but haven't published

anything. This might just be the excuse I need to get started. I've always wanted to write a book."

"How are you going to organize the story? Chronologically?"

"I could. But it goes back several years and I'm not sure it's the best approach. Something more dramatic, such as the *in medias res* technique I remember from my lit courses in university."

"What's that?"

"Starting in the present with the crisis and working backwards and then working back up to the crisis and moving forward to the climax. But I'm not sure how to work in the Luna side of the story."

"The translator?"

"Yeah. Jumping back and forth between her and Kitty might get confusing since they're two separate stories and they only come together in the end."

"Alternating chapters? That's one technique a lot of novels use. By the way, whatever happened to Luna? Did she find out about what Kitty did to Isham?"

"No. She kept sending frantic, threatening emails to both of them at the very time Kitty was launching her attacks on Isham. Jim told me Isham decided not to say a word to Luna about it for fear of reopening the can of worms."

"How could that be?"

"Kitty's ban on Isham mentioning anything about her to anyone. No matter how Luna reacted, Kitty could say Isham was again making things worse by spreading more disinformation about her. I think he was right to keep Luna in the dark. Luna just continued to rant at them with no idea of her own role in the tragicomedy. He also wanted to gain as much distance from Luna as possible in case she truly went insane."

"Did she?"

"I know no more about what happened to her than I do about Kitty or Isham."

"How could an educated woman talented at English and

capable of translating a book like that suddenly go mad?"

"It's a mystery to me too. But a major factor seems to be that this was their second relationship. She had barely gotten over their first affair years earlier and then she was plunged back into a new tormented relationship with this difficult man she was in love with again. It must have been a terrible humiliation and it just broke her."

"He reduced one woman to raving and another to rage, and they both reduced him to anonymity."

"It would be nice to say I could wrap up the whole story with a happy ending, such as they all got over it and made up and entered into polyamorous bliss together. As a novel I could end it that way. But reality is sexier."

Also by the author

Jeff Malmquist is unaccountably catapulted to the year 2060. He finds himself in New Gary, Indiana, a labor camp of one million Chicagoans, their identities hacked and incriminated as pedophiles through the collusion of a corrupt U.S. Government, the Russian cybermafia, and China. He escapes to Chicago, only to find himself in a full-scale replica of Ancient Rome in China, erected for the wealthy country's amusement and manned by a million enslaved Italians. As he struggles to orient himself in these synchronized urban labyrinths, he is plunged back to real Ancient Rome, before being flung yet further into the future: It's 2115 and the Chinese Empire rules the world. The former Western hemisphere is now the American Special Administrative Region, a vast Cantonese-speaking slave colony. Malmquist will soon be shipped to the most opulent city the world has ever known for an unspeakable fate.

A dystopian satire both bleak and funny, *The Kitchens of Canton* distills the worst of our present and future societies into a strangely seductive maze of a story.

"Kitchens is a 242-page mindfuck induced most likely by a combination of LSD, gender-fluid sexual experimentation and unbridled brilliance."—**Tom Carter, *Unsavory Elements***
"A wildly amusing and satirical premise sets the stage for a frenetic tale of time traveling and cross-cultural confusion."—**Chris Taylor, author of *Harvest Season***
"A dizzying, whirlwind tour across language, space and time...*The Kitchens of Canton* presents an eerie, if not implicative, vision of society's future."—**Quincy Carroll, *Up to the Mountain and Down to the Countryside***
"A picture forms of Isham Cook after reading even just two or three sentences from any of his books. He delights in the excessive, the sensuous and the extravagant."—**Arthur Meursault, *Party Members***
"An insightful, unconventional, and risqué view of present-day culture."—**Kirkus Reviews**

www.ingramcontent.com/pod-product-compliance
Lightning Source LLC
Chambersburg PA
CBHW031325170626
46807CB00002B/570